CW01647389

THE WINTER'S FAIL

SARA MADDERSON

Created with Vellum

For my Chris, Paddy and Tilly. You are my whole world.

PROLOGUE - NOVEMBER 2019

Dave, a corpulent fifty-something trader in a bright green polo shirt, stands up and leans over his cluster of monitors on the Loeb AG trading floor.

'Oi!' he hisses at the traders sitting around Emmy, addressing them in a broad East End accent. 'You 'eard what's 'appened?' He jerks his head at an empty corner office.

It's a quiet day and the equity markets are trading sideways. On days like this, everyone is grateful for a diversion. Heads bob up and Dave spits out the news he looks so eager to tell.

'They've only gone and suspended Beneventi!' he says. 'For sexual misconduct and *assault*.' He utters the last word lasciviously and nods for effect, his accent turning its *l* into a *w*.

'Fucking hell!' Martin, a consumer sector trader sitting next to Emmy, exclaims. 'That dirty bastard! Who's he supposed to have assaulted?'

Dave's head jerks in the opposite direction, towards the

institutional sales desk. He raises his eyebrows self-importantly and says in a theatrical whisper, 'Isabella Whitney.'

Emmy freezes like a statue in the verbal crossfire. She removes her gaze from Dave and fixes it to her screens, but the trading desk's team calendar swims in front of her eyes. She wants to crawl under her desk and simultaneously pump Dave for everything he knows.

Lorenzo Beneventi, owner of the currently empty corner office, runs the Equities division at Loeb and is therefore their ultimate boss. He is a beautiful, charismatic Italian. He's married, with two daughters. And he swept Emmy up in a thrilling affair with him almost as soon as she quit her aid work in India and succumbed to the dark side back in London—temping as an assistant at Loeb. If you asked her, she would say the sex is amazing, the chemistry is smoking and the need to sneak around with him behind the backs of everyone at work is intoxicating. In short, it's exactly the decadent, morally bankrupt behaviour she needs to put the devastation and trauma she experienced in India firmly out of her mind. But, if what Dave is saying is true, a wife and mistress aren't enough for Lorenzo.

Isabella Whitney, Dave explains, is claiming Lorenzo assaulted and propositioned her on a recent work trip. Isabella runs the UK Institutional Sales desk—she's a glossy, statuesque American who seems intense and straight-talking. Emmy doesn't know her well, having only been at Loeb for six months. But she doesn't strike Emmy as the type to cry wolf.

Everyone has now swivelled around in their chairs. Dave has the floor.

'What happens now?' asks Si, another trader (it's a predominantly male desk). 'Is he gone for good?'

'Apparently they've been investigating it for a while but

they seem to think 'e's guilty and now they're asking other women to come forward if 'e's assaulted them too,' Dave says.

Jesus Christ. This is not happening. She tries to equate what Dave is saying about Lorenzo with the man she's been sleeping with. There's no question he's bad news. He chatted her up brazenly at the onsite gym and then again in the kitchen area at the back of the trading floor, gold wedding band glinting in plain sight on his right hand. But she was heartbroken and disillusioned on her return from India, wanting to obliterate the memories that still won't leave her. When Lorenzo invited her for a drink at the Rosewood Hotel on High Holborn she accepted, and that was that. They went straight upstairs after a bottle of champagne. He's unhealthily good-looking, but the real attraction is his utter confidence that she's interested in him. He's as assured with women as he is running Loeb's Equities division. It gives Emmy a kick to know that she, a temporary desk assistant who has none of the career or financial prospects of the men and women around her, has their boss completely in her thrall a couple of times a week.

Faithful or principled he is not, but she wouldn't have had him down as a sex offender. That said, he's used to getting what he wants, and she suspects he enjoyed a challenge. Isabella Whitney would certainly provide that; she wears an array of diamonds on her ring finger and she doesn't look like she suffers fools. Could Lorenzo really have been capable of assaulting her if she didn't succumb to his advances as easily as Emmy did? He has a ruthless side to him, a side that means she's never quite dropped her guard or allowed herself to fully open up with him. She's been acutely aware that for him, their relationship is just sex; she's been careful to treat it similarly.

Most of the traders on her row of desks are standing up now, discussing Lorenzo's suspension, although Dave's intel is limited. Watching the mighty fall is a popular spectator sport in the City. A few seats down, a flash of movement and colour catches her eye. Lara, one of the few female traders on the desk, stands up abruptly, grabs her coat and bag, and stalks down the walkway between the chairs, face scarlet and eyes fixed on the carpet. When she's gone, Martin whistles.

Emmy breaks her silence. 'What?' she asks.

'Looks like someone's pretty upset. I wonder if he got his hands on her. I hope not—she's a good kid.'

A wave of nausea hits her. Lara couldn't be more than mid-twenties. God, what kind of man has she exposed herself to? She isn't sure whether to feel stupid, violated, or relieved that she's escaped any unpleasantness in her dealings with him. He's been quiet the last few weeks; he's spent less time in the office than usual, and they've only hooked up a couple of times recently. When they have, he's been more subdued, and more tender with her, than usual. Clearly, she needs to call time on this guy, thank her lucky stars that she hasn't become more embroiled with him, and chalk it up to experience. She takes a breath. She'll do a coffee-run for the desk and pull herself together, and everything will be fine.

1

MONDAY, 2ND DECEMBER

Everything would have been fine, except that since late November Emmy's nipples have hurt like mad, and her boobs are so achy that she can't sleep on her stomach. She's also had a couple of hairy moments on the tube and at work where her mouth fills with saliva and she feels motion sick. She's found herself hanging over the toilet bowl, spitting up before hurrying downstairs to the cafeteria to load up on bagels or croissants. Even thinking about her usual choice of scrambled eggs turns her stomach.

Finally, this morning, she takes the plunge and makes the dreaded run to Boots to buy a pregnancy test. To cheer herself up, she hits a Christmas playlist on Spotify and cranks it up on her AirPods. She's as obsessed by Christmas at thirty-seven as she was at seven, and now it's officially December, she's unleashed. *Fairytale of New York* rings in her ears as she locks herself in a cubicle in the office loos and proceeds to pee on a stick.

She has the answer in minutes. The digital display informs her she's *3+ weeks pregnant.*

Pregnant. Holy shit. The implications of the word are too much to absorb. Unlike her sister Rosa, she's shunned the traditional trappings of a western lifestyle as long as she can. And now she's back in London, sitting on a toilet in the middle of some capitalist hell-hole, with no flat or pension, inadequate savings and, seemingly, the beginnings of a tiny baby growing inside her—a baby whose father has been fired for sexual assault. Rosa will be horrified. Her mother will be furious with her. She can't conceive of telling Lorenzo, whom Loeb finally fired last week. He's called her almost every day since then and she's ignored the calls.

She's always wanted to be a mother, in the most primal way. Rosa, who is six years older than her, has produced two beautiful daughters, but Emmy sometimes gets the feeling that Rosa has done it to check a couple of boxes on the blueprint of what she believes to be the right type of life. Whereas Emmy, at thirty-seven, sometimes feels as though time is running away from her. The older she gets, the less confident she is about her choice to be a free spirit, even though freedom is what she still yearns for. If she's honest with herself, this lack of confidence in her chosen path is one reason she came back to the UK, but six months on she's still in limbo; she's failed to put down any roots here.

'I'm pregnant,' she tells herself. It's such a loaded word. Pregnant with possibility. Pregnant with hope. Pregnant with all sorts of unimaginable bloody problems. She stares at the stick and panic rises in her like reflux. She has no idea what to do next—she should presumably go see a doctor, but she doesn't know if she still has a GP, having been out of the country for a six-year stint. She's had no reason to use the NHS since she's got back.

She looks around and feels stupid. She's calibrating her reaction to this stick; it's as if she thinks she should produce some sort of adult, measured response. She should be either horrified or ecstatic but she feels neither. This is by far the most grown-up thing to have ever happened to her, and she's shirking a normal reaction, even now.

Her closest friends are all out in India; she's let most of her friendships in the UK lapse shamefully. There's nothing else for it; she'll have to call Rosa. Her sister's inevitable disapproval will be a reasonable price to pay for bringing someone who cares about her into this mess. Rosa's a proper grown up, with a Rangemaster oven and an abundant supply of spare loo rolls in her utility room. She'll know what to do.

She waves her hand over the sanitary bin—that's a contraption she won't be needing for a few months—and drops the stick into it. Such an inauspicious little stick; a farcically underwhelming representation of the game-changing news it brings. Spotify is now playing *O Holy Night*. It's her favourite carol; the sense of awe and sacred solemnity it evokes over the birth of a child never fails to give her goosebumps. She looks down at the pregnancy test packaging. From the sublime to the ridiculous. Inside this cookie-cutter office loo, she puts her head in her hands.

ROSA CLIP-CLOPS down Old Bond Street in her patent Louboutin booties. She's just partaken in a divine brunch at Dior's stunning townhouse with Cordelia de Castellane, creative director of Dior Maison. The event was very exclusive—there were fewer than a dozen influencers there—and de Castellane walked them through how to decorate for Christmas with Dior's beautiful china. She carries a large Dior carrier bag filled with toile-de-jouy goodies. Once she's on the train back to Surrey, she'll edit her photos, apply some dreamy filters and stick them all up on Instagram Stories. The endorsement from events like this is even more precious than the exclusive content they provide.

Her phone rings in her hand. Emmy. She double-taps her AirPod to accept the call and stops outside Ralph Lauren, its windows gloriously bedecked for Christmas with green, gold and scarlet in that sumptuous, over-stuffed way only Americans can truly pull off.

'Hi, Em,' she says, pulling up Instagram on her phone. She posted some preliminary shots already, and her inbox is full of direct messages from swooning followers. 'How are you doing?'

Her sister's breathing is ragged.

'Are you running?' Rosa asks.

'No, I'm crying.'

She scrolls through her Instagram comments. 'What's up?'

Something unintelligible.

'What?'

'I'm pregnant,' Emmy whimpers.

Jesus Christ. She exits Instagram and jerks her head up, as if answers lie ahead on Bond Street. Her baby sister is pregnant, but this can't be a good thing; she wasn't aware that Emmy was seeing someone.

'Oh, God,' she says now. 'Who's the father?'

'It's someone from work.'

A banker. Well, that sounds respectable at least. 'Is it serious, with him?' she asks.

'No.' Emmy's voice is muffled. 'He's married.'

'Oh, for fuck's sake, Em.' She pinches the bridge of her nose. 'Does he know—have you told him yet?'

'No. I just found out myself. And it gets worse.'

She steels herself. This sounds like a mess the proportion of which only Emmy can create. 'Go on.'

'He's been fired. He was suspended a few weeks ago for assaulting a couple of women at the firm, and for sexual misconduct more generally, and they fired him last week. He was super-senior; he ran the whole Equities division.'

'Oh my God! Did he hurt you? Are you ok?'

Emmy sighs down the phone. 'No, he didn't hurt me, thank God. I went into it with my eyes wide open. At the time, it seemed like a lot of fun. But it turns out he was even sleeping with a much younger girl on my desk; I mean, the guy's an animal. I've heard on the desk assistants' grapevine that his wife's divorcing him now.'

'Ok.' Rosa thinks. 'He's not an ideal father-figure. Does he have kids already?'

'Yes,' Emmy says. 'Two daughters.'

'So his wife's leaving him and he'll have to pay child support for his daughters and he's just been fired.' She opens up Evernote on her phone and types *Establish paternity rights + obligations* into a new note. 'That doesn't sound promising. We'll have to get some advice on what your and his rights are. How far gone are you?'

'I—I don't know. The test just says 3+ weeks. I guess I need to see if I have an NHS GP? I don't even know if I have one anymore.'

'We can do better than that,' Rosa says briskly. 'I'll call my obstetrician and see if she or a colleague can see you. They've got a practice right by Chelseas & Westminster Hospital—they're very good.' She types *Call Maternal Health Centre and register E w/ NHS GP?* into the same note.

'I can't afford to go private, Rosa.'

'I know. I'll pick up the tab for this. Let's get you scanned and then we can make arrangements to hand you over to the NHS. You must have an idea of how far along you were —when was your last period?'

Silence.

'Emmy?'

'God, I don't know,' Emmy says. 'I hadn't even thought about it. Two, three months?'

'Christ,' says Rosa. 'We need to get you checked out as soon as possible so you have options.' This is typical Emmy. How can she have missed two or three periods and not noticed? She still needs a babysitter; the idea of her as a mother is terrifying.

She takes a breath and addresses the elephant in the room. 'Do you know what you want to do? Do you want to keep this baby?'

2

TUESDAY, 3RD DECEMBER 2019

Stacey positions herself for the final serve of her coaching session. She plants her right foot firmly back, opens her arms into a Y and throws the ball up, whacking it satisfyingly over the net. Despite the cold, she's long since abandoned her white zip-up jacket. Her coach, Raphael, grins and volleys the ball straight back at full force, and they rally until he smashes it into the far corner, beyond her reach.

The rally is a form of foreplay. The whole session is, really. The lessons started because she wanted to keep honing her game over the winter, but as soon as she met Raphael—a young, hot, former pro from Paris—her agenda changed. Her me-days got an upgrade.

Tuesday is Stacey's me-day. If it's her weekend to have the kids then she's usually broken by Sunday night. Unfortunately, too much financial news breaks or leaks over the weekend for Mondays to be devoted to self-care. Instead, each Monday she helms the ship that is her FinTech company, Lokk, and then escapes to Beaverbrook the following day to unplug and find some time to think.

Beaverbrook has the giant advantage of being a mere twenty minutes from the kids' school, Hampton Park. It's a delightful, newish hotel and country club of which Stacey became a member before you could say Amex. The Brits are definitely improving in their ability to execute on a decent country club. She spends her Tuesday me-days here without fail. They used to feature a tennis lesson, swim and some serious work-time alone, before meeting up with some girlfriends for a late lunch or glass of champagne.

These days the routine is much the same, except that she's swapped the swim for sex in one of the Coach House bedrooms. It turns out sex with Raphael has a more galvanising effect on her neurons than a swim ever can. When he leaves, she cranks up her MacBook and settles back on her pillows with a chicken salad. Her brainpower at its peak, she fires off new ideas and unforeseen solutions and fizzes with creativity. She should put him on the payroll.

Today, he brushes past her as she retrieves her jacket.

'*Bien joué*,' he says. 'See you in a minute?'

'Sure thing, babe,' she says. 'Usual room. Gimme five, will you?'

In her room, she peels off her damp tennis whites and strolls into the walk-in shower, cranking the handle. A deluge of near-instant scalding water assaults her and she stands underneath it, enjoying the massaging effect it has on the crown of her head. She hears the bedroom door click and opens her eyes to see Raphael ridding himself of his own clothes before striding through to the bathroom. He walks in, lithe, dark and extremely hairy, and pulls her into his arms.

Stacey is physically wrung out from the lesson, but her nerve-endings are on high alert. She knows from their previous post-tennis romps that he's in his early thirties and eventually plans to return to Paris. He tells her he's never done this with any of his clients before; she's not sure she believes him, but frankly, she doesn't care.

'You played like a crazy woman today,' he says in her ear. He's holding her up, his arms wrapped around her lower back. 'All that energy. You were amazing. Did you save any for me?'

'I have plenty left for you,' she says. 'But it's the thought of this that gives me energy out on the court. It's so hot, rallying with you and knowing that you're going to screw me senseless afterwards.'

He holds her even more tightly and presses her towards him, his tongue taut in her mouth. She runs her palms down his sinewy back and over his deliciously pert, hairy butt. They've had a thing going for the past five or six weeks; she's pretty confident it's going to happen each week but it's still new enough for her not to be quite sure, and the kick she gets from turning up for a tennis lesson and hoping for far more afterwards is insane.

It's particularly insane after fourteen years of married monogamy. *This* is what she missed before she filed for divorce. Her married sex-life was perfectly good, but it's hard to maintain that sense of novelty when you've gotten into bed with the same guy almost every night for that long. Spoiler: he loves you. Spoiler: if you make a move, he'll probably say yes. It wasn't that she thought she could do better; it was that she wanted variety. She wanted that unbeatable edge you get from not knowing someone well, from being surprised by them, from getting to know their body and their kinks—before it all becomes too familiar again.

Raphael is now soaping up her breasts with one hand while his other hand moves lower, sliding down her slippery abdomen and between her legs. He's very sexy, very exotic, and very skilful. Someone has trained him well. She assumes French women don't accept laziness in their lovers. He starts talking to her, telling her what he's going to do to her next.

'French only,' she purrs. 'Let's go to bed.'

He laughs. '*D'accord. Allez.*'

Stacey throws a couple of bath-sheets on the bed and they tumble onto them, still soaking, their body temperatures still high after the tennis. She luxuriates on the bed, looking up at him as he crouches over her. He's divine, brown-black eyes boring into her. Water drips from him all over her body; her sensitised skin laps up the teasing droplets. She squirms. He bends to kiss her and then pulls away, murmuring a steady, intoxicating stream of words in French. She can't understand a single one, which makes it all the hotter. But she understands the look in his eyes and she understands the meaning of the body parts he's helpfully tracing with his fingertips. He may be delivering a litany of threats or a string of promises. She hopes it's both.

~

RAPHAEL, as usual, doesn't disappoint. She spends a glorious hour with him before giving him the boot, ringing for room service and settling down with her work in a fluffy robe. She opens her MacBook and leans her head against the headboard. She feels alive and energised. God, she shouldn't have given up on the single life so young—married at twenty-seven, then four kids over nine years, and working in finance the whole way through. She's finally living again; she's seized back control of her life while she's still young enough to enjoy it. And boy, is she enjoying this newfound freedom.

~

AFTER A COUPLE of uninterrupted hours of productive work, she dresses, makes up her face and heads over to the main house. She's meeting her friends in Sir Frank's Bar, an astonishingly beautiful salmon-pink room that doubles as a gallery for the work of Victorian botanical artist Marianne North. Hundreds of paintings line the walls, immaculately tiled. She spots her girls sitting on a velvet sofa under a section of the exhibition entitled *India & Ceylon*, and, waving, hurries over.

Evelyn spots her first and stands up for a hug. She's now Evelyn Macleod-Rutherford. It's been over eighteen months since her ex-husband and business partner, the celebrity chef Seb Macleod, came out as gay and turned her world upside down. These days, she's Commercial Director for Sorrel Farm, a beautiful organic farm and resort in Kent run by her closest friends. She married the farm's hot estate manager, Angus, this summer at the resort and Stacey has never seen her so happy. She and Evelyn go way back; they met years ago at a women-in-business networking event and hit it off immediately.

She looks fantastic. Her neat baby bump is barely visible under a soft cream sweater, and she's one of the very few pregnant woman Stacey's seen who can pull off leather pants and look ravishing. She's glowing—all that organic produce and the hot husband clearly agree with her.

'Hey girl,' Stacey says, pulling her in tightly and giving her a good squeeze before turning to the other woman at the table, Astrid.

Astrid Carmichael runs a beautiful and highly successful eponymous fashion brand. Her taste is impeccable and Stacey rues the day Evelyn introduced her to Astrid and her brand; she has a weakness for Astrid's four-figure work dresses. Today she's the perfect poster-child for her own label in a black silk-chiffon midi dress over some lust-worthy boots that Stacey immediately clocks.

Astrid kisses her warmly on both cheeks, and they all sit.

'This is such a treat, ladies,' Stacey says. 'How's the baby, Evelyn?'

'*She* is doing great, thank you,' says Evelyn, cocking her head to one side and beaming.

'Oh my God!' Stacey's hands go to her mouth. 'It's a girl! I am so happy for you guys—is Angus ecstatic?'

'He's over the moon,' Evelyn says. 'I am too—finally, another female. Our family is way too boy-heavy.'

She has a son, Eddie, who must be coming up for ten now, and Angus also has two older sons from his previous marriage. This little girl is going to get spoilt.

'Mmm, Angus with a baby daughter,' Stacey says. 'Hot. He'll be the most adoring dad. You seriously got yourself the perfect guy there.'

Evelyn smiles at her, her eyes kind. 'If I may remind you, you had the perfect guy too—it just wasn't what you wanted from life anymore.'

'True.' She knows Evelyn's still puzzled by her decision to walk out on fourteen years of marriage. 'But he's good, I'm good, and the kids are all thriving, so no harm done.'

'How is single life?' Astrid asks, pouring Stacey a glass of champagne from the bottle in the cooler.

'It's fabulous, actually.' She takes a sip and shrugs her shoulders. 'I had a tennis lesson this morning with my heavenly French coach, Raphael, and then he fucked me afterwards in one of the lovely Coach House bedrooms. It's becoming a bit of a regular thing.'

The others react in shock and delight; Astrid puts her hand over her mouth to keep in her champagne and Evelyn bends over double.

'Oh my God, you are a piece of work,' she says. 'Good for you. She's hilarious, isn't she, Astrid?'

Astrid looks coy. She tucks a (depressingly natural) platinum lock of hair behind her ear and shifts on the sofa. 'I may have had something very similar going on this term.'

'What?!' Stacey slaps her on the knee. 'Tell us everything.'

'I don't have a tennis coach,' Astrid says, 'but I've been sleeping with Tabby's PE teacher for most of this term—Callum. He's Irish, and I can't tell you how gorgeous he is. Here, I'll show you.'

She picks up her phone and holds it out, scrolling through an Instagram feed of a young guy who should be a model if he isn't already.

'Holy shit!' Stacey says. 'He is *smoking*. Astrid—this is incredible. Can you pass him onto me when you're done?' She taps into a few pictures. He's sensational.

'Actually,' Astrid says, 'we finished it a couple of weeks ago. I'm afraid he's just fallen madly in love with Tabby's new class teacher, and I've met someone too.'

'Shame,' Stacey says airily. 'But great news about the new guy—you were pretty down last time I saw you.'

'So, who is he?' Evelyn takes a sip of sparkling water. 'He must be pretty special to top *that*.' She nods at a photo of Astrid's gorgeous guy smiling into the camera.

'He's a business associate,' says Astrid. 'Unfortunately,

he lives in New York, but he's told me how he feels and he's waiting for my decision.'

'And...?' Stacey asks.

'Friday night is crunch-time,' Astrid says. 'We've got a big school fundraiser at the Savoy and he's coming over for it.' She takes a breath. 'I'm actually really excited to see him. We've been FaceTiming every night. He's called Gray Landau; he runs Constellation—the US luxury goods conglomerate?'

'Impressive,' Evelyn says. 'Mark was such a shit to you. It's about time you met someone who sees how amazing you are.'

Stacey's aware of the broad brush-strokes of Astrid's story. Her ex left her out of the blue for a much younger colleague a couple of years back; since Stacey's known her, she's been struggling with the pressures of running a large brand and bringing up a child alone. An outsider would never know it, however: Astrid projects a glamorous, serene image to the world.

'He's forty-eight,' says Astrid, 'so a big jump up from Callum. But I think I'm ready for a proper grown-up. I didn't want to rush my decision, but he's amazing.'

'I have to say,'—Evelyn smiles for effect—'I'm finding being with a proper grown-up very enjoyable indeed.' She wiggles her eyebrows at them.

'Oh, look at the cat that got the cream!' Stacey guzzles more of her champagne. 'But, to be fair, you had a secretly gay husband for ten years so we won't begrudge you some married smugness second time around. It's just great to see you so happy. And Astrid, I hope things work out with Gray.' She holds up her glass. 'Here's to new beginnings.'

'So, Astrid,' Evelyn says. 'Will we be meeting Gray on the twenty-first?'

Last Christmas, Evelyn's first at Sorrel Farm, she threw an enchanting party featuring carol singing around a huge fire pit in the walled garden and a delicious feast in the resort's main barn. Astrid's brand sponsored the event. They've made it an annual occurrence, much to Stacey's delight, holding it on the Winter Solstice.

'If it all goes well on Friday, then I'm hoping he'll come back for a few days before or after Christmas,' Astrid says. 'So fingers crossed I'll have someone to keep me warm by the fire pit.'

'It's already the highlight of my holiday calendar,' Stacey announced. 'Things kick off tomorrow with Mia's nativity play.'

'Oh, how sweet,' Astrid coos. 'Nativities always make me cry.'

A waiter interrupts, hovering at Stacey's elbow. 'Excuse me, Madam. The gentleman by the window has sent this over, with his best wishes.' He nods and proffers a bottle of Ruinart *Blanc de Blancs* and a business card.

Stacey swivels as the other two vainly attempt to hide their giggles. By the French doors sits a dark-haired god, long legs crossed at the ankles in front of him, his shirt open-necked under a lustrous wool suit. He raises his tumbler to her and gives her a slow smile, not without arrogance. She inclines her head and raises her glass in thanks before looking down at his card. *Antoine Haddad. Partner.* Below this, the name of a family office she knows by reputation, and a Mayfair address. Poor Raphael's days may be numbered.

3

TUESDAY, 3RD DECEMBER

Annabel's has once again pulled out all the stops for Christmas. The facade of the iconic Mayfair club is covered in an enormous conical structure designed to look like a stylistic Christmas tree. The peak of the white and gold edifice towers above the building itself and dominates Berkeley Square. There are tourists everywhere, taking snaps from the street and the gardens.

Rosa privately thinks last year's facade, which was green and featured red and white candy canes, was less tacky, but she can't argue that the white and gold colour scheme is easier to match with her outfit. She's here primarily to meet Volare for a strategy lunch, but Annabel's always offers a wealth of social media opportunities. She smooths down her perfectly waved hair and takes off her white faux-fur coat, draping it over her shoulders so her adorable little Alessandra Rich shift is visible. It's crafted from gold and white tweed with big, gold, eighties-style buttons. She has the sweetest white leather Louboutin ankle boots on. It was worth the pain and expense of having a car take her into London; she and her outfit are still immaculate.

She hands her large Volare tote bag to her intern, Trixie, and adjusts her micro hat box bag, also by Volare, on her wrist. Her five million followers will lap up this festive look outside one of London's most exclusive establishments. They'll go even crazier for the shots inside, where only members and their guests can go.

'I'm ready,' she tells Trixie. 'Go for it.' She strikes her pose, leg cocked, hands delicately clutching the tiny handbag in front of her. She's perfected her Mona Lisa half-smile, eyes open wide.

Trixie clicks away. 'Got some good ones,' she says.

'Good. Find a cafe and edit them while I'm at lunch—I'll send you the interior shots as I take them.'

She flounces off to a red-coated doorman who opens the front door for her. She's meeting Patrizia and Giacomo from Volare in the Rose Room for lunch. Despite her outward nonchalance, this place never fails to thrill her. The banisters of the main staircase is packed full of greenery thickly clustered with pink and purple baubles. Understated it is not; it's a decadent dream. What she loves most about Annabel's isn't its opulence but its dedication to beauty, to living life as fabulously as possible. It's a philosophy she shares, that life is better when you're surrounded by beauty.

The Rose Room is exquisite. A back-lit pink onyx bar glows softly, dominating the space. A barman in a sherbet-pink suit is shaking up a cocktail. She steps forward and asks him if she can take a video of it. He smiles his acquiescence. Happily, the cocktail he pours into the waiting coupe is the prettiest shade of pink. She turns and sees Patrizia and Giacomo already at a table. They stand to greet her.

'*Ciao*, bella,' Giacomo purrs, kissing her on both cheeks. 'You look stunning.' She can never work out if he's gay and enjoys a gentle flirtation, or if he's straight and his camp demeanour is his killer move, his method of getting women to drop their guard. He could, of course, be bisexual. Either way, he's not her type, but she enjoys his attention. Italian men have a talent for making women feel seen that is sadly deficient in British guys.

'*Ciao*, Rosa,' says Patrizia. She's sleek and impeccably groomed, with an aquiline nose and expensive-looking skin. The dynamic of Rosa's relationship with Patrizia is one that she notices she has with many other women—careful competitiveness underpinned by grudging mutual admiration.

Now, Patrizia gestures down Rosa's outfit with her index finger. 'This is fabulous, no?' she says to Giacomo. 'So chic. I love white for winter.'

'*Si, si*,' he agrees. 'It's perfection. The bag is to die for with this coat and dress.'

'My intern took lots of photos outside, in front of the Annabel's tree,' Rosa says, easing off her coat and taking a seat. 'I'll tag you later and include the shopping link in my Stories, obviously.'

The server appears with a bottle of Dom Perignon and fills Rosa's glass. They toast to Christmas and make small talk about Patrizia's son's first term at Bocconi University and their plans for the new year—they're all going skiing after Christmas.

When their starters arrive, Rosa picks up her phone. 'I've got all this as a PDF to send you, but I thought you'd like to hear some high-level figures.' She reels off numbers—the number of posts she's done for Volare this season and the engagement those posts have had, as well as the sales figures her affiliate platforms tell her she's generated for Volare's products through her Instagram account.

'The engagement on the handbags is much higher than

the luggage,' she says. 'They're more accessibly priced, of course, but it's also easier to have fun with them and showcase them out and about in town.'

'Perhaps, in that case, we should provide you with more of the 'igher priced bags,' Giacomo says. 'If your followers are responding to this product, it makes sense to up-sell them within the same category.'

'We can also offer you more opportunities to travel with the luggage,' says Patrizia. 'It's important that this product is seen as very aspirational, conjuring up the... the vibe of the discerning traveller. We have you scheduled to go to Paris with the luggage the week before Christmas, yes?'

'Yes, the eighteenth,' Rosa says. She's looking forward to it; a night with David in the Peninsula courtesy of Volare, in exchange for selling the Volare dream in the manner they just discussed. 'I've already planned my outfits for the trip.'

Giovanni claps his hands together. 'Fabulous. We are so 'appy to be working with you, Rosa. Most of the big British influencers—I mean, those with followers in the millions—are just trashy. You know? Fake everything'—he gesticulates down his body—'like fake eyelashes, lips, hair, breasts. Even fake asses! We do not want these people with Volare. And their followers—they all live in the council apartments, yes? They cannot afford Volare even if they want to. Nasty, nasty, nasty.' He grimaces and pretends to brush off the lapels of his jacket. He's definitely gay, Rosa decides. Every time he says *Volare*, he positively trills it, shrugging his shoulders in glee. It's endearing and flamboyant, even if he is a raging snob.

'This is why we need you, *amore mio*. You. Have. Class.' He raps on the table with each word. 'You have so much style and beauty, and the rich ladies, they flock to you! This is what we want. We want the ladies of South Kensington and Chelsea, of the Upper East Side, of Palm Springs, of Westchester... we want the ladies who understand good taste and true luxury. And you'—he blows her a kiss —'bring them to us on Instagram. We should do a little trunk show here, no? Hosted by you. Very exclusive, very chic.'

'I'd be delighted.' Rosa basks in the warm glow of Giovanni's acknowledgement of her status. God knows, she's put enough work and sacrifice to get to where she is. Endless primping and preening and dieting and getting up at the crack of dawn to look effortlessly glossy, so she can do a 'spontaneous' Instagram story from her car post school run. She's worked her absolute arse off and it's validating to have Giovanni reflect her status back to her. From her perspective, she's only just left base camp, but she finds it gratifying to know that others see her as being on top of the world.

He's right. Her following is densely populated with wealthy, image-conscious women who value, or even rely on, her style mandates. They're flush with cash and trigger-happy, buying on instinct when they see the looks she puts together. This results in a virtuous circle whereby Rosa is courted by designer brands and high-end platforms such as Net-à-Porter, who are confident she can sell their more premium pieces. It's altogether more fun than trying to flog product for the shitty e-commerce behemoths who are selling £9.99 dresses that make the wearer look like a porn star. She shudders to even think of those brands. The premium end of the market is her turf, and she adores it.

The only fly in the ointment is that Volare's aspirational branding has been accused of concealing some grubby secrets: the ill-treated and underpaid Chinese workers in their Prato factories and the reports that Italian customs officers have seized illegally imported skins of endangered species, destined for bespoke Volare luggage sets. More recent is the accusation by fashion watchdog Diet Prada on Instagram that Volare's Allegra tote bag, allegedly ripped off by a world-famous reality TV star for her collaboration with one of the shitty e-commerce brands, was in fact a publicity stunt. Diet Prada have alleged that Volare paid said star handsomely to come up with a fifty-dollar version of the Allegra and thus put the spotlight on the thousand-dollar original.

Whatever the truth, it's worked. The waiting list for the Allegra is now a year long. Rosa doesn't want to delve too deeply into Volare's underbelly. Giacomo and Patrizia have denied the accusations just as passionately to her as the company has to the press. It's privately owned by a Sicilian billionaire whose business dealings are also rather murky, so the company provides little transparency on its business practices. Rosa benefits handsomely from being Volare's ally. She'd rather keep it that way and focus on promoting Volare's glossy brand than poking around in its dirty little secrets.

4

TUESDAY, 3RD DECEMBER 2019

Emmy stands in the carpark at Esher railway station, overnight bag at her feet, shoulders hunched, trying to disappear inside her parka. This morning she begged off work and went to see Rosa's obstetrician at some swanky clinic in South Kensington. Once the doctor had Emmy on the bed, she inserted what looked like a long dildo, explaining that early scans are carried out transvaginally via an internal camera. She was sweet, but delivered her verdict with brutal efficiency as she pointed to the flashing peanut on the screen.

'You're eight-to-nine weeks along. How long have you known you were pregnant?'

'I just did the test yesterday,' Emmy confessed.

'Well,' she said, 'many women find the first trimester difficult to manage in terms of nausea and fatigue, so you've escaped that, at least. But you need to register with a GP as soon as possible if you're planning on giving birth on the NHS, as you'll be due the 12-week scan after Christmas, depending on their capacity.'

Emmy left the clinic with the certainty of a life growing

inside her and trudged towards Earls Court tube station. The enormity of what lay ahead exhausted her; even registering with the NHS sounded like a total faff. In India, she'd been a whirlwind of efficiency, but she was far less effective at looking after herself. She blamed Rosa and her mother, whose joint helicopter parenting had left her with a sort of learned helplessness. It had been one reason she'd had to escape, find her own feet.

She called Rosa and told her the news.

'God,' Rosa said. 'It's amazing that you've got this far without symptoms. Both my first trimesters were horrific.'

'That's what the doctor said.' Emmy didn't feel lucky, but she supposed she should thank heaven for small mercies.

'How are you feeling about it—are you really sure you want to go ahead with this?'

Emmy attempted to explain to her again that she had no inkling of wanting to give up this baby. She hadn't exactly digested the fact that by summer she'd be a mother, but she was thirty-seven. She'd come back to the UK searching for something, and perhaps this was it. She didn't know if she'd find love ever or in time to get pregnant, so she assumed that life was bringing her this baby because that was meant to be her next step. It was pretty straightforward, from where she stood. She just needed to roll with it. She had a far more accepting—or fatalistic, as Rosa liked to put it—view on the universe than her cynical sister.

'Ok,' said Rosa, exasperation in her voice. 'Well, good for you. But how are you feeling about it all? What's your plan? You're on a zero-hours temp contract right now—you won't get any paid maternity leave beyond statutory, which won't keep you and the baby, believe me.'

'I don't know, Rosa,' Emmy said through gritted teeth. The panic crept up through her body, churning her stomach and tightening her chest. The reality wasn't her and her baby against the world, it was a shitty bedsit somewhere or moving home to her mum's in Hampshire. What a God-awful thought. Her current flat-share wasn't an option.

'You realise what you have to do,' Rosa continued. 'You'll have to tell the father and get some kind of child allowance from him. It's the only option.'

'Rosa, will you get off my back, for fuck's sake? I need some time to process all this—God! I'm aware I need to make a plan, but please don't overwhelm me. This is fucking scary, you know?'

'Sorry, Ems,' said her sister in a softer voice. 'You know you're not alone. You have Mum, and me and David. We'll all help you through this. I hate thinking of you being up in London on your own. Why don't you take the rest of the week off—tell them you've had a family emergency? Come down tonight, after work, and spend a few days here. I have an obscene amount of gorgeous baby stuff that I was gifted for Dolly; it's all in the attic. We can have a look through and start getting you excited about all this. Just—let us take some of the burden off you, for a few days. Let us spoil you.'

~

ROSA PULLS UP with customary promptness a moment later and whisks her home in a luxurious Range Rover. When they pull up outside Rosa's undeniably stunning home, Emmy gasps. It looks like something from a Christmas movie, even from the driveway. Tasteful white fairy lights adorn the trees around the front garden and the apex of the porch. There are a couple of reindeer by the door, again illuminated in white, and they look magical rather than tacky.

'Bloody hell, Rosa,' she says. 'How on earth have you got

your decorations up so early? The garden looks amazing—Dolly must be beside herself.'

'Glad you like them,' Rosa says. 'I'm doing a promotion with Lavender and Sage, a very premium florist in Cobham. They've basically decorated the house and garden for Christmas—everything's fresh. Their team was here all of last Friday and Saturday. Wait till you see inside.'

'Does that mean you get all this for free?' Emmy clambers out of the Range Rover.

'Better,' Rosa says. 'They're paying me. The house is a great showcase for them; they know I'll be doing a fair bit of entertaining over the next month, and I'm contractually obliged to share a certain amount of posts and stories on Instagram. That's why they wanted it all up so early; gives them plenty of time to drum up business.'

Emmy shakes her head. 'You are such a jammy bitch. Unbelievable. Can I be an influencer?'

'It's a lot harder work than it looks and you know it,' says Rosa. 'Come on in. Everyone's dying to see you.'

She opens the front door, which Emmy notices has a beautiful green and white wreath on it, and they head in.

Emmy wants to cry. She feels like a walking cliché—the irresponsible younger daughter who gets knocked up and temporarily escapes the grime of London and her dingy flat-share. The second she crosses the threshold she's transported to a different world, a world of grownups. It's people like Rosa and David who should have kids, not people like her. Creating an aspirational lifestyle is Rosa's forte, and indeed her job. She's also just admitted to having had a team of professional florists decorate her house. But Emmy's not prepared for the effect it will have on her. It's like walking into a Christmas movie; she wants to collapse on the floor and beg them to adopt her and the baby. The gulf between where she and her sister are in life seems unbridgeable.

There's an enormous tree in the square hallway, decorated in white and silver, and the staircase snaking around it boasts garlands of greenery and fairy lights. Huge, creamy candles flicker softly in hurricane lanterns dotted around the hall, and another huge tree twinkles in the living room, beyond the open double doors. The house smells heavenly, of cloves and nutmeg and orange. It's toasty, and Rosa even has choral Christmas music playing softly through the Sonos system. The festoons of what is obviously fresh greenery—pine and eucalyptus—accent Rosa's neutral colour-scheme perfectly. Emmy feels like a creature from another planet.

'God, it's gorgeous,' she sighs, and throws down her bag. 'Can I just live here forever?'

A door opens upstairs and uneven footsteps pound overhead.

'Auntie Emmy!' Her little niece, Dolly, throws herself down the stairs at an alarming rate, hands grabbing at the carefully garlanded banister as Rosa flinches, and launches herself at Emmy, head-butting her exactly where she supposes her unborn child is.

'Hello, Squidge!' She goes to pick Dolly up and remembers she probably shouldn't lift heavy objects, even children. Instead, she crouches down and cups Dolly's deliciously soft cheeks. One of the greatest gifts of being back in the UK has been getting to know her youngest niece, who was born during Emmy's stint in India and whom she only met a handful of times before her return. She really is like a little doll. She dances on the spot now, jigging up and down while delivering a semi-coherent stream of consciousness.

'Dolly, do you need a wee?' asks Rosa, and Dolly freezes as though she's just had a profound revelation.

'Mmm!' she squeaks and scuttles off, her hand glued to her crotch.

Rosa laughs as Emmy gets to her feet. 'She still thinks that holding your wee in is something that requires your hand rather than your pelvic floor.'

'She's heaven,' Emmy says. 'Hi, Tallulah.'

Her other niece has wandered in. She's thirteen and coltish, all gangly limbs and tangled honey-coloured hair. She's wearing a school hoodie and hot pants. To be fair, it is tropical in this house.

'Hi, Emmy!' She hugs her aunt. 'Can I show you my latest dance routine?' She launches into a routine that looks not unlike a lap dance, but which Emmy has to admit is very good. She raises her eyebrows at Rosa, who rolls her eyes in response.

'I'm going to record it properly later and put it on TikTok,' Tallulah announces. 'Did Mom tell you I've gone vegan?'

'Good for you,' Emmy tells her. Rosa rolls her eyes again. Emmy's glad she has a good relationship with Tallulah. She's a great girl, but Emmy wouldn't want to get on her bad side. Rosa, unfortunately, finds herself there regularly.

Dolly is back from the loo, wiping her hands down her t-shirt.

'Auntie Emmy, would you like some dinner? Daddy has maked Thai curry.'

'Made curry,' Rosa corrects her. 'Honestly,' she says to Emmy as they walk through to the kitchen. 'Six grand a term, and that school can't even teach them to speak properly.'

Rosa's husband, David, is at the large marble island in

the centre of the palatial kitchen, tending to a wok on the hob. He puts down the spoon and strides over to Emmy, enfolding her in a warm bear-hug.

'Welcome, Em,' he says in her ear. 'And, um, congratulations?'

'I haven't decided if it's congratulations yet,' she whispers back. 'Still a bit shell-shocked.'

'We're all here for you.' He kisses her on the cheek and releases her. She's extremely fond of David. He's affectionate and good-natured, the polar opposite of her dear sister. Emmy's not sure how he puts up with his wife's constant sniping and put-downs, but he seems to let them roll off his back. He's also seriously attractive, with short black-grey hair and a gym-honed body—he doesn't carry any of that excess weight around his middle that forty-something blokes tend to accumulate. He and Rosa are an undeniably gorgeous couple. She just wishes her sister would give him a break every once in a while.

They sit down to dinner, David and Rosa handing out big bowls of Thai green curry with fluffy white rice. David's made a vegan portion for Tallulah. The kitchen is as tranquil as the rest of the house—a huge white space with copper pendant lamps hanging over the dining table. Here, too, the florists have worked their verdant magic; a plump runner of greenery squats on the wooden table.

'This is so Christmassy,' Emmy sighs. 'I've been trying to get in the mood with Spotify, but the house is like a different universe—it's like I've walked into Narnia.'

'Things are about to get more Christmassy tomorrow, aren't they, sweetpea?' David asks, poking Dolly in the arm.

'Yes!' she shouts through a mouthful of food. 'Tomorrow is my *nativity*! I'm an angel.'

Of course you are, thinks Emmy. Rosa has probably

bribed the school to cast Dolly in an Instagrammable role. Aloud, she says, 'That's amazing! Can I come and watch?'

'Sure,' Rosa says. 'It's right after drop-off—they're having to fit in two class nativities a day. She'll go to school in her costume, and they'll give us a coffee while they get the kids set up. We leave at eight sharp, ok?'

'Got it,' says Emmy. 'I can't believe I get to travel with a real live angel—that's so exciting!' She clasps her hands to her chest and looks heavenward. 'Bring it on, Dolly.'

5

WEDNESDAY, 4TH DECEMBER

Hampton Park school is something else. Emmy hasn't been here before; the carpark is large enough to serve a theme park or an airport. They follow a path around the side of the school buildings; to Emmy's left lie extensive tree-studded grounds, an elevated adventure playground visible through a copse. These are lucky kids.

The school hall, a utilitarian space that smells like all school halls everywhere, has been decorated with numerous strings of white fairy lights adorning the vaulted ceiling and the obligatory climbing apparatus is flattened against the walls. Parents mill about, greeting each other and chatting. There are a lot of dads indulging in mutual back-slapping. From somewhere by the stage comes a jaunty piano arrangement of *Ding Dong, Merrily on High*. Rosa pulls Emmy and David up towards the front of the hall and they find three spare seats in the middle of a row already filled with parents and grandparents.

'Rosa! David—hey guys!' A stunning blonde woman in the next seat greets them in an American accent, her hugs as effusive as her tone. There are lots of seriously glamorous mums here—especially given it's not yet 9am—but this woman is really gorgeous. She's tall and leggy and dressed in a spray-on black shift dress made of sparkly tweed, that comes across as expensive and seductive and don't-fuck-with-me all at once. She looks as though she should be on some glossy American legal drama.

'Stacey, this is my sister Emmy,' Rosa tells her. 'Em is staying with us for a few days. Emmy, this is Stacey—her daughters are great friends with Tallulah and Dolly. Stacey has four kids at the school.'

'Emmy!' Stacey greets her like a long-lost friend, reaching over to hug her hello. It's impossible not to warm to her. She also smells amazing. She beams at Emmy. 'It's so fun to meet you! You guys are so alike!'

Emmy clocks Rosa's frosty look and grins internally. It's true that there's a decent family resemblance, but while Emmy usually leaves her auburn hair to rampage in loose curls down her back, Rosa's is always carefully blow-dried and tonged in immaculate waves. Rosa is always telling her to make more of an effort with her appearance. Today she thinks she looks pretty good, actually, having borrowed a heavenly pale pink cashmere sweater from her sister's obnoxiously well-stocked dressing-room. Stacey, however, is on another level. Somehow it's reassuring to know this goddess is a mother of four—at some point, somewhere down the line, it's possible to emerge from the sleep deprivation and bodily fluids to a life where you can thrive. Right now, that life feels light-years away.

'It's lovely to meet you too,' she tells Stacey, and listens as she and Rosa launch into a complicated conversation about netball fixtures and pickup times and the clash between netball and the swimming gala the following week. David sits between the two women, on his phone, zoned out from their conversation.

The nativity play is gorgeous from start to finish—unintentionally hilarious and extremely moving. Dolly acquits herself beautifully as a tiny angel. Emmy suspects the pregnancy hormones don't help, but her ovaries are exploding. There are some high-energy songs she doesn't know, which the kids appear to shout rather than sing, but a few traditional crowd-pleasers make an appearance, and as the children sing *Silent Night* impressively softly, tears stream down her cheeks.

There's something about seeing dozens of tiny five-and-six-year-olds in nativity costumes that she's hard-wired to respond to. There are the confused-looking shepherds, the lopsided stars, the little guy waving frantically at his parents and the diminutive Joseph who seems more interested in the contents of his nostrils than in his wife and newborn son. Their innocence is so steadfast and so far removed from the morally grimy world she's just escaped at Loeb that it takes her breath away. Presumably this is why people have children—*this* is why she's going ahead with something that, on paper, seems ill-advised at best. It's astonishing to believe that in five or six years' time she'll be sitting in another (less expensive) school, watching her little peanut perform. The promise of this future feels weighty and solemn.

When the short performance has ended, a teacher—the head?—stands up and makes a big fuss about how well they all did, leading an enthusiastic round of applause for the children and their harried-looking class teachers.

Then she says, 'As usual, we're collecting for our chosen charity at the end of every nativity play. You'll see our wonderful Year Five volunteers at the back of the hall as you exit, so please give generously. This year's very worthy charity is Discite—the children have chosen it by ballot. Please welcome Jack Fisher to the stage to say a few words about Discite.'

She stands aside, and a tall, well-built guy bounds up to the stage. He's wearing a chunky, cable-knit jumper and he has thick dark hair which he brushes back with his hand as he grins at the crowd. He's absolutely gorgeous. On the other side of the stage, a little girl dressed as a sheep breaks rank, shouting 'Daddy!' She runs over to him as quickly as she can in the cumbersome costume and he melts, bending and scooping her up in his arms. She wraps herself around him like a koala, and he holds her on his waist with one arm. Emmy's ovaries get their second wind and her stomach does a flip. Jesus, the dads at this school are insanely attractive.

'Thanks so much to Year One—that was an *outstanding* nativity play!' he says in a voice that's cultured but not obnoxiously posh. He talks exaggeratedly, more for the kids' benefit than the parents. 'And a huge thank you from me and everyone at Discite for choosing us as your Christmas charity. We are so excited to have you helping us.

'For those of you who don't know,'—he addresses the parents—'Discite is a non-profit providing educational software via tablets for children in developing countries. So far, we're based in Tanzania, Malawi and the Uttar Pradesh province in northern India.' Emmy sits up straighter. This is her turf; these are her people he is helping.

He continues, 'Discite builds the software. We have a partner company that provides the tablets. And for every £12 we raise, we can send another tablet to a child who can't go to school, or whose teachers don't turn up for school.'

He turns to the children again. 'Can you imagine what

would happen if your teacher didn't turn up one day? It would be chaos!'

They giggle delightedly and squirm.

'These tablets fill a giant hole in the educational needs of developing nations,' he tells the room. 'We work with a network of NGOs, or non-governmental organisations, to get them into the hands of the children who need them the most. But you haven't come here to hear me talk, so please take a look at our website if you'd like further information. Thank you all.'

He raises his hand in an Obama-like manner; it's very sexy. Then he puts down his little sheep and gives her a smacker on the cheek, before she trots off. He bounds back down the steps and heads to his seat.

Emmy sighs and leans in towards Rosa next to her.

'I think I've just come,' she murmurs.

Rosa presses her lips together, her shoulders shaking with laughter.

'Keep that information to yourself,' she whispers back. 'Jack is Stacey's ex-husband.'

6

WEDNESDAY, 4TH DECEMBER

As the parents stream out of the hall, Rosa experiences an unfamiliar glow of wellbeing. The nativity play has centred her, temporarily removing her from what she will only admit to herself is the toxic world of influencers. When she sat in that hall and closed her eyes and let the sound of children's voices fill her heart, the exhausting outer world faded away for a moment. Even Emmy's crass comment about Jack amused her, though lord knows, she'll have to keep her away from him—the ink is barely dry on his and Stacey's divorce papers. It can't even have been a year since it all went through. Stacey is chatting happily away to Emmy behind her.

She puts an unusually affectionate hand on David's arm. 'Put some cash in the charity bucket, will you darling?' she murmurs, and drifts onwards in the seas of parents as he wrestles with his wallet. Dolly looked positively angelic, and she's ecstatic with the snaps she got of her this morning, standing in her costume in front of the living room Christmas tree, the florist tagged in the shots. Tallulah deigned to take one of Rosa and Dolly together—she's far better than David at taking photos—and it's a great shot, Rosa carefully coordinated in a winter-white cowl-neck, skinny jeans and her stiletto booties. Her fingers are itching to pull out her phone and see how many likes and comments the post has garnered so far. Mummy-and-Dolly shots always do well.

As the throng of parents moves painfully in the carpark's direction, the deputy head, Mr Norton, shoots forward and touches Rosa on the arm.

'Mrs Hamilton,' he says, eyes darting in alarm. 'Do you have a second? And Ms Fisher? It's about Tallulah and Martha.'

THEY SIT with Mr Norton waiting for the head teacher, Miss Quentin, to make her way back from the nativity. Rosa has asked Emmy to wait in the car, and David sits beside her, shifting in his seat. On her other side sit Stacey and Jack—Stacey grabbed Jack from the hall after Mr Norton's summons.

Miss Quentin shuffles into her office and shuts the door firmly. Her posture is so terrible that it makes Rosa instantly sit up straighter.

'I'm sorry to keep you waiting. I'm afraid it's come to my attention this morning that both Martha and Tallulah have posted videos to their TikTok accounts that they recorded on school premises, in school uniform.'

Rosa bows her head and mutters *shit* under her breath. Jack groans.

'This is a serious breach of school rules,' Miss Quentin continues. 'The Year Sevens had a session on our social media policy only a couple of weeks ago. They are all aware that the school strictly prohibits publishing any footage of the school or of themselves in uniform.'

'How do you know they've done this?' Stacey asks. 'Martha's TikTok account is private—we're very careful about vetting who follows her. So how can you have access to their posts?'

Miss Quentin colours. 'A parent came in with her daughter's phone first thing this morning and showed me. I can't say who it was, but her daughter follows both of your daughters—the parent showed me the same video on both feeds. There are five girls in the video, but Martha and Tallulah are the only ones who've posted it.'

'Is the video still up?' David asks.

'It is. I haven't spoken to the girls yet—I wanted to brief you first. I'll pull them out of class now and have them show you.' She pauses. 'I'm afraid I have no choice but to suspend both your daughters until end of day tomorrow.'

They all react, heads snapping up, palms out.

'Jesus!' Stacey says. 'Really, Miss Quentin? Isn't that an overreaction? It's a video. Let them pull it down and apologise. Give them a detention if you need to. But a suspension is ridiculous.'

'I'm afraid I have to insist.' Miss Quentin folds her arms. 'Wait till you see the video. It's shocking. The song playing in the background has explicit lyrics and the dancing—well, the dancing is scandalous. Very provocative. The girls need to understand the grave consequences of an act like this. Not only does footage like this do great harm to the school's reputation, but far more importantly, there are serious safeguarding issues at stake. We, and you, cannot protect our boys and girls if they are putting themselves at risk by circulating inappropriate content, no matter how secure you believe their accounts to be. This is an extremely serious infringement; we have to show a zero-tolerance policy for violations of this nature. Please excuse me while I fetch your daughters.'

She leaves the room. Stacey swivels in her chair. 'Can you believe this fucking mess?' she asks. 'What the fuck is wrong with our children? How can they be so goddamn stupid?'

Jack puts a hand on her shoulder, but she shrugs him off.

'I think that's what it is—stupidity,' says David. 'They're not bad kids; they just don't think. This is all just a game to them.'

'Well, we have to make them see that it's real,' Rosa says. 'They are so bloody lucky to be at this school; they have to start caring more about the community they're in and about the consequences of their actions on that community. Can we agree a punishment for them both, before we see them?'

'No devices for a month,' Jack suggests. 'They can watch TV, but no phones or iPads; no creating or consuming content other than good old Netflix.'

'Ugh,' Rosa groans. 'Agreed. It's going to be more painful for us than for them, but we really need to take a firm stance.'

'We need to have a good chat with them, too,' David says. 'Make them understand that their actions have consequences. One: this kind of behaviour reflects so badly on their teachers, who work so hard for them, and on the entire school. Two: I think we need to have the paedophile chat with Tallulah again.'

'Agreed,' Stacey says. 'But they're going to hate us so much for taking their phones away that I'm not sure they'll listen.' She turns to Jack. 'I'm supposed to be on my way into town already. Can you take her home with you? She was supposed to be boarding tonight, too. God, these children are so freaking painful.'

'It's fine,' he says. 'She can stay with me today and tomorrow. I'll put her to work in the office.'

A few minutes later, Miss Quentin returns with both girls. They amble in behind her, slouching under the weight of their bags and, hopefully, their shame. They eye their parents warily. Stacey stands up, crossing her arms, but Miss Quentin stops her before she can say anything.

'I think the first thing to do is to show your parents the video, so they know what's going on here.'

'I deleted it,' Tallulah says, squaring her shoulders. Of course she did; she would have destroyed the evidence at the first whiff of trouble.

'Martha?' Miss Quentin raises her eyebrows.

Martha sighs and pulls her bag off her shoulder, unzipping the front pocket. She's inherited her parents' good looks; she's tall and leggy, with a cloud of dark hair and huge green eyes like Jack's. She's a sweet girl; she adores and looks up to Tallulah. Rosa strongly suspects her own darling daughter to be the ringleader in this situation.

Martha pulls up the offending video and hands it to Miss Quentin, who hits play and turns the phone around. The parents lean forward in unison.

It's horrific—a tightly choreographed, and impressively well-edited, dance video in which the five of them gyrate and twerk to the music in full school uniform, the Hampton Park crest clearly visible on their sweaters. They've hitched up their skirts, and some rap song that Rosa has never heard blares out of the phone. She can't discern much of it, but suddenly the singer shouts *suck my dick* and everyone in the room flinches. She shoots a glance at the girls. They're frozen; seeing the video through their parents' eyes seems to be driving home the implications of what they've done.

Jack puts his hand up as if to shield his eyes. 'We've seen enough, thanks.'

'Right.' Miss Quentin hands Martha's phone to Stacey. 'Martha and Tallulah, you are suspended until end of day tomorrow. You may come into school as normal on Thursday. You'll be expected to complete tomorrow's homework assignments as usual; your teachers will email them to you. You can go with your parents now.'

Both girls start sobbing, alive to the shit-show that likely awaits them when their parents get their hands on them. Too right, Rosa thinks grimly. David goes to put his arm around Tallulah and Rosa wants to hit him with her weighty Volare handbag. She limits herself to a rap on his arm and a quick shake of her head.

'Let's get out of here,' she says tersely. 'Thank you, Miss Quentin. We're very sorry for the trouble that Tallulah has caused.'

THEY WALK in stony silence to the car. Rosa has already lost an unscheduled half an hour out of her day. She needs to get home and finish that update for Volare. In the car, she gives Emmy a one-line brief of what's happened. She thinks she sees a flicker of amusement cross her sister's face, but at least Emmy's smart enough not to voice any hilarity she feels. Instead, she grimaces and says, 'Oh dear.'

David pulls out of the school gates and Rosa lets rip.

'How could you be so stupid? Honestly, Tallulah, do you have any brain cells in there?'

In the back, Tallulah slides further down into her seat, arms crossed, looking pointedly out of the window.

'David.' Rosa needs his support here, needs a united show of parental wrath. He sighs as he navigates a right-turn.

'Tallulah,' he says, his tone softer than Rosa's. 'Just help us understand your thought process. We know you're not stupid;'—this with a disapproving glance at Rosa—'we're just trying to get to the bottom of how something like this could happen.'

'You're overthinking it,' Tallulah says sulkily. This is one of her newer comebacks. 'We were in extra early yesterday morning and I was teaching the others the dance routine I'd made up. Once they'd got the hang of it, Loralie said we should video it on my phone. I edited it during break and it was so cool that Martha and I decided to upload it last night when we got home.'

'And what about the rules?' asks Rosa, turning around in her seat as far as she can. 'What about the fact that you're in full school uniform, on school property, doing a really quite inappropriate dance routine to an explicit song?'

'There are so many rules,' Tallulah says, 'and we never know which ones they actually mean. Like, we're supposed to put our phones in our lockers during lessons, but Mr Turner never actually makes us.'

'Rules are there for a reason,' David says. 'To keep everyone safe.'

'That's such a load of bullshit.' Tallulah swings dramatically around to face the window again. 'You guys are such hypocrites.'

'Tallulah,' Rose says in what she hopes is a scarily quiet voice. 'We've talked about using language like that before. It's not acceptable. And we are not hypocrites.'

'You are. You're always telling me not to blindly accept rules without questioning whether they're sensible. And we weren't doing any harm, so we figured, what's the problem?'

'You could have done harm,' Rosa says through gritted teeth, 'on so many levels. I appreciate what you're saying about rules. But the rules at school are specifically created to keep you safe. You may think you're grown-up, dancing like that to a song like that, but let me tell you, there are a lot of people out there who would like very much to see twelve-and-thirteen-year-old girls dancing like that in school uniform, and they'd like it so much that they'd pull up to your school in a white van—the school whose front door you've so helpfully directed them to by wearing your uniform—and they'd lie in wait for you girls to come out and then they'd drag you off in their van and sell you on the dark web and we'd never see you again.'

Tallulah bursts into tears as David raises his hand in protest. 'Rosa—Jesus, rein it in a notch.'

'Stop, Mum!' Tallulah shouts. 'You're scaring me! Why are you being so mean?!'

'I want to scare you,' Rosa says. 'I want to shock you into understanding why rules that you think are tiresome and irrelevant are in place. They are there to *safeguard you* until you grow up enough to be able to look after yourself. This is not a game, ok, Tallulah? Daddy and I are very uncomfortable with TikTok in general. You are on thin ice with that app, young lady. As it is, we've decided, as have Martha's parents, that you've lost all your phone privileges for the next month. You can watch TV; that's about it. You can have it back on New Year's Day, and you're getting away lightly, believe me.'

'No!' Tallulah screams as if Rosa has just ripped off a

limb, and David jumps at the wheel, jerking the car. Emmy's in the other back seat, looking like she wants to disappear.

'Mum, Dad, you can't do that! Ohmigod I will *die* if I can't have my phone. I'm sorry I'm sorry I'm sorry; I won't do it again, I promise!' She buries her head in her hands and weeps dramatically. Rosa and David exchange a glance.

'It's not up for discussion,' Rosa says. 'Martha's losing her phone too, so you can be social outcasts together. Actions have consequences; remember that, Tallulah.'

7

WEDNESDAY, 4TH DECEMBER

Tallulah is in her room and she is *bored*. Obviously, she took Dolly's iPad as soon as she got home, but it's so lame; the only YouTube it has on it is the kids' one and it has no internet browsers. She can't download any new apps on it without Apple asking her parents' permission. She's been home for three hours now and Mom brought her up a sandwich earlier, but now she has *nothing* to do. Mom says when she's ready to do her schoolwork she can come down and do it on the big iMac in the living room so they can monitor her. They've taken away her laptop, her iPad, *and* her phone.

She's started calling her mother *Mom* recently instead of *Mum*; Martha does it because Stacey is American, and it sounds so much cooler. Stacey is a million times cooler than her mom anyway, hands down. She'll definitely get mad with Martha about getting suspended, but generally she's pretty relaxed. It's such a waste because Martha is a lot less brave than Tallulah when it comes to trying new things that might get her into trouble. She can't help it; she's usually really well behaved. Tallulah wishes they could swap moms. Then Tallulah could have a cool mom who let her do what she wanted and who was just really glamorous, and her own mom would probably prefer Martha anyway.

Everyone at school says Tallulah's mom is so glamorous, and it's true that her clothes are amazing. She gets so many free things it's just rude. Tallulah and Dolly get free things too, but usually they're stupid, like these matchy-matchy dresses that Dolly loves, but Tallulah thinks are lame. She always refuses to wear them. Then her mom gets really angry and shouts at her and says they all have to wear them because the brands who sent them will be upset if they don't.

She's noticed that over the past few months her mom has stopped asking her to wear things. Mainly she just dresses Dolly up and the two of them pose together - Mom calls them *Mummy and Dolly* shots. Hashtag-Mummy-and-Dolly. Ugh. Dolly's too small to find it lame and she's so pretty that Mom probably prefers to take photos with her anyway—she's more Instagrammable, as mom would say. She looks like an adorable little doll when Mom dresses her up, whereas Tallulah's hair is frizzy and has more ginger in it than Dolly's. Also, her nose seems to grow more quickly than the rest of her. It's, like, spreading across her face like it's swollen. Her nose probably worries her more than anything else. She's reassured by the fact that Dua Lipa has quite a prominent nose, but Dua Lipa also has incredibly strong eyebrows and amazing, plump lips so she can totally carry it off. It's so unfair that Tallulah's *nose* is growing and not her boobs. She's completely flat-chested, and she hasn't even got her period yet, even though she's already thirteen. It's so mortifying.

She scrolls through Dolly's apps. There are loads of spelling and times table apps that Mom and Dad downloaded for her, loads of princess dress-up ones and cake-baking games. Ugh. They're so *lame*. This is all Mom's fault. She can tell, just by the way her parents were behaving in the car on the way home, that her mom was madder than her dad. She was definitely the ringleader. If she hadn't started yelling and prodding Dad to say something, Tallulah reckons he would have just had a quiet word with her and given her a hug when they got home and told her that everything was going to be ok.

She loves her dad; she's just not sure why he married such a total bitch. That's the problem, really—Mom's a bitch. She's so beautiful and she's surrounded by all these amazing things that she gets gifted, and yet she never seems happy. All she does is complain and nag—she nags Dad as much as she nags Tallulah. And all she cares about is who's going to see her at the school gates in her new booties, and how many likes she has on Instagram. It's so lame. She needs to get a life and be more like Stacey or Emmy who, Tallulah has to admit, is extremely cool. Emmy probably doesn't care what anyone thinks of her; she probably doesn't even have an Instagram account.

Mom isn't just hypocritical about rules; she's hypocritical about money. She's always telling them not to talk about money and to be grateful for their 'blessings', but she's obsessed by it! Tallulah's heard her talking to Dad about how much money other parents make or how much their houses are worth. She gets really cross when people get a new car or move to a new house that might be bigger than theirs. She wants everyone to think she's rich and successful, but Tallulah knows there's no way they're as rich as people like Martha's parents. Martha's so lucky; her mom bought a new house that has a pool, and now *both* her houses have pools. *And* her dad has stables with three ponies and two horses. If Tallulah could have some ponies and horses and a dog like Martha to pet and talk to when she got sad, she'd probably never get sad in the first place.

Mom is so happy when people admire her. She went to this Dior thing the other day and apparently it was very *exclusive*—she didn't shut up about it all day. Thank God Emmy's come to stay; she's the only girl in this house who's normal.

Mom's biggest problem is that her whole life seems to be on her phone, and sometimes it's like she and Dad and Dolly are invisible. A small part of Tallulah gets this—she knows the warm glow of pleasure she feels when she gets lots of likes on TikTok. It's like it's *proof* that she's popular. But Mom chose to have a family, and it's not clear why she bothered. Except to have little props in her photo shoots.

There's a company called Volare that she's been working with. Their bags are amazing but Tallulah saw Diet Prada on Instagram talking about them importing skins from endangered species just to make handbags for rich people. It makes her blood boil whenever she thinks about it. Animals are far nicer than people, and she doesn't get why having a dead part of an animal on your body makes you cool. It doesn't. It's revolting (Tallulah no longer wears leather shoes). And she's also read about how the farmers of these animals treat the animals. They nail snakes to trees and *skin them alive*. They take hours to die. The entire world is still obsessed with Jesus getting crucified two thousand years ago, and no one seems to care that they're doing the same thing to snakes. She's tried to have a conversation with her mom about this, but Mom just tells her that it's very sweet that she feels so strongly, but that she's misinformed.

It's infuriating. Mom can't see what's in front of her own eyes, or she just doesn't care because all she cares about is being rich and glamorous and hitting six million followers on Instagram and likes, likes, likes. She's so fucked up. She needs to be taught a lesson.

8

WEDNESDAY, 4TH DECEMBER

Jack opens a bottle of claret, the cork popping softly as he releases it. He sniffs the cork, tilts the decanter and steadily pours the wine in, mesmerised by the thin film of liquid wrapping itself around the entirety of the vessel.

Today has been more eventful than he bargained on, thrown off course by Martha's TikTok stunt. He sent her up to her room to do some reading for a couple of hours, and after lunch they went across the courtyard to the office where he got his PA to delegate some basic data-entry to her. The PA, like many on the team, helps him with both Discite and his main focus, his software company AscenSoar.

Mia is hosting a playdate with her friend Dolly, though thankfully the nanny, Carlotta, is supervising that. At least Pitt and Augie are weekly boarders this year, effectively halving the number of kids he, Stacey and Carlotta need to juggle Monday to Friday. They've settled in well; it's far less heart-rending to send twins off together to school than a single child.

The buzzer for the main gate goes. That'll be Rosa,

coming to get Dolly. He hits it, before swirling the decanter around and pouring some wine into an oversized glass. He deserves this drink today. Thanks to Carlotta he got an infra-red sauna session in this afternoon, followed by a skin-tingling few minutes in his ice-bath. He's rehydrated, and the wine is a welcome next step. He takes his glass through to the hallway, his ancient golden lab, Marge, padding stiffly beside him, and opens the heavy front door. A woman who definitely isn't Rosa stands in front of him.

She's beautiful. An abundance of copper-coloured waves pour over a dishevelled parka, and her skin is flawless. He takes in her delicate bone-structure and a rosy-red, slightly crooked mouth. The security light above the door burnishes her hair and casts shadows from her eyelashes across her cheeks. As he's reacting, her face breaks into a delighted smile and two adorable dimples appear.

'Oh!' she exclaims. 'Hi!'

He's as gratified by the warmth of her greeting as he is confused, and he feels his face stretching into a smile to match hers as he searches her face. She looks familiar, but he would definitely have remembered meeting her.

'Have we met?' he asks, grinning. Marge walks heavily outside and leans her thick body against her.

'Sorry!' She extends her hand, and he shakes it. 'I'm Emmy, Rosa's sister. I saw you speak at the nativity this morning; that's how I recognised you.' She bends to stroke Marge. 'Hello, you.'

Marge, although blind, lifts her cloudy eyes in greeting.

That's it. This woman reminds him of Rosa, although whatever underlying features they have in common, the gods have worked some serious alchemy on her.

'Please, come in,' he says, standing back.

She takes in the hallway. 'This is incredible,' she says, tilting her neck right back.

'Thank you.' He rubs his stubble. 'I assume you're here to pick up Dolly?'

'Yes,' she says. 'Rosa's a bit... preoccupied. David was going to do pickup, but he had to jump on a conference call so I thought I'd make myself useful.'

'Has Rosa calmed down yet? Is Tallulah in one piece?' he asks, leading her through to the kitchen. At her puzzled look he clarifies, 'My daughter Martha was Tallulah's co-conspirator, I'm afraid. For TikTok-gate. She's suspended too; she's upstairs, licking her wounds.'

'Ah, I see.' She grins. 'It was an awkward car journey home from the nativity. Rosa went nuclear.'

'Stacey too. That's my ex.'

'I met Stacey.' She squirms. 'We sat with her at the nativity. She seems lovely.'

He's amused by her discomfort. 'She's highly entertaining, that's for sure. Now, I'm afraid the girls may be another quarter of an hour. They've been riding.'

'Riding?' She peers out at the blackness beyond the windows. 'Isn't it a bit dark?'

'We have an arena—it's more of an old barn with a sawdust floor, but it works well for winter. They should be just finishing up, but they need to untack the ponies and wash them down—it's part of the deal. Our nanny will bring them back to the house when they're done. Can I tempt you with a glass of wine? Cup of tea?'

He waves his glass; he finds he's pleased that the girls aren't back yet and he can enjoy Emmy's looks and company for a little longer. The more he studies her, the less like Rosa she seems. Their vibes are totally different.

'No wine for me, I'm afraid,' she says. 'I'm driving. But a

herbal tea would be lovely, thank you.'

'Coming up.' He opens a drawer full of various teas and infusions. 'Take your pick.' He fills a mug from the boiling water tap on the island. 'Let's go through to the living room. It's warmer in there.'

He leads the way; the fire has caught properly now, and a welcome mass of flames streams up the chimney. Despite its size, the room feels wonderfully cosy.

'Here you go.' He sets her mug on the coffee table and gestures to one end of the enormous sofa facing the fire, plonking himself down towards the other end. Marge follows them in and lowers herself down by Emmy's feet.

Emmy sits down, still looking around. 'I honestly think you've designed my dream home,' she says. 'It's extraordinary.'

'Thank you.' Her approval is like a warm blanket, but he's aware of feeling vaguely guilty. After all, The Lodge, despite its unassuming name, is a pretty lavish display of wealth. 'It's been a labour of love,' he goes on. 'But I'm not sure we'd win any points for originality. We went to Soho Farmhouse a few years ago and loved it so much that we commissioned some people who'd worked on that project to come and create something similar here.' He must stop saying *we*. Stacey walked out; this is his now.

'Well, I have no idea what Soho Farmhouse is,' she says. 'So it looks thoroughly original to me. You're so lucky to live here.' She wriggles out of her coat and he tries not to look at her slim, sweater-clad figure underneath. She's wearing the softest-looking jumper in palest pink.

'Are you visiting Rosa and David?' he asks.

She looks down at her mug and frowns. He wonders if it's remotely acceptable to ask his ex-wife's friend's sister out for a drink.

'I've just come down from London for a couple of days,' she says. 'For the rest of the week, actually. I didn't realise I'd make the nativity, so it was a happy coincidence. It was so adorable.'

'It was, wasn't it?' He smiles at the memory of Mia the sheep ambushing him on stage. 'Those things are like therapy.'

'I was interested to hear about your charity,' she says, looking straight at him. He can see now that her eyes are grey, the whites remarkably white and clear. 'I've only been back in London a few months,' she continues. 'I spent six years in India before that. So your cause is close to my heart.'

Something inside him thrills. He knew it—he could feel some kind of commonality with her.

'Seriously?' He leans forward. 'What a small world. What were you doing out there—where were you?'

She pulls the cuffs of her jumper down over her long, slender fingers and picks up her mug again, cupping it greedily. He feels irrationally jealous of the mug.

'I worked for a few NGOs,' she says. 'Mainly in Uttar Pradesh, though I moved around. I started in Delhi, and I spent the past couple of years in Kanpur. Well, I was based at our hub in Kanpur in theory, but I spent a lot of time travelling around the area; the more remote the village, the better.'

He stares. 'Doing aid work?'

'Yes. Mainly logistics and project management. The last NGO I worked for was a partner of The Gates Foundation, and I ended up in a liaison role, working with the foundation on allocating funds to the right projects, analysing success rates—stuff like that.'

'But you were out in the field?'

'Yep. This NGO's focus is family planning and maternal health, so quite a wide remit. There were plenty of spreadsheets, but we also spent a lot of time with women in the villages, especially in the more remote ones where sex work is one of the few options available to them, given the amount of truckers that pass through.'

'Jesus,' he says. 'That's intense.'

She nods in affirmation and speaks quietly. 'It's a very... complex situation out there. Culturally, I mean. It's not just a case of handing out contraception. There's such an ingrained culture of violence; these women still have so little status and respect. That's where the real work lies. And change has been slow. Anyway.'

She looks up at him, and her face brightens. 'That's why I was interested to hear about your non-profit,' she continues. 'So many of the women just want to talk about their kids when we meet with them—all they care about is giving their children an education, breaking the cycle. But I know how hard it must be for you to implement; it's such a decentralised mess.'

He's been studying her as she speaks; God only knows what horrors she's seen out there. And yet, she's a breath of fresh air. She's not tainted by that entitled materialism that everyone else he crosses paths with these days is. It's hard to place her, and yet the more she says, the more he catches a glimpse of what has formed her. He's undertaken a couple of trips to both India and Africa to get Discite off the ground, but his experiences have barely scratched the surface, whereas hers are part of her fabric.

'To be honest,' he says, 'it's a fucking nightmare, logistically speaking.'

She laughs, and he feels brave enough to ask, 'So, what brought you back here?'

Her face clouds over. 'Some things happened, and I couldn't take it anymore. I was too angry, and felt too helpless, so I bailed. I'm not proud of myself.'

'Nonsense,' he says. 'You stuck it out for six years and gave up a big chunk of your life to serving others—that's a damn sight more than most people round here. It's an incredible sacrifice.'

She shrugs. 'I did it for selfish reasons. I loved it. Mum and Rosa thought it was selfish too—that I turned my back on my family, and spent so many years so far away from them. But I would have suffocated if I'd stayed here.'

He knew the feeling. 'And so what are you doing in London? Still NGO work?'

'No, actually, I've sold my soul. I was so short of cash when I got back that I got a job temping at Loeb, the investment bank? The money's good, but things are a bit complicated there at the moment, so I'm trying to work out what to do. I'm not sure coming back to London was the right move for me; I feel completely lost. That's why I'm down here, really. I needed some headspace. I have a lot of thinking to do.'

She flashes him a shy smile and he blinks slowly, then holds her gaze. In that moment, he makes a decision. He's had a couple of very short-lived flings since the divorce, but Emmy is the first woman he's met who's genuinely piqued his interest. He's surprised by the strength of his reaction to her: they've been talking for ten minutes, and he'd really like to just pull her down onto the rug with him, dogs and small children be damned. It's not merely a physical thing; something deep inside him, the same part of him that's the driving force behind Discite, is drawn to her.

On the other hand, that same part of him—his soul, presumably, if he still has one—has latched onto Emmy's experience and is busy telling him that her arrival here is serendipity in motion. He thinks of the gulf that lies between the immense potential of their software, which he knows is world class, and the limited inroads they've made on the ground so far. The uptake in Tanzania has been encouraging, less so in Malawi, but in India it's still a total shit-show. Adoption rates are patchy, a frustrating proportion of the tablets they've gifted haven't even been activated yet, and their communication with the NGOs responsible for implementing them on the ground leaves a lot to be desired. Perhaps the universe has sent her here tonight to plug the gaping hole in this great white hope he has for the future of education. If that's the case, he needs to stop thinking with his dick and seize the opportunity in front of him.

'I'm not sure you're going to get much headspace around here,' he says carefully, 'but if you're at a bit of a crossroads, then here's a provocative question for you: would you consider helping us out?'

Her jaw practically hits the floor. 'A job, you mean?'

'Yes, basically. Well, a bit of consulting, at least. We're a software company—that's my background. Our software is brilliant. Where we're less strong is on the implementation side. We decided right at the start to stick with our strengths and focus on the software, so we outsource the distribution to NGO partners. But we haven't had anyone managing those relationships for a couple of months and it's a mess—no proper communication or accountability from the NGOs, we've got tablets going AWOL... our hardware partner is livid about it. And we can't have any kind of real impact if we don't nail the distribution part of the equation. We definitely need someone, for a few months at least, to build these relationships and tighten up our implementation strategy.'

'I don't know what to say...' She puts down the mug and strokes Marge, who rolls over, paws in the air. 'Would it be based here? Not in India?'

'Yes, here, of course,' he says. 'The offices for both my software company and Discite are right across the courtyard there. I suspect the pay won't be anywhere near as good as what Loeb can offer you, but we can help with accommodation if that's any use—we've got a couple of spare flats in the complex here. Unless you enjoy living in the Rosa-Tallulah crossfire.' He shoots her a grin. 'I realise this is very over-the-top, and you just came in to pick up Dolly. Sorry for coming on strong. But it's uncanny, you walking in here with the exact experience we need. I've been tearing my hair out over it all. I have no idea what your commitments are in London, though.'

'Let me see.' She counts on her fingers. 'A zero-hour contract at Loeb, a messy personal situation there which I won't go into, and a box-room in a friend's flat in Lewisham, currently. So as you can see, it would be hard to tempt me away.'

Her face breaks into the most beautiful smile, and his heart constricts. *Think of the marginalised children of India*, he tells himself. *Having someone to advocate for them is far more important than where your next date's coming from.*

'Why don't you come in tomorrow morning, if you're free, and you can see the set-up?' he suggests. You can meet the team and have a play with the product. Thursday mornings are team yoga and breakfast at eight-thirty if you're game?'

'How very Millennial of you,' she says. 'I'd love to.'

9

WEDNESDAY, 4TH DECEMBER

Emmy floats back to Rosa's house. Granted, the Range Rover practically drives itself. The past few days she's been wiped out by this time in the evening, but tonight her energy levels are a match for Dolly, who's high as a kite after her riding lesson. On the short drive home Dolly delivers an impressive and high-pitched monologue about her naughty pony, Merlin.

When they get back, Emmy sashays into the kitchen where Rosa is chopping broccoli while David unloads the dishwasher. Tallulah has presumably been banished to her room.

Rosa looks up. 'You were gone a while—did you find it ok?'

'I've been offered a job,' Emmy announces.

'You already have a job.'

'Well, a temping job, yes, but...'

'Don't tell me.' Rosa puts down the knife. 'Jack?'

'Yes.' She feels herself blush and curses inwardly.

'Really. Jesus, you're a fast worker. So,'—Rosa looks to

check Dolly's left the room—'you don't want to get in his pants anymore?'

'Rosa!' Emmy exclaims, looking over at David, who sniggers and puts his hands up as if to say *don't mind me*. 'He's ridiculously attractive, but if he's going to be my boss, then of course I wouldn't go there.'

Both Rosa and David guffaw, and David slaps the counter.

'You're good value; I'll give you that, Em,' he says.

'What?' Emmy asks.

Rosa points at her still-flat belly.

'Who knocked you up? Your boss, wasn't it?'

'That's different,' Emmy argues. 'It's a massive firm, and I had absolutely nothing to do with him at work. He was just a random colleague... who happened to run the trading floor. But if I'm going to work for Jack, then of course nothing's going to happen.' *Even if I want it to.*

'So, what's this job then?' David asks.

'I'm going in tomorrow morning to find out more,' she says. 'He just had the idea while I was there. Apparently, they depend on NGOs on the ground to get the tablets rolled out, and they're having a lot of trouble with their NGO relationships in India. We were talking about my experiences out there and he asked if I'd be interested in helping them out, getting proper distribution processes established.'

'Do you think you're qualified to do that?' asks Rosa.

'Should be. I'll know more tomorrow. I was on the other side when I was out there, but a lot of my job was liaising with The Gates Foundation, so I can certainly put myself in the NGOs' shoes. He's even offered me digs on the premises.' She winks at Rosa.

'God, you are so jammy,' Rosa says. 'And what about the small matter of...?' She gestures at Emmy's belly again.

'I haven't mentioned it. Don't look at me like that! I'm not even nine weeks gone. It sounds like this gig is more of a temporary thing, anyway; he wants someone to get the relationships up and running. I'll declare it, obviously, when I've had my twelve-week scan.'

'Ok,' says Rosa, raising her eyebrows. 'If you say so.'

'His house is amazing, isn't it? It's like a hotel; I couldn't believe it. And the fact that they have an indoor arena! It's like another planet, being down here.'

'It's a far cry from India, that's for sure,' says David, taking a sip of wine and pouring a glass for Rosa.

'The house is incredible,' Rosa says. 'They used to throw the most amazing parties there—I miss their Christmas party. It was strange not having it last year.'

'What happened between them?' Emmy asks. 'They must have made an attractive couple; Stacey's stunning.'

'She really is.' Rosa cradles her wine glass. 'She just got —bored, I guess. They'd been together since their early twenties. They've got Martha and Mia, and twin boys in Year Six called Pitt and Augie. The boys are weekly boarders at Hampton Park. Also, Stacey's extremely intelligent—what does she do exactly, David?'

'She founded a FinTech company—something to do with risk management for asset managers,' David says. 'She was in hedge funds for years, but she and Jack met at Oxford, I believe. She was there on a Rhodes scholarship—she's a seriously impressive woman.'

Super high-achieving, and absolutely gorgeous, Emmy thinks with a pang.

'So, she got bored?' she asks, to get the conversation back to Jack.

'Apparently so,' Rosa says. 'Jack didn't see it coming; none of us did. They seemed very much the golden couple. But she told me she just felt as though she was being buried alive and she needed a taste of freedom. So she walked out —told him she didn't want to be married anymore.'

'Jack behaved very reasonably, in my view,' David says. 'He was devastated. But he didn't put up a fight and the whole divorce went through quickly—it must be over a year since they split up.'

'And he kept the family home?'

'Well, his businesses are based in the grounds,' David pointed out. 'And Stacey said she wanted a fresh start and, quote, a *sexier* home.' He makes a face.

'David's opinion of Stacey has plummeted since it happened.' Rosa shoots him a look. 'But to her credit, they seem to have kept a good relationship and they juggle the kids well. She's quite the woman about town now; she's always full of hysterical stories about the guys she's dating. I admire her, in a way. She was brave enough to recognise what she wanted in life and she went for it.'

EMMY LIES in the bath after dinner. Rosa's tub is amazing; she's run an enormous bubble bath for Emmy and lit candles all around the room. Emmy feels like she's in the womb. Her sister can be so cutting and prickly, but her thoughtful actions often speak louder than her words.

She thinks about Jack. She nearly fell over when he answered the door; David hadn't mentioned whose house she'd be picking Dolly up from. She knows she made a tit of herself, beaming at him when she saw him, but she couldn't help it. He was so gorgeous it was ridiculous. And that house! It was like a dream come true. It was very attractive, watching him saunter around his beautiful home, fishbowl wineglass in hand. To be fair, he would look attractive in any context. What on earth was Stacey thinking, walking away from him? Didn't she realise she'd hit the jackpot?

She's fairly confident she wasn't the only one this evening who felt a connection. While Jack was charming and hospitable, there was something else there on that sofa—an intimacy—despite the fact that she'd rocked up just minutes earlier. She caught him looking at her in a way that went beyond mere hospitality. She's seen that look in men's eyes over the years and she suspects she was looking at Jack in exactly the same way. But she can't deny that the chances of her experiences having been such a perfect match for this charity's needs were tiny, and she tells herself she's glad he chose to follow up on the professional, rather than the romantic, potential between them.

The excitement of seeing him, and of potentially getting stuck into such a well-suited opportunity with Discite, has conveniently distracted her from her inconvenient pregnancy. She's constantly aware that a tiny, strawberry-sized baby is suspended deep inside of her, but it's a passive knowing rather than an active consciousness. She can see herself forging ahead with this non-profit work over the coming months, but she has to keep reminding herself that she'll be following a very different path in tandem—the path to motherhood. Maybe she can just go with the flow. That's one good thing about pregnancy; aside from eliminating certain foods and activities and taking her folic acid, there's not much she actually has to *do*. She can bury her head in the sand for a few more weeks, or even months, if she wants.

She squeezes some heavenly Jo Malone shower gel into

her hand and soaps herself up. Her stomach is still pretty flat; maybe a little bloated, but nothing more. She could weigh herself, but she has no idea what she weighed before she got pregnant; it's not something she's ever obsessed over. One thing she's noticed is that despite the exhaustion and the nausea, her sex drive seems to have ramped up—highly inconvenient when she's shunned Lorenzo and has no other prospects on the horizon.

She presses her nipples tentatively. They are bloody agony, but a heat rushes through her nevertheless. She remembers the jokes about horny pregnant women. Turns out they're not so funny when you're a single mother-to-be. She rests her head on the edge of the tub and allows herself to think about Lorenzo. She's been keeping him at arm's length, ignoring his continued calls and refusing to think about him. Her feelings towards him are messy. She feels stupid and grubby and naïve. She's also seriously pissed off with him for getting her pregnant. The only explanation is that one of the condoms must have ripped. If he noticed, he didn't say anything, and she was certainly none the wiser.

Now she tentatively allows herself to remember the good bits of their relationship, if you could call it that. It may have been a fling with few emotional entanglements; he may have turned out to be a dodgy bastard. But while it lasted, it was one of the most sexually charged experiences of her life. Lorenzo showed up for each of their rendezvous full of passion; she's never felt so desirable as she did through his eyes. He worshipped her body; he lavished praise on her and he consumed her. She recalls his brown eyes, almost black with desire as she contorted herself for him; she remembers his mouth on her. When she was in those bedrooms with him at the Rosewood, he obliterated everything else—and that was precisely what she needed after India.

Phew. She's overheating in this bath; she flings her arms and legs up to the side and savours the hit of cool air on her wet skin. Fleetingly, she considers calling him to arrange a hook-up or, at the very least, to get him to talk her over the edge on the phone. It's the least he can do after landing her in this mess. But she remembers the other women, the fact that Lara admitted to screwing him and Isabella accused him of groping and propositioning her. He's bad news, and the worst kind of person she could have picked to be father to her child. It's best to steer well clear of him.

10

THURSDAY, 5TH DECEMBER

This morning, the enormous gates of Jack's home are open and Emmy cycles straight through on Rosa's bike. She's not sure the bike's ever seen any action—it's pristine. The journey's only taken her ten minutes, though she can't deny Jack's offer of accommodation is tempting. The house is straight in front of her, as beautiful in daylight as it was yesterday evening, while over to the right of the flagstone courtyard is a huge barn-like construction with picture windows. Placards by the double doors are labelled AscenSoar and Discite.

She pulls up and sticks the bike in a rack in front of the building. Inside, the entire ground floor looks to be one giant space. To her left are several rows of white desks where a few people are already working; on the right is a communal area with sofas and a kitchen at the end. The sofas have been pushed to the extremities and yoga mats laid down; a group of workers mills around.

She and Jack spot each other at the same time—he breaks free from the group and comes towards her with a wide smile. He's barefoot, wearing running shorts and a zip-up hoodie; Emmy tries and fails to take in his legs, covered with dark hair, and her stomach flips. She fiddles with her helmet, wondering if she should shake his hand, or kiss him, or something, when he stops just shy of her body space and opens his arms wide.

'Welcome!' he says. 'Thanks for coming.'

'I'm glad to be here,' she says, suddenly shy. 'This is a great setup you have.'

'It's very easy for me,' he says. 'Shortest commute ever. But if you take up my offer of accommodation, yours would be even shorter.' He points upwards. 'There are a couple of flats upstairs. Carlotta, our nanny, has one for the occasions she needs to be here, but the other one has your name on it. I'll show you in a bit.'

He leads her over to the gaggle of people. 'Most of the team works for AscenSoar, my for-profit company. Discite has a small dedicated team, but it relies on pro-bono hours from the AscenSoar engineers too; we have a formal agreement in place between the two companies.

'This is Natasha, my head of fundraising.' A willowy brunette offers her hand sullenly. She's in sleek black yoga gear that's heavy on the mesh panelling.

'And meet Klaus, one of our senior engineers,' Jack says. 'Klaus, Emmy may be joining us in an NGO liaison role. She's come in to check the place out, so be nice.'

Klaus grins and shakes her hand vigorously. At least not everyone's as hostile as Natasha. 'Hey, Emmy!' he says. 'Welcome!'

'Right,' says Jack. 'Let's get started, shall we?' He catches the eye of the yoga teacher, who looks as though she's wandered straight out of an ashram. Emmy likes her immediately.

'Oi, everyone!' Jack cups his hands around his mouth and shouts down the room. 'If you're joining the yoga class, we're getting started.'

Emmy puts down her helmet and takes off her jacket, trainers and socks, joining Jack at the front. He gestures to a mat next to him and grins. 'Enjoy.'

He's taken off his hoodie and chucked it into a corner of the room. She tries to ignore his presence next to her as she settles into some slow sun salutations with the rest of the group. She's glad she's had breakfast already. She's quickly established that the best way to avoid morning sickness is to stuff herself with carbs as soon as possible after waking, especially if she's planning on exerting herself.

The session progresses into a vinyasa flow and she moves fluidly through the positions. Jack, she notices, does the same. They settle into a wide-legged forward fold for a few moments.

'Now,' the instructor says, 'if inversions are in your practice, you can place the crown of your head on the mat and come up into a tripod headstand. Otherwise, just stay where you are.'

Emmy grounds her forearms and head into the floor and slowly, steadily, lifts her legs until they're straight. She's not entirely sure whether she's allowed to do inversions when pregnant, but this seems harmless enough and boy, does it feel good. As the blood rushes to her head, she feels a deep sense of peace and the anxious, frazzled feeling she's had since she peed on that bloody stick appears to leave her. She makes a mental commitment to resume her daily yoga practice, so sacred when she was in India and all but forgotten since she's been back.

They're sideways on their mats now, and Jack's right in front of her. He's in a tripod headstand too; his t-shirt has ridden up and she has an uninterrupted view of most of his back, the muscles working as they support his bodyweight. She runs her gaze up his body, very slowly so as to keep her balance. His bum is clenched under his shorts and his deliciously hairy legs are straight, his feet pointed. He's perfection along classical lines. There it is again, that flicker that runs up her entire abdomen to her throat like someone's plucking a guitar string.

At the end of the practice they indulge in a savasana so heavenly that she could happily fall asleep on her mat. She grudgingly pulls herself up to seated to bid the instructor *namaste*.

'How did you find that?' Jack asks, getting to his feet. 'You're very good.'

'Thanks,' she replies. 'It was wonderful; I've been really crap at keeping up my practice since I got back from India, so this was a useful kick up the arse. Nice headstand, by the way.'

He flashes her a grin. 'Ha. Thanks. I try to keep it up too; I'm way too overexcitable for my own good, so yoga and meditation are two tools I take seriously to preserve my sanity. Fancy some breakfast?'

JACK DEVOTES the rest of the morning to persuading Emmy of Discite's potential and of her suitability to his team. He's lined up several people to sit down with her and show her the ropes. He is invigorated and clear-minded after his yoga practice; he's been up since six doing his usual priming activities of meditation, cardio, weights and a cold shower. The yoga has grounded him, though he shouldn't have put

Emmy next to him; throughout the session he found himself hyper-aware of her presence beside him as she moved gracefully through the flow. She's surprisingly strong and has beautiful form.

Having her here lends a frisson to what should be a normal Thursday. He tries to see the office through her eyes: the large, sunlit space and the buzz of contended, motivated people chatting over breakfast. Hopefully she's enamoured enough to give them a shot. He's not in the habit of offering people jobs in the time it takes to drink a cup of tea; he needs to get her properly vetted, but he has a strong relationship with his own instinct and his gut reaction is that she'd fit in well culturally and that she's the biggest missing piece in making the Discite puzzle work right now. What he's trying not to think about are his ulterior motives for having her come on board.

He helps her load up on breakfast from the kitchen counter and walks her around the office space, painting the broad brush-strokes of how the AscenSoar and Discite teams are structured. He finds he's glad to have an excuse to be by her side.

'Do you want to have a look at the space upstairs—see what you think of it?' he asks.

'Definitely,' she says, and he shows her out the front door and round to a separate entrance at the side of the building. He takes the stairs inside two at a time, unlocking the right-hand door at the top.

'Here we go!' He leads her into a large room under the eaves and gesticulates. *Dial it down, Jack; you sound like a game-show host.* They had a couple of flats installed up here when they designed the offices a few years ago. They're a decent size and their interior designer furnished them neutrally but comfortably; this morning the low winter sun shines through the easterly window and illuminates the whole room.

Emmy's walking around, staring. 'This is gorgeous!' she tells him.

He shrugs, slightly awkwardly. 'Glad you like it. There's a little kitchen through there, and the bedroom and ensuite are beside it. Come and have a look.'

He follows her into the bedroom. The bed is made up with crisp white linen; beside it the walk-in shower is visible through the bathroom door. She drops onto the bed and pats it like a kid.

'This is seriously luxurious,' she says. 'Why don't you rent this place out?'

'It's useful to have it available. We can put guests up here, bribe people we're trying to hire...'

She grins and throws her hands up. 'Well, I'm sold on the accommodation part, anyway. This beats Lewisham. Let's hope your charity's just as impressive, eh?'

'Come downstairs,' he says, 'and you can meet my baby properly.'

~

SHE FOLLOWS him down to a corner of the office with swivel chairs big enough to curl up in. His lovely golden labrador pads after them and settles down at her feet with a heavy sigh. Jack hands her a tablet.

'This is the product,' he says. 'We call it the Disco tablet.'

She turns it over in her hands; its chunky red shell is pleasingly robust. She taps the screen and it comes to life with some cute little avatars on the home screen.

'How did you come up with this?' she asks. 'Is it similar to what AscenSoar does?'

'A little,' he says, sitting back in his chair and raking a hand through his dark hair. 'AscenSoar is designed to work with teachers and for teachers. The whole case for the Disco tablet revolves around independent learning. We need the kids to be able to teach themselves, whether they're at school or they're at home with no access to a school or teachers.'

She's playing with the tablet as she listens, tapping through a basic maths sequence. 'So, what's the secret?' she asks.

'Personalisation,' he says, 'and gamification. The kids need to be able to learn independently without a teacher assigning tasks, so personalisation is key. The software constantly modifies the exercises based on the kids' answers. But I think gamification is the real secret. I got the idea from my boys, Augie and Pitt. They're eleven.

'They detest rote learning,' he continues. 'Spellings, times tables, anything like that is a bloody nightmare to teach them. We had so many years of fights and tears over homework. They just wouldn't persevere. You'd tell them they'd got an answer wrong and they'd storm out of the room. One day, another dad told me about a times table app, so we downloaded it onto their iPads—this is going back a few years. Here's the thing. All computer games are really about the game saying *No; No; Wrong; Fail; Try Again; You're Dead*. And yet the kids come back for more, time and time again. We tell them they're wrong; they cry and scream. A computer game does it and it makes them even more goal-oriented—it's astonishing.'

She looks up from the tablet. He has an enormous grin

on his face as he warms to his theme. He's beyond adorable, but he's also compelling.

'I've seen my kids teach themselves Minecraft and Fortnite,' he continues. 'And they will try and try until they get to the next level; giving up is not an option in these games. For all their faults, the resilience they build is amazing. So we've shamelessly gamified the programmes on here. We've spent a lot of time and money on the interface—the avatars and so forth. And we've made it heavily reward-driven. When the kids complete a level they can upgrade their character's skin, they can earn currency and they can enter locked realms. It's all designed to keep them moving forward.'

'I'm sold.' Emmy holds her hands up. 'On the product, anyway. It sounds incredible. So, where are the problems on the ground coming from?'

Jack tells her his fears that he's neglected the distribution side in favour of the software itself, which is his area of expertise, and he's been swamped by the demands of AscenSoar which is growing rapidly. He shows her the list of NGOs they've already partnered with in India; some names are familiar to her and the list looks long—that's a lot of relationships to manage. He's worried the NGOs aren't focused enough on the take-up and usage of the tablets; in some areas they aren't being used much or at all, and he has very little colour on why.

Much of the problem seems to stem from basic communication issues—the NGO partners don't have someone at Discite sufficiently dedicated to their needs and they haven't had enough support for the roll-out on the ground, so they've gradually stopped checking in and providing feedback. It'll be a messy situation to unravel, and will probably require some awkward conversations and a good deal of *mea culpa* on Discite's part, but it doesn't sound like rocket science. On the contrary, it sounds like the scrappy kind of challenge she loved out in India, and a shit-load better than booking plane tickets and submitting expenses for entitled bankers.

'This is something I can help you with,' she tells Jack. 'I'd love to be a part of it.'

11

SATURDAY, 7TH DECEMBER

'Right,' Rosa says. 'You can have the pick of my wardrobe, except for the Chanel. You may as well take advantage while you still have your waist—your skanky old harem pants won't cut it tonight.'

They're standing in Rosa's enormous walk-in closet, which features an array of hanging rails and beautifully lit shoe racks. The amount of clothes her sister owns is quite astonishing, and the fact that she's been gifted most of them even more so.

'It sounds bloody awful,' says Emmy. 'And I'll be the only sober person there.'

'Don't be silly. There'll be lots of designated drivers. And it will be fun. The Freynes give seriously fabulous parties—almost as good as the ones Jack and Stacey used to give.'

Emmy rolls her eyes.

'I saw that.' Rosa sweeps a stray scarf off the ottoman in the centre of the space and puts it in a drawer. 'They'll probably both be there tonight—separately, of course. Did you speak to Loeb yesterday?'

'Yep,' Emmy says. 'I've cut the cord.'

'What did they say?'

'The HR woman was pretty sniffy about me walking out with no notice until I told her I was pregnant with Lorenzo's baby. I've never seen anyone try to get rid of me so quickly. They really don't need another woman coming forward. Plus, I was on a temp contract. So it's all good.'

'I hope you know what you're doing with Discite,' Rosa sniffs. 'It sounds like a recipe for disaster to me. You've accepted a job with him and he has no idea you're pregnant, or that you've got a stonking great crush on him.'

'It's a temporary consulting role, not a job. I'm on a day rate. And I'm nine weeks pregnant—I shouldn't have to tell any boss I'm pregnant before my twelve week scan. I'll be able to get these distribution headaches turned around for him well before I pop. And I don't have a crush on him; I just think he's incredibly hot, that's all. I'm not in the market for a guy with four kids, believe me.'

'Well, that's a relief,' says Rosa, 'because I very much doubt a divorced father of four is in the market for a girlfriend who's up the duff by someone else.'

It's a flippant comment, but it stings. Emmy hasn't had the chance to think much about the fact that this pregnancy will dramatically curtail her chances of a relationship. She doesn't want a relationship—not after the Lorenzo debacle and not when she hasn't a clue what she wants from life or where she wants to settle. Still, it hurts to know it's out of her hands.

'Come on.' Rosa heads to a rail of dresses and pulls out a couple on hangers. 'We need something worthy of that hair.'

Rosa's hair stylist, Philippe, came by this afternoon and tended to them both. Rosa's hair looks like a glossier version of what she manages on her own every day—perfectly tonged tresses. Emmy begged him not to make her look too over-the-top, and he took pity on her and simply gave her a great blow-dry, teasing her curls into long, silky waves that are sleek without looking too high-maintenance. She has to agree that her hair looks glorious, though she can't imagine how Rosa can bear to devote so much time each day to keeping hers tamed.

'What are you wearing?' she asks.

'I'm going festive scarlet.' Rosa points to a dress hanging on a wardrobe door knob. It's short, with a huge flouncy V-neck and an oversized bow across the chest. It looks like something Barbie would have worn in the eighties, but weirdly, it works. 'It'll look great on camera against the white decorations downstairs,' she continues.

'It's gorgeous, but I'd rather something a little lower key,' Emmy says.

'Please. As if I'd let you steal my thunder, anyway. I was thinking black for you. Your hair looks so shiny from that conditioning treatment.'

She picks out a black minidress with capped sleeves. It's plain except for diamonté buttons along the shoulder and a feathery trim around the hem that is very Barbara Streisand. 'I love it,' she says in surprise.

'It's Miu Miu,' Rosa says. 'It'll be perfect.'

STACEY PICKS up her phone and inhales. She types a message to Jack and hits send before she can change her mind. *I'm bringing a date to the party tonight. Just wanted to let you know in advance x.* He texts straight back. *Got it. See you later.*

She's asked Antoine, the guy who sent over the bottle of champagne at Beaverbrook, to be her date. She met him yesterday for lunch at his club, 5 Hertford Street, and surprised herself with how much she enjoyed his company. He's erudite and sophisticated, educated between Beirut and Paris. The family office on this business card is, as she suspected, his own family's office; namely, his family's wealth is so great that it requires having its own asset management company to manage it. Antoine and his two brothers handle the investment side of things.

It's unusual for her to mix her worlds: her dating life and her and Jack's friends in Surrey, but she has a couple of reasons for inviting Antoine down to Surrey tonight. First, she wants to sleep with him and she'd rather do it on her turf than his. Jack has the kids this weekend, so she has her house to herself. Antoine made it clear at lunch yesterday that he's extremely interested. He told her he hadn't been able to take his eyes off her in the Beaverbrook Bar, that she'd been glowing. She desisted from telling him the reason for the glow—her session with Raphael.

The second reason is a little more complex. She feels she needs to justify her decision to walk out on Jack to their social circle. No one understood it when she left him—Jack is the golden boy, after all. But more pertinently, they were the golden couple. They had four kids and two stellar careers and seemed blissfully happy together. She's aware that many of their friends, even the women (especially the women) thought it churlish of her to walk out on a wonderful guy and a strong marriage, to turn their kids' lives upside down. Some of them advised her to beg him to take her back.

But they never saw inside her marriage or her heart; they knew her on a superficial level. They saw the Stacey who juggled school run with getting into London to run a thriving business; they saw the side she and Jack presented at parties and barbecues and fundraisers. While many of them may love or settle for that life, for Stacey it was Groundhog Day, going through the motions with no hope of a twinge of excitement beyond school-gates gossip or a win at work. Once Mia went to school, it struck her that she'd be repeating this cycle for the next fourteen years with little else to satisfy her. Staying married felt as pointless as persevering with a book she wasn't enjoying.

Everyone called it a midlife crisis, of course. She told Jack she wanted a divorce a few months after her fortieth birthday. It was Evelyn Macleod who'd unwittingly put the idea into her head. When her marriage with Seb was breaking down, Stacey found herself feeling envy alongside the sympathy and concern she had for her friend. By coming out, Seb gave Evelyn a get-out-of-jail-free card. She had the chance to walk away and make a fresh start, which she did, very successfully, with Angus.

Evelyn is so in love with Angus, it's like a movie. Stacey likely had that with Jack once, a long time ago, but it was when they were far too young to appreciate it. That love bloomed and then mellowed over time until it became like an old pair of slippers that had likely passed their expiration date but were too comfortable to take off. She suspected she'd felt like that for a while, until Evelyn's second chance threw Stacey's own desires into sharp relief.

So, she threw off the well-loved slippers and emerged, barefoot, back into the world. The first night she stayed in her crazy, glass-fronted rental house on her own, she felt none of the trepidation that divorced women often describe at having to fend for themselves: she felt deliriously, completely free.

There were still the whispers though. *Poor Jack. How could she have done that to him? He's such a catch. I wonder if she regrets it.* Tonight was about silencing those whispers and, most likely, creating new ones. She'd show the parents from school that her gamble was paying off and she was living a life of romance, excitement and sexual freedom they could only dream of. It wasn't about oneupmanship. It was about demonstrating that the desire to put herself first, after decades of servitude to her family, was achievable and justifiable. The sky had not fallen. Her kids would be fine. And she wouldn't go to the grave feeling as though she'd lived half a life.

She just wanted to make sure that none of that occurred at Jack's expense, hence the text to him. The funny thing was, she was pretty sure Jack was fine. The divorcees from school moved in quickly, but he batted them all away and seemed to focus all his energy on Ascensoar, Discite, the kids and on his health and fitness. He was investing more time in himself; he'd even gone on some insane alpha male trip to Poland with Wim Hof and a load of other crazy Type A guys to sit in ice baths and chant. He was a wonderful man, the best husband and father she could ever have chosen. But he would never have conceived of leaving her.

One night, when he'd got over his deep shock and grief at her request for a divorce, he admitted that she had a point. Their relationship had settled into something that wasn't the stellar experience they both demanded in every other aspect of their lives. It was still love, but it wasn't a great love. Their sex life was fine, average, but they were two people who'd always fought for all aspects of their life to be far above average. Jack's reaction was to suggest seeing a counsellor together, but Stacey gently told him that was missing the point. The point was that if they craved excitement and newness and intoxication, they wouldn't get that from each other after nearly twenty years.

Eventually, Jack agreed with her perspective. The difference between them was that he would have settled, unquestioningly, for staying married to her forever; he would have been content and loyal, but he wouldn't have dreamt of demanding a second chance for himself. By taking the plunge on behalf of both of them, she hopes she hasn't ruined his life but rather offered him the opportunity for a new one.

12

SATURDAY, 7TH DECEMBER

The Freynes know how to throw a party. Jack feels a momentary wave of relief that he can simply turn up and enjoy the festivities. A couple of years ago he would have been knee-deep in preparations for their annual Christmas cocktail party as Stacey barked orders at the caterers, decorators and kids. He secretly enjoyed it, despite his protestations.

Now, a member of the catering staff greets him at the door of Laurence and Lottie's impressive new-build in a private estate in Weybridge. His plan was to arrive early and slip out early, but there's already a decent crowd. He hands the woman his coat and heads through to the vast kitchen-cum-living room.

Laurence spots him. 'Bro!' He engulfs Jack in a hug and points to the bar. 'Looking sharp. Go get yourself sorted with a drink. The house speciality tonight is pomegranate martini.'

Laurence and Lottie are good mates, parents from Martha's year group who often made up a fun foursome for dinners and barbecues. Like many of their friends, they were uncomfortable in the aftermath of the divorce, but they've taken their cue from Jack and Stacey and seem to be coming round to the idea that the Fishers aren't about to reenact *The War of the Roses* if they invite them both to the same social event.

He recognises most of the faces in this room; it's a close-knit community of Hampton Park parents, cultivated over years of Saturday morning football and lacrosse practice, school fundraisers and organised fun. These people make up the bulk of his social circle these days, though the dynamic has undeniably shifted since the divorce. He suspects it's been harder for Stacey; there's been more judgement thrown her way.

There are more and more divorces as they move through the school; most of the parents in Mia's class are still together, but in Year Seven it's a different story. He expects David and Rosa will be here and finds himself hoping Emmy will join them. These are his friends and he cares about them, but the school social circle can be stifling and she's a breath of fresh air. He requests a pomegranate martini and watches the barman mix and pour it with a flourish.

'Hey, Jack.'

It's Stacey's voice and he turns around. She looks incredible, as usual. She always goes all-out for these things; he suspects she views it as a competitive sport with the other mothers and, without fail, she comes up trumps. Her golden hair is like a halo and she's wearing a slinky, bronze dress. She looks like an Oscar. He puts a hand on her back to kiss her hello and finds it bare.

'Hi Stace,' he says. 'You look lovely.'

She preens. 'Thank you. This is Antoine Haddad. Antoine, this is my ex-husband, Jack Fisher.'

He drags his eyes to the left to take in her date. The guy's a finance dude—you can spot them a mile off. He reeks of money. He's dark, rangy and younger than them. His hair is slicked back and he's drenched in cologne, but he looks undeniably good. Not that any of that matters—it's none of his business whom Stacey dates.

'Good to meet you, mate,' he says. 'Are you local?'

'No, I live in London,' Antoine replies in a French accent, 'but it's nice to have a change of scene.'

They make polite small-talk for a few minutes before Jack leaves them to it. It's hard to muster up any enthusiasm for this guy. He has a wolfish look in his eyes that Jack knows is intended for Stacey. He's heard through the grapevine that she has an active dating life, but it's horrifying to imagine, so he'd rather give her and her dates a wide berth. He orders another martini and makes his way through the room.

He spots David first, then Rosa. And next to her, Emmy, but not as he knows her. Her hair is blown out in silky, coppery waves and she's in an extremely short black dress and heels. Her legs are endless. He hasn't seen her out of yoga pants or jeans before. She looks incandescent. Fuck. He swallows and makes his way over, thoughts of Stacey's date forgotten.

~

EMMY CATCHES Jack's eye as he weaves through the crowd of people—he's taller than most people here. He's smiling straight at her.

David reaches him first, wrapping him in a bear-hug. 'Get in here!' he says, ruffling Jack's hair. David had a few beers while watching the football this afternoon, and he's on excellent form. 'Oh shit, sorry, mate,' he continues as Jack holds his martini glass away from the hug, pink liquid slopping over the sides. Jack kisses Rosa, complimenting her on her dress, and then comes to face Emmy.

'Hi,' he says softly, kissing her on both cheeks. 'You look wonderful—you scrub up well.'

'It's all Rosa's doing,' she says, grinning at him. She certainly feels wonderful. For all her judgmental thoughts about how seriously Rosa takes her appearance, it's a delightful novelty to feel glossy and chic, and she wants to bask like a cat in the admiration in Jack's eyes.

'She does scrub up well, when she makes an effort,' Rosa says, giving her some side-eye. 'So, Jack. Emmy's your new employee *and* your new tenant. Thanks for taking her on.'

'It's me who should be thanking her for taking us on.' Jack takes a sip of his drink, his eyes still on Emmy. 'I hope you're not too horrified by the state of our affairs. When are you going to move in?'

'I'll hop up to London on the train tomorrow,' Emmy says, 'and put my clothes in my big backpacker's rucksack. I haven't accumulated much stuff since I got back. Then I'll just bring it into work on Monday, if that works.'

'We're looking forward to having you,' says Jack.

A woman gestures excitedly to Rosa and she and David move off, with Rosa murmuring to Jack that they'll catch up later.

There's a DJ at the other end of the room, and he now has *Last Christmas* blaring. Jack moves a little closer to her. 'So,' he says. 'You on the G&Ts?'

She holds up her glass. 'Tonic only. Designated driver.'

He laughs. 'That's so harsh!' He doesn't know the real reason she can't drink. 'They're getting their pound of flesh from their guest, aren't they?'

'I don't mind. I'm not a fan of having a permanent hangover in December.'

'I know what you mean.' He brandishes his near-empty glass. 'These things are dangerous; I need to be careful.' Someone bumps him from behind and he stumbles into her, his hand on her bare arm. 'Sorry, creepy boss.'

If only. He couldn't be less sleazy. He looks particularly handsome tonight in a smart navy shirt and jeans, his dark hair still slightly mussed up from when David tousled it. He's standing so close to her she can smell him, and his beautiful eyes crinkle as he smiles down at her. They're a greeny-hazel, dark-lashed. It's no use. She'll behave herself and do her job, but she can't lay aside the feelings he's arousing in her. The problem is, she'd put money on the fact that he feels the same way. She smiles up into his face. 'You're not creepy. This is an impressive party—you guys certainly know how to put on a show in Esher.'

He looks around. 'It's a sociable crowd. Stacey and I moved down here when Martha was a toddler. The schools are excellent, but we were pretty young and we thought we'd be saying goodbye to our social life. Once she started school, though, we got sucked in. Most of the people round here are go-getters; they work hard and play hard. It's intense, but I'm grateful for these guys. A far cry from Kanpur, though, I imagine?'

'It is—I think that's what I'm trying to compute. I mean, everyone at Loeb is loaded, too, but I didn't socialise much at work. I was mainly with my uni friends. But even Lewisham is the height of luxury compared to Kanpur.'

'Do you miss it?'

She sighs. 'I do. So much. It's hard to explain—it's a kind of visceral loss; I feel it in my bones. It's not rational—my quality of life's much better here. Especially once I get my mitts on your luxury flat! But I felt more alive there than I do here. I think it was the scale of the place; the sky; the sense of space... and the people. The suffering is awful, but the flip-side of that is you get this profound human connection that I just don't feel here—everything's so sterile. The buildings, the weather, the stiff upper lip that we all put on... I feel like I'm missing out on what life's all about when I'm not there.' She shrugs. 'It's weird, I know.'

'It's not weird,' he says. 'It makes perfect sense. I have that feeling too, sometimes, that we don't get tested enough in this society, that we're not really living to our true potential. I've spent a lot of time navel-gazing and trying to work out how to fill that gap.'

'What did you come up with?' she asks. 'Honestly, if you've worked out the magic formula, then I'd love to know.'

'I don't think there is one,' he says, 'except to live big and dream big and serve others. That's what I'm trying to achieve with Discite. It's also why I try to get out of my own head as much as possible and have amazing experiences. My drug is skydiving—I do it wherever I can.'

'Really? I've never done it—I would *love* to. A group of us looked into it when we were in Nepal, but it was way too expensive.'

'I've done it in the Himalayas,' he admits. He shakes his head. 'It was fucking amazing; hands down one of the most spiritual experiences of my life. If you ever get the chance to do it—I'd say, go for it. Doesn't have to be Nepal.'

'I will,' she says. 'You've sold me on it—one for the bucket list. I'll start saving.' There's not much chance she'll skydive anytime soon with a baby on the way, but she recognises the value of tucking away some dreams for herself, even if it takes years to realise them. One day, she'll soar through the sky, weightless.

'So,' he says, 'if you don't mind my asking... why did you leave India, if you loved it so much? You said something bad happened?'

Her eyes prick with tears.

'Oh, God.' He holds up his hand. 'I'm so sorry—me and my big mouth. You don't have to talk about it.'

'It's ok,' she says. 'It's not really a cocktail party story, but I'll give you the main gist of it. I mentioned that we worked with a lot of sex workers, right?'

He nodded.

'Well, there was one group of women we were working with; we ran a community centre where they could come and get contraception and have a rest—just somewhere they could be safe. They could bring their kids, too. Sometimes, they'd nap on the floor while their kids ran around and played. One morning we got word that several of the women had been rounded up by the police. Most of them got taken into custody, but one of them was raped by at least a couple of the policemen and they beat her to death afterwards.' She hangs her head and presses her temples with her fingers.

'*Fuck*,' says Jack. 'Jesus, I'm so sorry, Emmy. What was her name?'

'Rekha,' she says. 'She was twenty-four. And she had the most beautiful little boy. It was just so disgusting; I lost the plot. I couldn't keep working in a system like that, where these women were invisible and completely worthless. I'd been feeling helpless and frustrated for quite a while and this was the last straw—I packed my bags and came home.'

'I'm so sorry,' he says again. 'It must be intolerable to keep plugging away in the face of tragedy like that.'

'It's just the feeling that you're constantly swimming against this enormous tide,' she says, 'and you don't have a hope in hell of making one bit of difference. It's exhausting.'

'I know.' He rubs her shoulder gently. 'It is exhausting. But don't think you haven't made a difference. Every single life you touch makes it worthwhile. Don't forget that. The only thing you can do is take it person by person. And I know we'll reach far more people with you on board; that's why I'm so happy to have you with us. It's obvious how deeply you care about this cause.'

She looks into his kind, concerned face and feels wiped out all of a sudden; she'd give anything to collapse against his chest and have his arms around her. She's cocooned with him here; in their heads they're a world away from the oblivious, joyful people getting drunk around them. Instead, she nods and gives him a grin to indicate she'll be fine.

'Ok,' he says. He removes his hand from her shoulder. 'I'm sorry for reminding you of the things you're trying to forget. Most depressing Christmas party conversation ever. Do you want to come with me and I'll introduce you to some people? Or we can go and laugh at David's dancing. I could use another drink, and you need to have some fun.'

13

MONDAY, 9TH DECEMBER

The searing heat of the water permeates Stacey's scalp as she stands under the oversized shower head. The heat is so revitalising that she sighs audibly. It's been an intoxicating weekend with Antoine, and now she's back in mommy mode. Jack dropped the kids off after their tea last night, and their raucous chatter instantly filled the house. They'd decorated Jack's place for Christmas and were full of tales of rediscovering beloved decorations and eating all the foil-wrapped chocolate shapes he had intended for the tree. Mia was exhausted when she got back —she'd been out with the ponies most of the day, according to Jack—and went out like a light last night.

It's still odd, sharing them, but she'd be lying if she said she didn't enjoy the precious child-free weekends that their custody arrangement gives her. Their definition of joint custody is pretty loose, but it works for them. She laughed when friends asked, during the early days of the divorce negotiations, whether they were fighting for each other for custody. As if either of them would battle to have full custody of four kids! No, this arrangement has given them both space to find their footing in their single lives while also giving them access to their kids. It's a shame they see so little of the boys now that they're at school, but Jack is brilliant at going along to their mid-week fixtures.

Her weekend with Antoine was everything she'd hoped. He joined her for a glass of champagne at her place before the party, taking in the minimalist luxury of her home and the resplendence of her flood-lit pool, gleaming turquoise beyond the patio doors. She keeps it heated all year round—the geothermal heat pump has been a great call. The house and garden are a huge departure from the rustic warmth of The Lodge. She needed a clean break when she left him; this is more her style.

'You have a beautiful home,' he told her as they sat with their drinks in the double-height living area. 'I can see why you left London.'

'This would probably buy me a small flat in Mayfair,' she agreed.

'You are a very intelligent, very impressive woman,' he said, 'and I told you yesterday how sexy I found that. And now I find you have a pool, too. I think we need to take a dip together later, you and I, under the stars.'

While a small part of her brain imagined her girlfriends' sniggering reaction if she relayed this line to them in Antoine's French accent, in the moment she found it deeply gratifying. Another part of her brain began to shoot clear messages straight to her groin as he gazed into her eyes. He moved his arm along the sofa and proceeded to run his fingertips lightly up her bare spine. She parted her lips involuntarily, and he shook his head and tutted. She couldn't take her eyes off his mouth.

'Not yet,' he said. 'If I kiss you now, I promise we will not make it to that party.'

The result was that she spent most of the party squirming with desire. She was conscious of her skin tingling beneath her backless dress and her silk panties. She spent most of the party introducing Antoine to people who were great friends and catching up with them. Usually, she would have been in her element to see everyone, but tonight she couldn't get out of there fast enough. After a couple of hours, enough of the women at the room had cast lascivious, yearning looks at Antoine that she felt as though she'd made her point: she'd emerged from the ashes of divorce triumphant, with a guy on her arm who was younger, wealthier and hotter than any of the husbands here.

She whispered to Antoine, 'Let's go take that dip.'

Back at her place, things ratcheted up quickly. She grabbed some fluffy white robes and another bottle of champagne. Out by the pool it was freezing, and steam rose thickly from the surface of the water. Good. She'd cranked up the heat a couple of days previously in anticipation of this weekend.

Antoine slid her dress down over her shoulders and arms, kissing her hard as he did. It slithered to the ground and she stood in her panties and heels, feeling not unlike a Bond girl. It was absolutely frigid—she shivered and laughed as she unbuttoned his shirt. His body was lean, his pecs defined. They completed the undressing as quickly as they could and dove into the bath-like water. Fuck her blow-dry.

He guided her over to the side of the pool and pushed himself against her. She moaned and wrapped her legs around him, pulling him closer. He was even sexier than Raphael; it felt more intense. It was the power thing, she decided. Raphael was adorable, but ultimately he was a tennis coach and she was a guest. The power was all in her favour. She spent her days ordering people about at work and ordering kids about at home. She just wanted someone to take control of her. That was where Antoine had the edge: he was a seriously wealthy, powerful man who knew what he wanted and was used to getting it, and she was delighted to put herself in his capable hands. She suspected this dynamic was giving him the same kick—she was likely far less of a pushover than the women he usually dated; ergo conquering her would be a bigger triumph.

Now his hands were everywhere, his long fingers probing inside her, and she could hear the hunger in his voice as he delivered a steady stream of words into her ear that made her blush even as the sensation spiralled up and up and she clung to him, gasping and sinking her teeth into his shoulder.

He released her and pointed to the shallow steps leading out of the pool. 'Go and lie over there. I don't want you to come just yet,' he said. He pulled himself out of the water—he was magnificent—and picked up his jacket. He drew out a couple of condoms and a brief look of uncertainty crossed his face.

'These are safe to use in the pool, yes?' he asked.

She hid a smirk. This guy had clearly seen far fewer Spring Breaks than she had in her prime. 'They sure are,' she said. God bless latex. He rolled the condom on and strode back into the pool. She lay back on the steps, in the water from the waist down. Her upper half was freezing.

'Look how hard the cold makes your beautiful nipples,' he said, and pinched them both hard. That was it; she had to have him inside her that very second. She wrapped her legs around him again and he thrust into her faster and faster, his mouth open on hers, his arm around her back to tether her to him. As they came, she felt as though she was floating, like the Lady of Shalott, on the surface of the water.

~

NOW, in the shower, she tilts her head this way and that, her breathing quickening as she recalls Antoine's impressive roster of tricks on Saturday night and Sunday morning. She'll cancel her tennis lesson at Beaverbrook tomorrow, but she'll keep her room reservation. It turns out Antoine's there most Tuesdays too, and she'd rather do a PT session in the gym (it's probably wise to book a female PT) and then reunite with him. Raphael's a lovely boy, but Antoine's a proper power-player, a worthy adversary. Hmm, it's heavenly to fantasise about him in the shower and idly browse some images of what he may have planned for their rendezvous tomorrow.

Her hair wet, she pumps a generous dollop of her favourite botanical shower gel into her hand and begins to wash herself. She works up her arms and over her breasts and then crosses them to wash her armpits. She stops dead, fear hitting her right in the throat. What's that under her right arm? It's a rubbery hardness, protruding from the side of her breast—just above where her bra underwire would usually finish. How the hell has she not noticed this before? She massages it carefully with her fingertips. It's a lump. It's a fucking lump.

14

MONDAY, 9TH DECEMBER

This is not at all how she wants to start her week. Finding the lump has thrown her into a spiral of panic. The first call she makes is to Elaine, her executive assistant, asking her to compile a list of options for next steps. She leaves Carlotta to do the school run, hugs the kids and heads straight into the office. Once there, she and Elaine make a plan. There'll be no wasting time with a GP appointment—she'll get the best advice out there.

Thanks to Elaine's efficiency and Stacey's ability to pull strings, she has an appointment at eleven with a breast consultant on Harley Street, where she'll also have a mammogram and an ultrasound. She's cancelled her date with Antoine at Beaverbrook tomorrow. He was very sweet and concerned on her behalf, but right now she can't even think about him. Their flirtation seems trivial compared to the barrel she's staring down. She even feels a little bad for him—he's presumably seeing her for a bit of fun and some great sex; he doesn't need her to put a health scare like this on the table after two dates. She thinks about calling Evelyn, but she doesn't want to bother her. Elaine offered to come with her, which touched Stacey more than she could say, but she'd rather be here alone. Besides, she's left Elaine with tonnes of work to do.

Weirdly, the person she most wants to call is Jack, but she won't do it yet. There's no point worrying him until she knows what she's dealing with. She sits in the waiting room of what is a typical Harley Street building. Soft lighting and tasteful Christmas decorations do little to detract from the soulless vibe. A woman sitting opposite, at least ten years younger than Stacey and wearing athleisure wear, grips her husband's hand. The third woman in the room has a silk scarf on her head and the bloated, hairless face of a chemo patient. Fuck. Don't look at her.

She thumbs unseeingly through *Harper's Bazaar*. She prides herself on being a badass, a go-getter, but this little lump has scared the shit out of her. She closes her eyes and conjures up magical, multi-sensory memories of her children this morning. Mia's deep, throaty chuckle, mouth wide open and head cast back, her bottom tooth now wobbly enough to be pitched at a revolting angle. The shadows under Martha's eyes—Stacey suspects she was reading well after the lights went out last night. She's always a little off when she comes back from a weekend at Jack's, as if it's an effort to recalibrate herself. It probably is. Pitt and Augie's *smell*. They're still young enough to smell delicious, and when they hug her they sandwich her between them. It's heaven. Thank God she has them next weekend; the single night between them being at Jack's and going back to school just isn't enough.

They're so real and vibrant. Whatever the doctor says today, she'll head home early and surprise the girls on the school run. She needs to be with them this evening, to be around their warmth and energy. She'll make chicken noodle soup, and they can watch a girlie movie.

The memories of her children are like sunlight on water, but below the surface, darker thoughts attempt to rise from the depths and pull her down. Cancer. Surgeries; chemo; losing her hair, losing her energy and her appetite for life; not being able to look after her children properly. Losing the battle. Dying and leaving the kids motherless. Leaving Jack to bring up four grieving children on his own. How will he handle Martha getting her period? What if the kids stop remembering how much she loves them? She'll have to write so many notes to them: love letters that immortalise her love for them long after she's gone.

Stop it. *Stop it.*

HER CONSULTANT, Mr Dominic Henshaw, is professional and polite. He carries out a manual examination of her breasts and assures her he can feel no other lumps aside from the one she's discovered. They proceed with the mammogram, which is intense but blessedly brief. She stands topless and shivers as a cold machine squishes her breasts, before lying down for an ultrasound. While she's still on the bed, Mr Henshaw numbs the area where the lump is and gives her a local anaesthetic. While they wait for it to kick in they make stilted small talk and Stacey gives him her potted history: four kids, divorced, runs a FinTech company. She's way less chatty than usual, lying here in this stark, darkened room.

He inserts the needle for the biopsy and talks her through the procedure as he goes. He's matter-of-fact and doesn't patronise her. After he's put the samples in their pots and applied a little paper stitch and a dressing, she dresses and follows him to sit at his desk.

'I can't give you a formal diagnosis until I've had the biopsy results back,' he says. 'But, it looks like this is a fibroadenoma.'

Stacey looks at him blankly.

'Fibroademonas are benign tumours,' he clarifies.

The room shifts and she has a buzzing in her ears; the deafening silence that follows the release of good news.

She puts her face in her hands. 'Jesus,' she says. 'Phew. Thank God.'

'Now,' he says. 'It's not quite that straightforward. Yours is particularly large. We should run some hormone tests to check if you have elevated oestrogen levels. Unfortunately, because this is the first time we've observed it, we have no way of knowing how fast it's grown. But when they're this size, we like to take them out to be safe.'

'Right,' she says. She needs to get her head around what questions she should ask, but her brain isn't fully operational. It was stupid to have come here alone. She should have had some moral support, but who would she have asked? Jack?

'How would you take it out?' she asks now.

'Under general anaesthetic. You'd be in and out of hospital within a few hours; we use a keyhole procedure so the invasion is minimal. I carry these procedures out at London Bridge Hospital. Where are you based?'

'Um, Esher, in Surrey,' she says.

'I see. Well, assuming it's convenient for you to come to London Bridge, I can operate on you myself. I would highly recommend that you have someone to escort you safely home. Do you have someone who can be there with you?'

'I do,' she says. There's only one person for that job.

SHE CALLS Jack as soon as she sets foot out on Harley Street. London feels like a different place now—full of promise, optimism, bustle. She entered this clinic under a menacing cloud and it's as though she's stepped out into dazzling sunshine. She may even stroll over to the Connaught and buy herself a celebratory glass of champagne.

'Hi Stace.' He sounds distracted; the echo suggests he has her on speaker and he's tapping away on his keyboard.

'Hey,' she says. 'I have something to update you on, and also a favour.'

'Shoot,' he says. He's great like this; he doesn't strop or throw a hissy fit when she asks him to help out. He most likely thinks she's asking a favour involving children's logistics.

'Everything's ok, but I need to go into hospital next week, for an outpatient procedure.'

There's a scuffling noise as he puts the phone to his ear. 'What procedure?' he asks. His voice is much clearer now. 'Is everything ok?'

'I really think it is, but I have to have a breast lump removed. We won't know for sure, but the doctor seems confident it's benign. It's just pretty... big, so he wants to get it out ASAP.'

'Jesus, Stace.' He breathes down the phone. 'When did this happen? What did he say?'

'It's all happened really quickly,' she says. 'I found it in the shower this morning, and I've seen a consultant on Harley Street just now. He's very highly regarded. He seems optimistic that it's a'—she looks down at the leaflet he's given her—'fibroademona, which is a benign tumour and apparently very common, but he won't quite know for sure till the biopsy results are back at the end of the week. But he's going to take it out next Tuesday, the seventeenth? Apparently it's a quick procedure; they use keyhole surgery. But I'll be under general, obviously. It's at London Bridge, and I wondered—'

'I'll come with you, of course,' he says quickly. 'I'd hate you to have to do that on your own.'

Her eyes prick at his words, and she closes them. She's felt desolate all day, uncharacteristically fragile.

'Thanks,' she whispers. 'It's just the getting home part, after I come round. I wasn't sure how I could do it alone.'

'You don't have to,' he says. 'I'll be there. We'll always be a team, Stace.'

15

TUESDAY, 10TH DECEMBER

The AscenSoar management accounts for 2019 are up on Jack's screen and the tiny numbers dance in front of his eyes. As they go into year-end, he's spent hours with his Finance Director, Peter, examining where the uplift from their original projections came from and what that means for their 2020 forecasts. They're ending the year with revenues twenty percent higher than they'd initially forecast and net profit twenty-five percent higher. This isn't just a huge coup for the AscenSoar team, it's a big deal for Discite too, as AscenSoar pays a proportion of its earnings as a charitable donation to Discite. And God knows, Discite can use all the funding it can get.

He rubs his eyes and minimises the spreadsheet. He'll take another look at the accounts later, with fresh eyes, but now is the moment he's been looking forward to all day—his three o'clock sit-down with Emmy. Yesterday was her first proper day as part of the Discite team, and she's also moved into the flat upstairs. Each time he considers her proximity to him, a warm glow spreads across his body and something indefinable lifts his spirits. She's got under his skin, but this doesn't worry him. It makes him happy.

Her presence on Saturday night transformed the Freynes' party from a regular fun, boozy get-together to something verging on magical. He's aware he didn't catch up with as many of his mates as he should have; he stuck to Emmy as closely as she'd let him. They ended up dancing to the excellent DJ with Rosa and David; David was four sheets to the wind at this point and threw some impressive shapes to Dancing in the Dark while Emmy and Rosa laughed at him. He was pretty hammered himself towards the end of the party, and when maintaining a friendly distance from Emmy became too much of a strain, he took himself quietly off home. On Sunday, entertaining four kids on a hangover took up most of his headspace.

It's been a busy couple of days on the AscenSoar side, but he finds himself looking over regularly to where she's sitting with the other full-time Discite employees. He hopes Natasha's playing nicely. She's not exactly a girls' girl, and she's made it abundantly clear in the past that she has a thing for him. He has a hunch she picked up on the vibes between him and Emmy last Thursday—even by her standards, she's given Emmy the cold shoulder. Natasha's an attractive woman, but she's way too young for him—not even thirty—and the bitchy ice-queen thing isn't really his type.

The men on the team, on the other hand, are being very attentive. Klaus actually blushed when Jack showed her her desk yesterday morning, and he could swear Sanj makes her a cup of tea every half an hour. The idea of them jostling for her attention makes him bristle, although he tells himself he has no claim on her. That said, he'd put money on the fact that she feels something too. She looks at him in a way that makes him believe he has every last drop of her attention, as though she's trying to absorb him. But what to do about it?

He heads to the kitchen area to make two cups of tea—take that, Sanj—and swings back by Emmy's desk.

'Ready for our catch-up?' he asks. Out of the corner of his eye, Natasha flicks her hair.

Emmy smiles up at him. 'Let's do it,' she says.

They sit side by side on a comfy sofa away from the banks of desks, a coffee table in front of them. Emmy puts her laptop on the table and her long fingers around her mug, and the gesture elicits the same longing that it did when she first did it at his house. She looks pale but beautiful, in a fine black sweater and jeans, her coppery hair tied back and fine gold hoops swinging from her ears. For the millionth time in the past few days, he questions whether he was right to offer her a job instead of a date. This had better be worth it.

Marge materialises—she has the layout of the office down pat—and settles herself at Emmy's feet. He's noticed she gravitates towards Emmy whenever she senses her, and he takes Marge's approval as a major endorsement. She rarely warms to relative strangers. Perhaps, like him, she's drawn to Emmy's calm. She exudes a quiet sense of peace, of not sweating the small stuff, that he can only admire. Emmy reaches down and strokes Marge's cheek with the back of her fingers; the old girl nuzzles into her.

Jack grins at her in what he hopes is a neutral, friendly, boss-like way. 'So, how have your first few days gone?'

'Well, I think,' she says. 'Everyone's been really nice. And it's a very relaxed culture here; it couldn't be more different from Loeb.'

'I can only imagine,' he says. He recalls that she said

she'd had some personal issue there; he's curious to know what it was. 'We've definitely tried to cultivate an informal atmosphere.'

'It's lovely,' she says. 'Anyway.' She leans forward and briskly opens up her laptop. Clearly she's not in the mood for small-talk. 'Let me show you what I've been working on.'

He leans in too and studies the spreadsheet. It's the list he sent her of NGOs they've targeted, those they've partnered with, and adoption rates.

She gestures at the screen. 'It seems to me we need to have different conversations with different NGOs. One. There's a long tail of NGOs who handle a tiny number of tablets. We may want to cull these relationships or see if we can expand the number of tablets under their jurisdiction. Two. We can sort by the percentage of activated tablets to total tablets for each NGO. Three. We can sort by utilisation rates for each tablet and see which NGOs are achieving the highest productivity rates and the greatest learning advances.

'With your blessing, I'd like to reach out by email to everyone in the bottom third on each of these measures and set up an introductory Skype, so I can assess next steps for each NGO and also get qualitative feedback from them on how they find the tablets, what the take up and reaction from the schools and families is like, where they suggest room for improvement in terms of the distribution and how user-friendly they find the software. Does that sound ok?'

'It sounds wonderful,' he says.

'Excellent,' she says. 'I don't think there's any substitute for talking things through face-to-face with the people on the ground; the colour we'll get will be invaluable.'

'Agreed. It sounds like you're on it.' For the first time in a while, he's excited when he thinks about their distribution network rather than his stomach sinking at the mere thought of it.

'Once that's done,' she says, 'are you also happy for me to look into other possible NGO partners we haven't approached before? I'm keen to tighten up that list, but if there are big guys we've overlooked, then it may be worth adding them as targets. I should have a few contacts out there who can put me in touch with the right people if we want to engage.'

'One hundred percent,' he says. 'Go for it. You have free rein on this, but I'm here if you need me to get involved.'

She gives him a bright, professional smile that hurts his heart a little. Fuck. She'll be great in this role.

~

As soon as Jack walks away, she slumps and rubs her forehead with her hand. She's fired up about the opportunity; she knows she can clean this distribution mess up and get the tablets working harder for the kids. But she could smell him when he was sitting next to her; she recognised his scent from the party. She could feel his body heat and the pull of his presence right beside her. Shit. It's going to be exhausting, holding herself together around him every day.

16

TUESDAY, 10TH DECEMBER

Tallulah tiptoes into the kitchen as quietly as she can. Mom's doing spellings with Dolly at the table and she's left her phone charging in a dock on the island. It's now or never. Tallulah has been working on this plan all weekend. Because her phone is still confiscated and she has no idea where it is, she had to use Dolly's iPad and work on iMovie, which is super lame, but never mind. She takes the phone off the dock and steals out of the room.

Back in her bedroom, she enters the passcode for Mom's phone—the code is Tallulah's birthday. It's been that forever. Once it's unlocked, she puts it down and AirDrops the video file from Dolly's iPad to the phone. She goes into Mom's Instagram account. It's insane—she has, like, three hundred new notifications. Tallulah checks them out. They're totally lame comments—*You're so beautiful! I love your style! Your little girl is beyond adorable!* Mom's been posting #MummyandDolly photos again. Ugh.

She wipes her frizz off her face and takes a deep breath. She didn't expect to feel this sick. It's probably just because she's scared of getting caught. She uploads the video to

Mom's Instagram Stories. Phew. A weird feeling hits her stomach, like Dad went over a speed bump too fast. She did it.

She can't resist a little peek at Mom's phone before she puts it back. Her WhatsApp is super lame; loads of chats from school and emojis from Trixie, Mom's intern, who's quite cool but way too into Mom. She checks out Mom's Amazon app and scrolls through her orders. Organic tampons—gross; lots of pink stuff that's probably for Dolly's stocking; a silicon spatula. An Apple Watch—like the one Tallulah has requested for Christmas, but *nicer*—it's the beautiful rose gold one that she didn't think she had a chance of getting. Her stomach flips even more and her eyes prick with tears. Her finger hovers over the Instagram app. No. Leave it. It's too late, anyway.

She puts the phone on silent mode—otherwise Trixie will call Mom immediately and give the game away. This video needs to get picked up by as many of Mom's stupid followers as possible. She sidles back into the kitchen and puts the phone back on the dock.

~

'Ten out of ten!' says Rosa, clapping her hands. Dolly beams at her. She's persevered so well with her spellings; this week they're all homophones. Wear and were; flour and flower; knot and not. Lately Rosa's been trying to spend more time being present with the girls after school—well, with Dolly at least. Dolly's a delight. She adores having Mummy-and-Dolly time and throws herself into any joint activity with Rosa, even if it's homework, poor little thing.

At least it's December; there are a few gorgeous kiddie events that Rosa and the girls have been invited to once they break up from school at the end of the week—not least ice-skating at Somerset House. Even Tallulah should enjoy that one. Her eldest daughter is so prickly at the moment. Rose is at the end of her tether. Stacey says Martha's actually been more relaxed since they confiscated her devices a week ago; Rosa certainly hasn't had that experience with Tallulah.

'Right, sweetie!' she says to Dolly. 'I'd better go get dinner sorted.' She kisses her soft, golden head and drifts over to the island where she picks up her phone.

She freezes.

The home screen has gone crazy—she scrolls down the lock screen.

Eight missed calls from Melissa, her agent.

Three missed calls from Patrizia.

Missed calls from several other friends, mainly mums from school.

WhatsApp informs her it has sixty-seven notifications.

What the hell?

She opens WhatsApp and goes straight to Melissa's messages. They're panicked and inarticulate.

Rosa check ur Stories

Pick up! I need 2 talk 2 u

Rosa u've got to delete the story! Call me

OMG Rosa Diet Prada's picked it up

ROSA!! WHERE TF R U

What. The fuck. Is going on. She swipes up to exit WhatsApp and opens Instagram. Her feed looks normal. Her finger hovers over her Stories icon and she swallows and presses it, tapping through each story from the past twenty-four hours. There's the tour she did of her Christmas decor downstairs and a few videos of her talking through some looks she's styled in front of her dressing room mirror. So far, so good. Then up pops a bright pink page with WHY

YOU SHOULD CANCEL MY MOM in pop-art lettering. Oh, Jesus. Her jaw drops open, and she has the vertiginous sensation of hanging over the edge of a precipice. She taps to move to the next page of the story. It's a video. Tallulah's sitting on her bed. She looks heartbreakingly young as she takes a deep breath and wipes some frizzy tendrils off her face. When she exhales her shoulders sag down, but she squares them, looks straight at the camera and starts to speak.

Hi. I'm Tallulah and Rosa is my mom. You don't see me very much on here cos I'm not the cute, Instagrammable one.

Rosa presses her free hand to her mouth as she watches what is likely to be a giant car crash unfold.

I've been reading about cancel culture, Tallulah continues, *and I think you should cancel my mom. My friends and I want to follow people on social media who inspire us and match our values. My mom has no values except looking pretty and making money. She doesn't care about you and she doesn't care about me. She definitely doesn't care about our planet. All she cares about is how many likes and followers she gets, and which parties and fashion shows she's invited to. She only makes friends with people she thinks are stylish or can get her stuff.*

Horror is creeping over Rosa like a cluster of spiders let loose across her skin.

I just think we deserve more than that, you know? There are five million of you following her, and she's using her platform to sell handbags instead of making a noise about the stuff that matters. The absolute worst thing she's done is hook up with Volare. They're like the most disgusting company ever.

Fuck. Fuck. Fuck.

They're just like Mom. They only care about what things look like; they don't care about whether they're hurting people or animals or the planet.

The screen shifts from Tallulah's face to an image. Rosa squints to work out what it is and recoils in disgust.

This is a snake farm in Vietnam. They nail—yes, nail, the snakes' heads to a tree. They're basically crucifying them. Then they can skin them more easily while they're still alive. They also pump them full of water so they can skin them too. And then they dump them in a pile and leave them to die, which sometimes takes days. PETA says Volare is one of the companies that's using snake farms like this—so people like my mom can have her cute little snakeskin handbag.

The video returns to a red-eyed Tallulah.

I'm sick of this stuff. I'm sick of people like Volare and Mom thinking they can do whatever they want for fashion. It's too high a price to pay. You're the customer. You're the follower. You get to decide what you want. Cancel companies like Volare. And cancel influencers like Rosa Hamilton who don't use their platforms for good. It's not ok, what they do. It's not ok.

Tallulah is sobbing by the end of this performance. The screen flashes to a page tagging PETA's Instagram account—it's the end of the story.

'Aargh.' A strange, strangled noise rises from Rose's throat alongside a bit of bile. She stares at her phone, attempting to process the implications of what she's just seen. She can't. All she knows is that she has to get it off her feed *now*. She jabs at the action buttons on the stories, deleting them one by one. There are six fifteen-second stories in all. She scrubs them all from her feed and warily presses the messages button which stores all the replies to her stories. There are thousands. The first page or two all look the same: *This is disgusting; you should be ashamed of yourself; at least someone in your family has some morals; unfollowing you now.*

She exits the app and braces herself to check her WhatsApp messages. A quick scroll shows that most are from industry friends and mums from school, telling her to check her Instagram and asking if she's alright. She can smell the schadenfreude wafting off the messages. The most worrying ones are from Patrizia. She doesn't want to let Patrizia know she's read her twelve messages just yet—she needs to buy some time—but she can see the first two lines of the latest one and it says *Why are these lies still up? Get them down now and call—*

The only people she has any intention of calling right now are Melissa and David. But first she has to deal with the small, frizzy-haired Judas upstairs. The blind rage that's rising inside terrifies her—she could cheerily wring that girl's neck right now. She goes to put down her phone and remembers Melissa said Diet Prada had got hold of the story. Shit. She goes back into Instagram, and what she finds makes her cover her face with her hand.

Diet Prada has reposted all six of Tallulah's stories and embellished them with thumbs-up emojis. They've also taken a screen-shot of Tallulah mid-flow and created a post about it on their main feed. Fuck. This is worse than she could have imagined. Diet Prada is a watchdog that feels more like a vigilante, and it's the bane of fashion designers and influencers. They're merciless. While they originally focused their encyclopaedic industry knowledge on spotting designers who've knocked off other designers, they now call out anything they deem to be inauthentic or immoral.

She scrolls through the carousel of images and videos on their feed. Tallulah looking teary; Rosa at the Volare summer party holding a snakeskin clutch bag; Tallulah's crucified-snake shot. The final video is a subtitled gif of a teary Tallulah saying on repeat, *it's not ok. It's not ok*. Great. Nothing spreads more quickly than a gif. The caption reads:

OMG. British mega-influencer @RosaHamilton is cancelled by her own daughter. In what seems to be a hijack of her mother's Instagram account, thirteen-year-old Tallulah Hamilton calls her mom out for having the wrong values and associating with brands such as Volare. Diet Prada is among the voices campaigning for more transparency from Volare, which has been accused of a variety of unsavoury acts, from using and illegally importing the skins of endangered species, to secretly endorsing cut-price knock-offs of their goods, to being bankrolled by the Mafia. Hats off to Tallulah for her chutzpah. Influencers of Hamilton's standing need to be called to account for the values they champion on their platforms. At the time of posting, the footage is still live on her account. We wouldn't like to be Tallulah when her mom finds it...

Rosa puts the phone down. Right. Where is that little bitch? It's time to go and deal with her daughter.

17

TUESDAY, 10TH DECEMBER

She storms upstairs and throws open Tallulah's door. Tallulah's on the bed, an open ring-binder on her lap. She shrinks into the pillows when she sees Rosa. Her eyes are wide.

'Mom—' she begins.

'Don't you *Mom* me, you little shit!' The words are vitriol; the delivery is a bark. Her breathing is shallow. Some part of her relishes the fear visible in Tallulah's eyes. She's fucked up majorly; she's waltzed in and attempted to decimate her mother's career with absolutely no idea of what she's doing. Rosa's glad she's scared of the ramifications of her actions. You came from my fucking womb, she thinks. I tore myself to deliver you; I've never been the same down there since. And this is how you repay me?

She looks at this girl who she's brought up and loved and lost countless nights of sleep for over the past thirteen years, and she wonders how the hell it's all gone so horribly wrong. How can she have raised a daughter who hates her so much that she sets out to destroy her?

'Why did you do it?' she spits. 'Do you have any idea how much damage you've done?'

'It was the only way you'd listen,' Tallulah whimpered. 'You don't listen to anything I have to say. You don't even see me except when I get in trouble at school. The only thing you care about is Instagram, so I thought if I went on there you'd finally hear me.'

Rosa's in no mood to listen. 'Look, you stupid. Little. Girl. This is not about you acting out to get my attention. This is a *big* deal. My Instagram feed is a job. It helps to pay for this house and your fancy school. It pays other people's salaries, and it generates thousands and thousands of pounds of sales for companies. And those companies pay people's salaries too. This is real life, and it is *not* a game. You have no authorisation at all to meddle in it.

'Would you go into Daddy's computer and try to sell some of his investments? No. I didn't think so. Well, this is exactly the same. You have threatened my entire career, which I've spent years and years building up, all because you didn't think you were getting enough attention. The world does not revolve around you, Tallulah, whatever you may think.

'I don't even want to look at you right now. You can eat dinner in your room and stay there till I'm ready to deal with you. You make me sick to my stomach. Just stay the hell away from me. I have to go and try to salvage my brand and my relationship with Volare.'

She leaves Tallulah staring at her and flounces out of the room, slamming the door behind her. God, that feels good. Downstairs, she settles Dolly in front of Netflix and calls David.

'David?' Her voice is eerily high-pitched. 'David? You need to come home *now*.'

'What's wrong?' he asks. 'I'm just pulling into Esher station. The markets were dead so—'

'It's Tallulah,' she says. 'She's hijacked my Instagram account and posted a video of her telling people to cancel me and also calling out Volare for animal cruelty. I've deleted it but it's already been viewed like thirty thousand times and now a few other accounts have picked it up.'

'Fuck,' he says.

'And I have all these missed calls from Melissa and Volare and I don't know what to do—I mean, I'm under contract with them! Can they sue me for breach?'

'Don't speak to them,' he says. 'Well, give Melissa a call if you like, but don't speak to Volare. I'll be home in ten—just sit tight and we'll work it out together.'

'Ok.'

She hangs up and runs a hand across her forehead. Thank God for David. In situations like this, she doesn't feel like a grownup; on the contrary, she has no idea what she's supposed to do about Tallulah or Volare or Melissa or her hard-won, five-million-strong group of followers. The amount of energy she's spent ensuring that they have the picture-perfect view of her life is dizzying, and Tallulah's just blasted her facade wide open for everyone to see her dirty laundry. She's just been painted as an evil, animal-hating, money-grabbing cow who's also a bad parent. She takes a peek at Instagram again. This morning she had five-point-one million followers; now it's four-point-nine. She's lost two hundred thousand followers already. Fuck.

Melissa calls again. Rosa puts a steadying hand on the kitchen island and picks up. 'Melissa—' she begins.

'Where the fuck have you been? Rosa! This is a fucking disaster!'

'I know, I—'

'You need to get it down!'

'I've just taken it down,' Rosa says.

'I'm just scrolling through your activity,' says Melissa. 'Fuck, it's had so many shares. Did you have any idea your daughter was planning this?'

'No! Of course not!'

'Shit,' Melissa says. 'PETA's reposted it and they're calling Tallulah the new Greta Thunberg.'

'Oh, for fuck's sake,' Rosa snarls. 'Talk me through my options—what should I do right now?'

'Ok, so I called my boss while I was waiting for you to get back to me,' Melissa says. 'There are two priorities, really. One, stem the flow of follower losses and critics, and two, make good with Volare.'

'Have you spoken to them?' Rosa asks. 'I've had a few missed calls from Patrizia—Tallulah must have put my phone on silent after she did it; I was doing homework with Dolly and I didn't notice.'

'I took a quick call from Patrizia,' Melissa admits. 'It wasn't pretty. She's fucking livid. She wants to speak to you, but I told her it was best to go through us right now. She mentioned that their lawyers were looking at the contract to see if you're in breach.'

'Oh, God,' Rosa gasps, balling up her fist and pressing it to her mouth as the panic rises through her body.

'I doubt they would sue, from experience,' Melissa continues. 'But they will require some serious love and a full apology from you on social media, distancing yourself from Tallulah's actions and refuting her accusations. You'll need to express a firm belief that the accusations of animal cruelty are false and that you stand by the brand's values. Until we've got that arranged, I would stay quiet on every other front. Don't take calls from the media; don't post anything on Instagram or reply to any messages for now—just sit tight till we've got things sorted with Volare.'

'Ok,' Rosa says in a small voice. 'I'll do that.' The last thing she wants to do is go anywhere near her bloody phone.

David's key turns in the front door and she's not sure she's ever heard a sweeter sound. She stumbles into the hallway and collapses into his arms, his stubble grazing her temple, the scent of his skin and his puffy coat hitting her nostrils, even though it's muddled with the smell of the commuter train. She's held it together, but now that he's home she can be weak and terrified and pathetic.

He holds her tightly, his breath warm on the top of her head. The relief of seeing him has burst the dam and she cries great, heaving rasps into his chest, her entire body shuddering.

'Oh, my darling,' he says, and tightens his arms around her. After a minute or two, when she's got a grip of her breathing, he releases her and cocks his head and says, 'Do you want to show me?'

'I deleted it,' she says, 'but everyone else has picked it up.'

They walk through to the kitchen where their housekeeper Maggie is pottering, preparing tea for the kids. David gives Dolly an enormous hug.

'I'm going to go upstairs and have a chat with Mummy,' he tells her. 'Maggie, can you keep an eye on Dolly, please?'

He grabs a bottle of white wine from the fridge and, picking up two glasses, gestures upstairs.

'Right, you,' he says when they're in their room. 'You need a large drink and a bath. I'm going to run you one.'

While it's running, they sit on the bed together and Rosa

pulls up Diet Prada's Instagram stories. David watches the video wordlessly.

'Say something,' Rosa demands when it's finished. David never speaks without thinking first, which is presumably an admirable trait but which can be extremely irritating when she wants him to join her in overreacting to something (usually the kids).

'I mean, it's totally out of line,' he says. 'It's horrifying, and it's unacceptable. But—'

'But what?' How can there possibly be a *but* in this context?

'But she's barely thirteen. Don't you think people will see it for what it is—a pissed-off teen who's got an axe to grind and is tech-savvy enough to hijack your phone? It's highly unfortunate, but perhaps it won't impact your brand that much?'

His attempt to comfort her has had the opposite effect: he's not taking it seriously. She's furious, and he should be furious too.

'You have no idea how things work in fashion,' she hisses. 'She may be just a pissed-off teen, but everything she said has undermined my image, my integrity... you have no idea how important it is to be authentic these days. If she's saying everything I do is a front, then she's basically calling me a fake. And then brands won't want to work with me, and I'll lose followers. It's all a bloody house of cards, you know. I make one false move and it all comes tumbling down. I've already lost at least two hundred thousand followers since the video went live.'

'Jesus,' he says. 'Ok, let's move into the bathroom and you can tell me what Melissa said.'

They walk through and he pulls off his tie.

'What are you doing?' she asks, taking off her sweater.

'I'm getting in with you,' he says. 'You need some TLC.'

He dims the lights. He's lit a few candles and gone heavy on the bubble-bath. He settles himself at one end of the tub and she lowers herself in, wincing at the heat. She lies back between his legs, head on his shoulder. He hands her her wine glass and wraps his arms around her.

'Alright,' he says into her ear. 'What was Melissa's advice?'

'I need to eat humble pie with Volare, basically,' she says. 'Make a public apology, assure all my followers I'm a fan of Volare's values. That kind of thing. It'll be hideous, but I know it's the only option if I'm to salvage this contract.'

David is quiet. She can almost hear the cogs whirring.

'Yes?' she says. She takes a sip of her chilled wine while she waits for him to process whatever he wants to say, and the liquid burn down her throat in that heavenly, numbing way she needs right now.

'Do you think there's any truth in what Tallulah said?' he asks slowly. 'Because, honestly, if they are involved in shit like that, then do you really want to get back into bed with them? Is this your chance to jump ship?'

She hasn't thought of that at all.

'How far into the contract are you?' he asks.

'I'm six months in and it's a year long,' she says.

'Ok… and when did this animal abuse come to light?'

'In the past month or two, I think.'

'I would just consider your next step very carefully.' He puts one hand up and strokes her hair; she leans back into him. 'I know how hard you work, darling, and I know this contract has been a huge coup for you. But Tallulah has, like it or not, thrown everything up into the air and you've got one chance to make sure you come back down on the right side. Forget the money; do what's best for you and your followers. Most likely they'll tell you what they think you should do. If I were you, I'd listen.'

She's considering his logic, a perspective that she hasn't for a second considered until he offered it, when she feels something sticking into her lower back. She sits bolt upright and swivels around, her mouth open in shock. Her husband is gazing at her with *that* expression on his face. His eyes are soft, his smile is lazy.

'David!' she says. 'My life is falling apart right now. I need your help! What I do not need is a boner!'

'Sorry, darling,' he says. He doesn't look remotely sorry. 'It's just—I'm lying here with my beautiful wife naked against me. And it's been a while, you know?'

'It hasn't been that long,' she says.

'Three-and-a-half weeks.' He raises his eyebrows at her. 'Last time we had sex was after the Andersons' dinner party. That was the sixteenth of November.'

The Andersons' dinner party feels like ages ago. David was by far the hottest and wittiest husband there, and she showed her appreciation by leaping on him when they got home.

'We've had sex since then!' she protests.

He shakes his head at her, not unkindly. 'Nope. But don't worry about it. I know how stressed you are at the moment. Just ignore it; it'll go back down in a minute.'

He caresses her shoulder, and she settles back down against him. Jesus. Not only has she totally fucked up her relationship with Tallulah, but she's facing business ruin and now it turns out she's been neglecting her husband as well. She's usually religious about making sure they have sex once a week. It's good for their marriage and even though she hardly ever thinks about sex as she goes about her daily life, she always has a great time in bed with him when they do get around to it. Besides, she's read somewhere that regular ejaculation is important for a healthy prostate and David can't be too careful now he's hitting his late forties. God. One more failure to chalk up; one more thing to add to the to-do list. She mentally pulls up a new note in Evernote. *Make David come once a week. Keep an eye on his balls for lumps.*

She turns her face towards his jaw. 'I'm so sorry,' she says. 'I had no idea it had been that long.'

'It's ok, seriously,' he says. 'We'll get our groove back.' He kisses her forehead.

'It's just that tonight I can't even think about sex, you know? With all this shit hitting the fan.'

'I know,' he says. 'Although, maybe it's exactly what you need—a bit of release. Just saying. I'm here to please.' He wraps one arm over her chest again and runs his other hand up and down her arm.

He's so gorgeous, and so loyal. She's well aware she can be a bitch to live with. He's her biggest cheerleader and he is always on her side, even when she falls glaringly short. She closes her eyes and feels the solidity of his chest as it rises and falls against her back. Lying here with him in this hot, fragrant bath, candles flickering behind her eyelids, she feels a false sense of security.

'I wish I could just lie here with you here, and make all the real-life shit go away,' she says.

'Maybe there's another way of looking at it,' he says.

'What do you mean?'

'Well, we're lying here in our beautiful home, together. We have two healthy daughters—ok, one's a bit of a handful but they're good kids, overall. Yes, I know how hard you've worked on this brand and I know there's money and reputation and jobs at stake here. I wouldn't want to understate that. But, maybe this is real life and what's on that little phone is less real. If you went over to Hampton and threw your phone in the Thames tomorrow, the sky would not fall. You've got me. I'm not going anywhere. We'll figure everything else out—our beloved firstborn, and your business. We'll do it together.'

It's an appealing thought: her family is real and everything else is, if not fake, then at least peripheral. She takes a large gulp of wine and feels a rush of love for this man. Maybe he's right; maybe she needs a release. She puts down her glass and draws up her knees, reaching behind her. She feels him stiffen and shift; his palm skimming down between her breasts and over her stomach.

'Speaking of doing things together…' she says.

18

TUESDAY, 10TH DECEMBER

Tallulah's pillow has a wet spot on it. Drip drip go her tears, plopping down over her nose and cheeks. Her nose is snotty and she can't be bothered to move; she stays huddled up in a ball on her bed and stares at the pink neon light on her wall that spells *Tallulah*. It's her favourite possession. Mom and Dad got it for her thirteenth birthday.

She thinks again of what she's done and of the rose-gold Apple Watch sitting on Mom's Amazon order page. Her stomach churns, a weird mixture of hunger and sickness. She should have got a snack when she had the chance, but she's not sure she could eat one now, anyway. This feels far worse than she thought it would. All week, she's been imagining how satisfying it will be to wipe that smug smile off Mom's face. So many times, she's wanted to scream when a nice mom approaches Mom in the school carpark and compliments her on her outfit or her Instagram feed, and Mom just smiles in a way that's totally *thank you and you'll never be equal to me so don't even try*. That's the smile she wanted to wipe off.

But when she saw Mom's face all tight and white and heard in her voice how much she *hates* her, all the satisfaction just went away, like—poof!—and now she kind of wishes she hadn't done it. The main reason is that under the anger, Mom looks *scared* and that's horrible. Parents aren't supposed to be scared; they're supposed to get cross but to be in control, and Mom looked out of control. It was stupid to think Mom would listen to her, that the video would suddenly magically make her see sense. Now she's so angry she won't listen to anything Tallulah says ever again.

There's a soft knock at the door. 'Can I come in?' Dad asks.

'Sure,' she says cautiously, but when he pokes his head round his face is kind and soft instead of angry.

'Why are you in a robe?' She pushes herself up onto her elbow.

'I just had a bath with your mum,' he says, and comes to sit on the edge of her bed.

'Ugh.' She wrinkles her nose. That's so *gross*. Grown-ups shouldn't take baths together. It would be so embarrassing if any of her friends at school found out about that.

'Hey.' He nudges her arm. 'Give me a break. She's very upset, you know. And very hurt by what you've done. And she's worried about her job. Wanna tell me your side of the story?'

She looks down at her hands and picks at an annoying little hangnail. 'I dunno,' she mutters.

'Well, you were a heck of a lot more articulate than that on the video. I've seen it,' he says as her head jerks up. 'So shoot.'

'I guess I was angry with her. And I wanted to hurt her.' She sneaks another look at his face, but he's just nodding. 'I was just so sick of her thinking her job was more important than us.'

'Your mum puts a lot of effort into both her job and into looking after you guys,' Dad tells her. 'I think she does a brilliant job of juggling.'

'But she makes it really obvious that she finds her job more interesting. She's always on her phone. Like, always. And she always looks so pissed off when we interrupt her.'

'Look,' Dad says. 'I'm just going to say this. We love you girls so, so much. But sometimes being a parent is hard. And sometimes it's dull. There's a lot of heavy lifting, and your mum does far more of that than me. Processing you guys, making sure you've got your netball kit, nagging you to do your homework, nagging to you to anything in fact! Make your bed, tidy your room, eat more of your dinner, get off your iPads—it's not always a riot, believe me! Maybe Mum can't be blamed for wanting to escape into the wonderful world of Instagram sometimes.'

She shrugs. In her head, her need to teach Mom a lesson had felt clear and all-consuming. Now it's muddied with other unwelcome emotions—guilt, and doubt.

'But,' she whispers, as though she's confessing a sin, 'sometimes I don't think Mom's a very good person. Like, she's too shallow—she doesn't care about the right stuff and she doesn't do enough good in the world. And once I started thinking that about her, I couldn't stop thinking it and it just got bigger and bigger.'

Dad takes her hand and squeezes it. 'Ok. Well, let me reassure you. Your mother is a wonderful person. Not everyone has to be an activist during their time on earth. Mum has lots of amazing qualities. Whatever you may think, she's a great mum—she fights for you girls and champions you whenever you get the chance. She takes her responsibilities very seriously. She's hardworking and ambitious and she really believes in herself—she believes she's capable of anything, and I hope that's something that you and Dolly take from her because it's really important.

'She's also got the most extraordinary eye for beauty; she really sees all the wonder in the world. I remember when I started dating her; we couldn't walk down a street or through a park without her pointing out all the beautiful things around us, from trees, to buildings, to birds. Before I met her, I'd just walk around London, oblivious. She taught me to look at the world as a magical, wonderful place. You've inherited that from her too.'

Tallulah imagines Mom and Dad walking down the street as Mom exclaims over a beautiful cherry blossom. It's a bit lame but also quite cute.

'But she's not like that now—she's grumpy and stressed out. I stress her out.'

Dad laughs and throws up his hands. 'Welcome to adulthood, Lulah! Why do you think she's stressed? Too much on her plate. Pesky children who argue with her and don't help enough around the house.' He wiggles his eyebrows at her. 'It's a lonely life, being a mother. She probably doesn't feel properly supported by any of us. So maybe the question should be: how can we help her more? How can we make sure she's less stressed and she has more time to enjoy her family? Huh?'

She's feeling outmanoeuvred and she's not quite sure how this has happened.

'She still chooses rubbish companies to work with,' she says grumpily. 'Like Volare.'

'Bear in mind,' Dad says, 'that as far as I understand it, none of that animal abuse came to light until after she signed the contract with them. Your mum may not be quite as passionate about animals as you are, but she's a good person and she has a powerful sense of justice. Give her some time to work out what she needs to do on that one. She's in a legal agreement with them, so it's not as simple as you think it is.'

'Okaaaay,' she says. She's not convinced.

'So, Missy.' He ruffles her hair and she pushes his hand away. It's frizzy enough already. 'This little stunt of yours is pretty serious, you know. Your mum and I both work very hard at our jobs. What were you trying to achieve—or did you even consider what damage you might to do Mum's career? Because I know you, Lulah, and you're not a spiteful person. You're kind and generous and empathetic. You feel other people's pain so deeply. It's one of the things I love most about you. I can't imagine you wanting to cause your mum pain.'

The ache in her tummy is back, or maybe it's not her tummy. Maybe it's her heart. She doubles over. She's disappointed Dad. It's even worse than hurting Mom. An image of Mom's pinched, scared face flashes into her head.

'I didn't really want to mess up her career,' she admits. She digs her fingernails into the padding of her thumb to distract herself from the pain in her heart. 'I just wanted to give her a really bad fright.'

19

WEDNESDAY, 11TH DECEMBER

The house is dark and David's steady breathing is the only sound when she wakes suddenly at 4am. Her brain assaults her with an instant download of the enormous shit-show that awaits her. She couldn't face her phone last night, but now it taunts her from her bedside table. She edges back the covers and puts on her dressing gown, creeping downstairs with the offending device. As she descends, the smell of pine and eucalyptus grows stronger. She flicks on the lights on the Christmas trees in the hallway and living room and goes to make a cup of coffee. It's peaceful, womblike, when it's lit only by the trees.

She settles on the sofa and, grimacing, turns the phone on. The hostility and fear she feels towards this small piece of kit is quite extraordinary. WhatsApp notification banners flip across the top of her screen at an alarming rate. She'll check the extent of the meltdown on Instagram, then she'll face her WhatsApps and emails. She scrolls through the Activity tab on Instagram; despite her having deleted the offending stories, comments are still pouring in, most of them offensive and judgemental.

She clicks through to see what posts she's been tagged in. Shit. Most of the fashion press have picked up the story on their own feeds: *Vogue, Grazia, Bazaar*, to name a few, as well as the *Daily Mail*, naturally. The *Business of Fashion*'s post is as lengthy and thoughtful as she would have expected. She'd rather have something short and bitchy, but their editor is ex-McKinsey and they're known for their cerebral take on fashion news.

Rosa Hamilton is the latest influencer to fall foul of cancel culture, the BoF writes. *In a highly articulate coup, her thirteen-year-old daughter, Tallulah Hamilton, made an impassioned speech on her mother's Instagram stories, pleading with Hamilton's followers to hold her to account over her contract with Italian luxury goods company Volare, which has recently been under fire for its treatment of endangered species and lack of corporate governance ... It's not a crime to enjoy and feature beautiful things, but Tallulah makes a valid point. Influencers with sizeable platforms do have a responsibility to their followers to be mindful about how they use their voice and what values they choose to portray ... While her daughter's post will likely have made uncomfortable viewing for Hamilton, she would do well to heed Tallulah's advice and reconsider the calibre of her brand partnerships as well as the causes she champions via her not inconsiderable platform.*

The article finished by reverting to the current debate around what cancel culture actually is: *Cancel culture has been deemed both welcome activism and the infringement of public figures' right to freedom of speech. The idea that we can or should call to 'cancel' those with whom we disagree should not be accepted automatically. Of course, our ability to cancel those in the public eye who come from a place of white privilege is questionable. Events of the past twelve months have suggested that many of these public figures simply lie low to lick their wounds for a short while before issuing a public* mea culpa *and springing back to their previous status with alarming speed.*

The BoF is essentially saying she'll be fine because she's white and privileged, a stance that's dismissive, insulting and reassuring in equal measure. It's interesting that they're on the same page as David regarding Volare. He's told her he'll speak to some colleagues today to get more background on the company before she makes her next step. Last night, despite the bleakness of her situation, the road seemed clear: grovel wildly and fix her relationship with Volare as quickly as possible. This morning, she has no fucking idea what she should do.

Scrolling through WhatsApp is like wading through a bloodbath. There are messages from school mums, industry friends, fashion designers, photographers, and even journalists who have her number. Everyone wants a piece of her; her pain is merely a juicy scandal that they all want to claim proximity to. There's a nice one from Stacey. *Why are teenage girls such sneaky little douchebags?* she writes. *If you want to avoid school for a day or two then give me a shout, Jack or I can help with school runs x.*

She hasn't even considered the school run. Usually, the carpark at drop off is fun, a way to socialise, gossip and one-up the other mothers. Rosa is frequently accosted by mothers wanting to compliment her on her outfit, get the gossip from the latest celebrity event Rosa's attended, or ask for a favour—an introduction or a prize for the next fundraiser. Rosa is always gracious, but usually dismissive. Today the shoe will be on the other foot and she'll be the source of the gossip, the one they point fingers at. No one will have had that much fun since Moira Gordon's husband ran off with his young colleague. God. There's no way she can face that crowd today. Diet Prada has nothing on the private school mothers of Surrey. She wants to stay here with her beautiful Christmas trees and eat mince pies all day.

Next, she checks her emails. There are a lot more journalist requests—her email is far more discoverable than her phone number. Worse, there are several from PR companies representing major brands. Chanel has uninvited her to the children's Christmas party they're throwing at Claridges next week, and Mulberry has pulled its invitation for her and the girls to go ice-skating at Somerset House. The language of both emails is frosty and judgemental. *In light of recent events, we feel it is no longer appropriate for you to attend our event next week ...* Jesus. They don't waste time. How is she going to explain that one to Dolly?

The implications of these about-turns are more painful than the sting of missing out on the events themselves. She's a card-carrying member of the exclusive club that is the British fashion industry. She's a front-row regular at London Fashion Week, and she goes to the British Fashion Awards on the arms of various designers. This status comes from years of back-breaking work and now the industry is discarding her, washing their hands of her before any of her tarnish can rub off on them. She's built her entire persona and career on external validation, and now that's being seized. It's as though she's a drug addict who's being forced to go cold turkey. They can't do this. It's not fair. The Business of Fashion may be dismissive of how real cancel culture can be for people like her, but it feels pretty fucking real right now. It feels icy cold.

David comes down a couple of hours later to find her lying on the sofa in her dressing gown, weeping as she tortures herself by reading all the press coverage of her fiasco. She looks up at him mournfully as he sits on the edge of the sofa.

'I can't do the school run. Those vultures will be out for my blood—I just—I can't face it, David.'

'It's ok.' He pats her dressing gown. 'I'll do it. I can work from home today, keep you company. I'll get the girls up shortly.' He nods at the phone. 'Facing your demons, are you?'

She sighs and puts it face-down. 'They're all out for my blood too—the whole industry is a pile of fucking lemmings. The fashion press are all over it, a couple of brands have dropped me like hot cakes, and everyone is weighing in with their opinion, both friends and randoms.'

'The moral high ground is always an attractive place to be, right?' David asks. 'As long as you're up there, judging others, you're temporarily excused from being judged yourself. It's just herd mentality—very primal; very disappointing.'

'It doesn't make it any easier,' she says.

'I know, sweetie. Listen, after you passed out last night I was WhatsApping with Miguel, our luxury goods analyst. He's very suspicious of Volare's credentials. They're being heavily bankrolled, but it's not quite clear by whom. They've reported fantastic sales numbers, but as they're private, no one has any insight into how accurate they are. And the word is that the big guys like LVMH and Kering wouldn't touch them with a barge-pole as an acquisition target because there's so much opacity surrounding their governance and operations. They talk a good game, but I'd be careful, darling. Maybe take today to consider whether you really want to get back into bed with them.'

20

THURSDAY, 12TH DECEMBER

Emmy is settled on the very comfortable sofa in her flat, catching up on *Strictly* reruns on BBC iPlayer. It's the final this Saturday; Kelvin and Oti must have it in the bag. She's worked her way through far too many Pringles; she half-heartedly considers whether it's worth the effort of getting off the sofa to put a ready-meal in the oven.

Her phone pings: it's a message from Jack.

Just got home to find the most enormous chilli in the AGA. Fancy coming over and helping me eat it?

She sits bolt upright. God, yes. Work this week has gone brilliantly, despite the toll the baby's taking on her energy levels. Jack seems delighted with the progress she's making, but she's found it a struggle to keep her feelings for him under control. He dazzles her. He's so vital, so dynamic, bounding around the office with the enthusiasm of a puppy. She's watched him buoy people up and juggle a multitude of issues from strategic to logistical. He can shift gears in an instant, assimilate information in seconds, and spit out solutions that are as elegant and fully conceived as if he's spent hours on them. She's in awe of his talents, and it's such a bloody turn-on to watch him in action that it's like torture.

She replies: *I'd love to. Give me 10.*

Excellent, he writes. *The door's open; just come on in.*

She leaps off the sofa and springs into action: brush teeth, spray on deodorant and perfume, run brush painfully through hair, and slap on enough makeup to hide her pallor while not looking like she's tried. She's in yoga pants and a snug sweater; they'll have to do. Her stomach is still completely flat; it continues to be hard to believe that a tiny being is slowly, steadily putting itself together somewhere inside her. She pulls on her Uggs and heads across the courtyard.

When she came to work last Monday with her rucksack full of belongings, she found the courtyard and surrounding garden had been bedecked with white fairy lights. They're on now and it looks magical. She pushes open the heavy front door and finds the interior decorated too. It's so different from Rosa's immaculate white scheme—there are warm reds and golds everywhere, with traditional wooden decorations hanging from the staircase. A soft statue of St Nicholas dressed in burlap stands at the foot of the stairs. Bing Crosby croons from somewhere. The effect is delightfully heart-warming.

'Hello?' she calls.

'Through here!' shouts Jack.

She heads into the kitchen and laughs. He's standing at the AGA in a colourful Fair Isle sweater, rows of Santa heads competing with snowmen, snowflakes and Christmas trees. 'Very festive,' she says.

'I thought so,' he replies. 'I'm just back from my annual Christmas lunch in town with some uni mates. Christmas jumpers obligatory. I think I surpassed myself this year.'

He walks over to her and wraps her in his arms, kissing the top of her head before releasing her. 'Hello, you,' he says.

The brief, heavenly display of affection throws her. She can tell, by the way he moves and smells, that he's had a fair bit to drink.

'Boozy Christmas lunch?' she asks.

'They always are. I was more restrained than some of my mates. And I ate enough to soak it all up, hence my alarm at finding this enormous chilli when I got home. Carol kindly stuck it in the AGA a few hours ago.'

She's met Carol, the housekeeper, briefly when she came over to introduce the cleaners to Emmy. 'Well,' she says, 'I'm happy to help. I was eating Pringles and catching up on *Strictly* when you texted.'

'Ooh, *Strictly*,' he says. 'Mia will be up to ninety on Saturday—she's obsessed by Oti and Kelvin. Stace'll have to vote three million times and you can bet Mia'll be dolled up in full ballroom regalia for the final.'

'Does Stacey have the kids this weekend?'

'Yup,' he says. 'That's why we decorated last weekend, when they were here.'

'It looks gorgeous. So festive.'

'Thank you. We had a lot of fun doing it. I've confined all their homemade decorations to the den. Mean Dad. Can I get you a glass of wine? I've opened a Malbec to go with the chilli.'

Why not? She hasn't drunk since her pregnancy test and half a glass won't do any harm. She'll just sip it; it's easier than finding an excuse for why she's not drinking. As usual, the enormous secret she's carrying hangs like a spectre over her when she's with him.

Oblivious, he pours some red into two glasses and hands one to her.

'Cheers. Have a seat. We can go through to the living room in a minute.'

'Cheers.' She eases herself up onto a barstool at the island and watches as he pours some rice into a pan, adds water and puts it on one of the hot plates on the top of the AGA. She takes a tentative sip of her wine. Part of her hopes she'll be the kind of pregnant woman to go off the taste, but no. It's sublime, silky and full-bodied. The kitchen is cosy and smells of slow-cooked chilli; Bing is still singing and Jack is... well, he's sheer perfection, even in that ridiculous jumper. And she's the one who gets to be here this evening, enjoying his company. She feels utterly content. A silly, happy grin spreads over her face and it's too much effort to rearrange her features into some semblance of neutrality.

Rice on, he comes back to the island to retrieve his wineglass. He leans over and plants his elbows on the counter next to her, takes a drink and puts down his glass. He's looking at her the entire time, mirroring her smile, and she holds his gaze. He opens his mouth and hesitates before speaking.

'God, Emmy,' he says. 'I have just enough Dutch courage in me to do this, but—I can't stop thinking about you.' He puts his hand on hers and strokes it with his thumb. 'I'm wondering if I have a chance with you? If I'm freaking you out, just tell me where to go.'

Her head fills with blood as it hits her that this is happening; Jack is interested, and she doesn't have to hold herself in any more, smile politely or speak professionally. She's unleashed.

'You have a lot more than a chance,' she says, and she leans forward and kisses him on his beautiful mouth. He melts into her and swivels her round on the barstool to face him; she opens her legs to get him as close to her as she can. He has one arm wrapped around her and the other in her hair. He tastes of wine and heaven, and all she can think as their tongues twist together is *thank God thank God thank God thank God thank God*.

Jack comes up for air. 'Thank fuck,' he gasps, and she laughs. 'Oh, Jesus, thank fuck. I've wanted to do that since you turned up here to collect...'

'Dolly,' she says.

'Dolly. You've turned my brain to mush. God, look at you,' he says, and kisses her again, crushing her to him as she runs her hands over him, exploring him. His hair is soft; his back and shoulders are sculpted under her palms. She slips a hand into one of the pockets of his jeans; his bum is glorious. Every bit of him is glorious. She can't believe she's got free rein over him. Her other hand rummages under the hem of his jumper and finds the smooth skin of his back; she pulls him even more tightly into her so there's no space between them at all.

He moves his mouth to drop kisses down her neck, his hands smoothing her hair off her face. 'Are you sure you're ok with this?' he murmurs.

She laughs and pulls herself free, cupping his face. 'Jack. I wanted to jump on you as soon as I saw you at the school nativity. You're just lucky Mia got there first.' His face lights up and she continues. 'I feel the same as you; I can't stop thinking about you. I didn't know what to do about it. The party was—'

'The party,' he says, 'was brutal. I just wanted to scoop you up and kiss you. That little black dress...' He runs a hand down her thigh. 'Mmm. You are breathtaking; do you know that? I came so close to asking you out that first night, but I ended up offering you a job instead.'

'I love the job,' she says, and kisses him. 'But this...' she shrugs. 'Is it ok, that we're doing this?'

'We'll work it out,' he says. 'We're both adults. Right now, the only thing I can think about is that you're right here with me, in my home, and I'm able to kiss you.' He leans into her again as a buzzer sounds. 'You've quite literally been saved by the bell,' he says. 'That's the rice. Having invited you over for chilli and then promptly forced myself on you, I'm now going to do the honourable thing and feed you.'

THEY BRING their wine and bowls of chilli through to the living room, where another large tree throws off its evocative scent and the fire crackles away. They sit on the thick white rug, backs against the sofa, leaning into each other. The fire casts out a wonderful heat, and the chilli is excellent. Jack has his arm around her and eats his food with a fork, the bowl balanced on his thighs. Marge pads silently into the room and lowers herself down so her enormous head is across Emmy's shins, before shifting contentedly and emitting a deep sigh. Emmy giggles.

'She's such a traitor,' Jack says. 'She's given me zero attention at work since you came on the scene. You've really got a fan there.'

'She's gorgeous.' She reaches forward and pats her head, enjoying Marge's weight on her. 'I'm getting very attached to her, but I'm sure she's just here for the chilli.'

'That too,' says Jack. 'Make sure she doesn't get any—that's one mess I don't want to have to clear up in the morning.'

When they've finished eating, he puts their bowls on the coffee table. Emmy rubs the rug with her socked toe.

'This is the most amazing rug,' she says. 'It's so thick and soft; it's like a bed.'

'Mmm,' Jack says. 'We can put it to the test, if you're game.'

She jerks her head up to look at him; his eyes are dark and his face is serious as he slides his fingers inside the neck of her sweater and strokes her collarbone, back and forth. His expression makes her stomach flip. She came over here bearing hopes she didn't dare articulate to herself, but now she knows exactly what's going to happen. Her gaze darts to the door. 'Is anyone else in the house?' she asks.

'Only Marge,' Jack says, 'and she can't see a thing. But still—I'll take her out to the kitchen.' He hauls himself up and grabs their bowls. 'Come on, old thing; that's my girl.'

She watches the fire, the thrill of anticipation creeping over her skin. He's back a few minutes later, switching off the chandelier overhead. The room is dim, lit only by the fire and the soft fairy lights on the Christmas tree. He sits down on the rug beside her and strokes her cheek, gazing at her as though he can't quite believe she's real. Then he hooks the back of her neck and pulls her towards him and she's lost in him. He's beguilingly novel and blessedly familiar all at once. She swings a leg over and straddles him. Within a couple of minutes, he's tugging at her sweater and off it comes over her head.

'I didn't exactly dress for this,' she manages, some part of her brain registering that she's wearing old, greying M&S underwear and definitely hasn't shaved her legs since the party. She's also full of chilli and Pringles; she mustn't be too athletic or she'll get a stitch.

'It's not your clothes I'm interested in,' he murmurs. 'And you could argue I haven't dressed for seduction either.'

She giggles. She's still sitting on him; she wrestles with the blasted Christmas jumper, but he's leaning back against the sofa. Suddenly, he sits upright and reaches behind his head, pulling the jumper and his t-shirt over it in that way that guys seem able to do. Quick as a flash, he's tossed them away and unhooked her bra. He runs his hands firmly up her back and slips her bra straps off her shoulders. As soon as his fingers hit her nipples and start to play with them, red-hot pain and red-hot desire shoot through them simultaneously. They're still agony, but the increased sensitivity means they're erogenous in a way she's never experienced before. She gasps and flinches.

'Oh, God,' he says. 'Sorry—is that sore?'

'No, no,' she says; 'they're just a bit sensitive, that's all. Don't stop—it feels amazing.'

'You're amazing,' he says. He pulls away and studies her face, her breasts. 'God, Emmy,' he whispers. 'I'm blown away by you.' He kisses her hard and increases the pressure of his hands on her nipples, tweaking and pinching them until she thinks she may pass out. Her hands, meanwhile, are delighting in his skin, grabbing his biceps, roaming over his shoulders and caressing his back.

He pulls away and twists backwards, grabbing a couple of cushions off the sofa and chucking them onto the rug. He holds her around the waist and eases her off him and down onto the cushions so he's crouching over her. He smiles at her, a slow grin of wonder that makes her face split as she smiles back at him.

He runs a finger under the waistband of her yoga pants. 'I remember you wearing these during yoga. I wanted to peel them off you even then.'

'Mmm,' she says. 'Yoga. I was ogling your back during your headstand.'

'Were you now?' He smirks, bends and gives her a smiling kiss. 'Well, clearly we've wasted an appalling amount of time already. Time to play catch up. Ok if I take them off?'

She nods and raises her bum off the rug as he slips the yoga pants off along with her knickers, leaving her stark naked.

She squirms. 'I absolutely did not expect to end up naked on your living room rug this evening.'

He shakes with laughter. 'Fuck, me neither. I'm thrilled with myself. If I'd known chilli was such a winner, I'd have spent my teens whipping it up for unsuspecting females. Now, let me look at you.'

As he speaks, he's on one elbow, running his other hand up and down her abdomen, from her neck to her breastbone to her stomach. He slips it between her legs and watches for her reaction. Her groin fills with heat. She pushes into his hand.

'Jack,' she moans, staring up at him. In answer, he lowers his face to hers and kisses her, gently at first and then harder, more hungrily. She pulls blindly at his belt buckle, undoing it and unzipping his jeans. He reaches behind and tugs them and his boxers off.

'Come here,' she says, and pulls him down on top of her, wrapping her legs around him and revelling in his erection, which is sticking into her pelvis. The fire throws off a wall of heat and her skin prickles with sweat. She closes her eyes and squeezes her thighs and holds him as tightly as she can. The sensation of him on top of her, his skin touching hers the entire length of her body, is overwhelming.

'Hang on a sec, gorgeous,' he murmurs and reaches over to his jeans, pulling out a foil packet.

'Where the hell did that materialise from?' she asks, laughing.

He has the grace to look embarrassed. 'I may have run upstairs for a couple when I put Marge in the kitchen.'

'I must stop being such a foregone conclusion,' she says.

He holds the packet up. 'Sure you're up for this?'

'Seriously,' she groans. 'Try and stop me.'

He puts it on the rug. 'I have unfinished business to attend to first.' Freeing himself from the grip of her legs, he raises himself up and showers kisses down onto her body. She luxuriates on the rug, feeling wanton, the heat from the flames licking her skin, and abandons herself to pure sensation as he slips a couple of fingers inside her and proceeds to go down on her in the most skilful way she's ever experienced. Not only that, but one of the more welcome side-effects of pregnancy is the amount of extra blood supply her body seems to be pumping to her sex organs. The result is that she falls apart, climaxing so hard that she shouts out—a guttural, unfamiliar noise that shocks her but appears to delight him.

He comes up to hug her and folds his arms tightly around her as she tries to catch her breath, her heart racing. 'You're incredible,' he growls into her neck. 'I can't get enough of you.'

She rolls with him so he's under her and straddles him, enjoying the view of his magnificent body. Desire is etched all over his face as he watches her and waits for her to make her move. Once she's got the condom on, she eases him inside her and begins to move. This is for Jack—she wants him to have the same transcendent experience that she just had—but as they move, she knows that it's just as much for her. Here is the man who has captivated her for what seems like a lifetime rather than a few days, everything about him becoming so mesmerising and so dear to her so quickly. Since she stepped over his threshold this evening, their relationship has escalated beyond her most fervent dreams and he's right here, beneath her, inside her, skin on skin. He's looking at her as if she's a vision and he pushes himself up to sitting so he can wrap one of his arms around her and kiss her while she unravels him. From the way his face crumples as he comes, to the passion with which he kisses her, she suspects he's had a similarly mystical experience.

He collapses back onto the cushions and she flops on top of him as he encloses her in his arms. Beneath her, his ribcage rises and falls as he catches his breath.

'That,' he whispers, 'was spectacular.'

'I know.' She nuzzles into his neck. 'I feel the same. You're heaven.'

They lie there and she's in a veritable stupor of emotion and contentment. Right now, nothing else exists for her aside from Jack, nothing else matters. There's a tiny heartbeat somewhere inside of her she can't even feel, a heartbeat that she'll have to acknowledge to herself and admit to him at some point, but not tonight. It can wait.

21

FRIDAY, 13TH DECEMBER

Emmy awakens to a shrill beeping sound that makes her sit up in bewilderment. She's in Jack's enormous bed and the room is very dark. He stops the racket and puts an arm around her, pulling her back down into their blissful cocoon.

'Sorry,' he says into her hair. 'It's my alarm.'

'What time is it?' she mutters. It feels like the dead of night.

'Five forty-five. I need to get up.'

'Ugh. What on earth for?'

'I have to do my morning routine,' he says. 'It takes me a couple of hours each morning.'

'What morning routine?' She wraps her top leg around him, drawing him towards her. 'Mmm,' she murmurs. 'You're so warm.'

He laughs and runs a leisurely hand up her thigh and over her backside. 'I'd rather you thought I was hot, but I'll take warm. I have to work out—weights and cardio, do my meditation, sauna, stuff like that. It's my priming sequence.'

'What do you mean, priming?' she asks.

'Getting ready for the day ahead. I like to prime my mind, body and soul so I can start my working day firing on all cylinders.'

She moves her hand down over the hairs on his chest, following the line of them that trails down his stomach, echoing the kisses she rained down on this trail last night when they moved up to Jack's bedroom.

'So that's your secret,' she mumbles. 'I'm pretty confident I could prime your mind, body and soul for you more effectively than any workout. But I need more sleep—my hours of service don't start yet.'

He shudders. 'I have no doubt you could, you little beauty, but I do need to sweat out this booze, for everyone's sake. We've got Deutsche Bank coming in for the morning to discuss the possibility of their becoming corporate sponsors. So,'—he drops a kiss on her shoulder—'I've got to get out of here before I succumb to temptation. Tell me—do you offer a priming service on Saturday mornings?'

'I just might,' she says, releasing him from her grip.

He kisses her. 'Excellent. I'll have to lure you over here again tonight, then.' He pulls back the covers and jumps out of bed, turning on the bedside lamp.

She squints at the light and scowls at him. 'Are you always this perky in the mornings?'

He grins. 'Oh, this is me on a hangover.'

'God,' she groans, and buries her head in her pillow. 'We have no future together, in that case.'

AT WORK, she's capable of very little other than staring blankly at her screen between shooting plaintive glances at

Jack. He's been holed up in a glass-fronted room most of the morning with a group of men in suits and Natasha, who looks vampish in a sleek red dress. She's pretty sure Natasha dislikes her. She's also pretty sure she has a thing for Jack. Jack himself is in a blazer and open-necked shirt, looking quite the disruptive entrepreneur. He shot her a wide grin when he came into the office earlier, but she hasn't had any other interaction with him since he left her in his bed.

She's beside herself with happiness, longing and torment. She still can't believe the events of last night actually happened. Whatever feelings she had for him before then have rocketed into the stratosphere, now that she knows what they're capable of together. It's hard to focus on anything else apart from the memory of him—his face, his hands, his smell, his body, his mouth on hers. She's drunk on him.

Shortly after midday the suits file out of the office, Jack and Natasha leading the way. Once he's seen them off, he heads back to his desk. A moment later, her Slack desktop app shows a message from him.

I wanted to make you aware, with no ulterior motive at all, that there's a copious amount of leftover chilli in my fridge for lunch.

A second later, another one pops up.

FYI, some women seem to find my (Carol's) chilli a valuable trading commodity.

She giggles and looks up to find him smiling at her across the room. Her heart does a little dance; he's adorable.

Fresh chilli, maybe, she writes. *If you're suggesting I'd put out in exchange for leftovers, then you've grossly undervalued me.*

He's right back with: *Really? It's not worth anything to you? Carol's chilli gets better with age—like me.*

There's nothing she wants more right now than to be sitting in his kitchen, alone with him.

Well, she concedes, *it may have some small value. But you'll get a lot less bang for your buck with leftovers.*

Are you sure you're comfortable using the word bang *in this conversation? I'll take any kind of bang you're offering.*

She laughs out loud and shakes her head at him.

See you at the house in 5? he asks. She nods. Just try to keep her away.

She skulks out of the office a minute after him and makes a run for it across the courtyard, slipping in through the front door. She finds him and Carol in the kitchen.

'Hi,' she says shyly.

He winks at her. 'I can take it from here, thanks Carol,' he says.

'I'll be off down to the shops then,' Carol tells him. 'Have you thought about what you'd like for dinner?'

'I don't know.' He smiles at Emmy. 'Emmy, what do we fancy for dinner?'

The trivial domestic question hits her straight in the heart. It's Friday lunchtime and she's here, with Jack, discussing what they should make for dinner. The prospect of a cosy evening in with him dances in front of her.

'You have some nice chicken legs in the fridge,' Carol offers. 'I can get some olives and rosemary if you want to make chicken *cacciatore*?'

Jack raises his eyebrows at Emmy, and she nods happily.

As soon as Carol has headed out the back door with her shopping bags, he crosses the kitchen, hugging her and twirling her round.

'How was your morning?' she asks as leans into him.

'Fruitful, hopefully,' he says, 'mainly thanks to Natasha. She wowed them all. I was a bit of a waste of space; I kept trying to focus on how many more kids we could educate with Deutsche's backing, but all I could think about was how fucking incredible it felt to be with you on that rug last night.'

She smiles and feels a warm rush of relief that she's not the only one who's spent the morning pining.

'It was pretty incredible in your bed later on, too,' she says.

'It was,' he agrees. 'I should have stayed with you this morning. I'm sorry. I'll make up for it tonight.'

'Did you plan it that way?' she asks. 'Last night—did you think we'd end up in bed together when you invited me over?'

'I don't know what I thought.' He smiles sheepishly and tucks a strand of hair behind her ear. 'All I know is that I was on my way home in a cab, thinking of you and feeling miserable. Then, when I got back and saw your light on, I just thought, *Jack, what are you doing? You want to see her; just ask her over, for God's sake.* The wine gave me the courage I needed but I didn't dare have any expectations; I just wanted to spend the evening with you.'

Then he kisses her and whatever angst she's had over whether he still feels the same way today dissipates.

When he pulls away, he says, 'What are you doing tomorrow?'

'Aside from priming your mind, body and soul, you mean?'

He grins. 'That's the priority. But do you have any plans for the rest of the day?'

'Nothing until the *Strictly* final. I promised Dolly I'd watch it with her. Why?'

'I've had an idea. Can I take you out for the day? It's a surprise. It might be a little OTT, but I think you'll enjoy it.'

He wraps his hand around the nape of her neck and she leans back into it.

'An OTT day out with you sounds amazing,' she says. 'Yes, please.'

'Excellent.' He kisses her forehead. 'I'll get the chilli on.'

22

SATURDAY, 14TH DECEMBER

Emmy rides beside Jack in his Tesla. Michael Bublé belts out Christmas classics and Jack's free hand is on her lap, his fingers entwined with hers as he drives. There's an ease and familiarity between them already. For someone who's recently divorced, he's incredibly open with his affections and verbal about what he thinks of her. As a result, she's been luxuriating in the glow of his attraction and of the appetite he seems to have for her company.

He's singing along to *Santa Claus is Coming to Town* in a surprisingly smooth baritone. The fact that he enjoys cheesy Christmas music is the icing on the cake—the guy is perfect. He looks boyishly carefree behind the wheel of his beautiful toy. They had a relaxed kitchen supper last night followed by a long bath, and their lovemaking this morning was lazy and intimate. They've only been together for two nights, and yet she feels as though she's falling down a Jack-shaped rabbit hole where all is well with the world.

The only blemish on her happiness is her pregnancy: this enormous secret she worries will change everything once she confides in him. While she's committed to having this baby, she hasn't exactly embraced it so far, and yet it's an inextricable part of what she has to offer Jack. She's played out the conversation ad nauseam in her head, and she can't conceive of how he'll react. The thought of telling him, and putting this fragile, brand-new romance at risk, makes her sick to her stomach. She gazes at him and promises herself that she'll come clean by the end of the weekend.

He catches her looking at him and grins back at her, tightening his grip on her hand. 'We'll be there in a minute,' he says.

She has no idea where he's taking her or what they'll be doing. He told her to dress casually. She's hoping for a nice walk and a good pub lunch, although that doesn't explain his reference to his proposal as OTT. They've only been in the car for about twenty minutes, and they're now driving down an inauspicious-looking country lane.

He slows the car. 'Here we go,' he says, and points.

There's a pair of gates and a large sign: SKYDIVE UK.

Oh, fuck, fuck, fuck.

He turns to her. 'I know it's not the Himalayas, but you said you'd love to try it. We can do a tandem skydive here; I'll be right next to you the whole time. What do you think?'

His smile is open and trusting; he looks like a little boy who's just handed his mother a flower he's picked. Thoughts crowd her head.

He's organised this to make her happy—it's one of the most thoughtful things anyone's done for her.

It probably cost a bloody fortune.

He's—unwittingly—forced her hand. She has to tell him now, and crush him, and ruin this beautiful surprise he's prepared.

'Can you pull over for a sec?' she asks. Her throat is tight and dry.

'Of course.' He looks startled. 'Are you ok? If you have cold feet, we can cancel—it's not a problem. I know it's daunting, the first time.'

He stops the car and she twists around to face him properly. Her stomach is churning and her forehead has broken out in an instant sweat. She squeezes his hand.

'Jack,' she says. 'I have to tell you something. I've been trying to find the right time, but I've been so happy the past couple of days I didn't want to rock the boat.'

'What is it?' he asks.

'I can't go skydiving,' she says. 'I'm so sorry. I'm ten weeks pregnant.'

23

SATURDAY, 14TH DECEMBER

He pulls his hand away from hers immediately, as if it's burnt. That, and the look that flashes across his face, tells her all she needs to know. As well as the shock, she registers distaste. He's disgusted.

His eyes scan her stomach. 'You're *pregnant*?'

'Yes,' she says. She tries to keep her voice steady. 'I only found out last week, and I came down here immediately—I didn't know what to do.'

'Are you'—he gestured gingerly, avoiding her eyes—'in a relationship?'

'No! Of course not. There's no one else, Jack.'

'Then who's the father?'

'It's someone from Loeb, but he's very much out of the picture. I'll have to tell him eventually, I suppose, but I haven't decided yet. It's a bit of a complicated situation with him.'

'Complicated, how?' he asks.

She squirms. There's no way of making this sound good. 'He ran the Equities division. He was married.' She braves eye contact, but his glare is stony. 'Um, a few weeks ago he got sacked for sexual misconduct.'

'They found about you two?'

'No; he got accused of assault and then several other women came forward; it turned out he'd been propositioning people, and he was even sleeping with a girl on my desk.'

'Jesus Christ,' Jack says. 'I read about that in the FT. Italian guy, right? *He's* the father?'

'I'm afraid so,' she says. 'It's such a mess.' She studies the back of her hands.

'Did he hurt you?' he asks in a strangled voice.

'No,' she says. 'He didn't hurt me; it was completely consensual. Very poor judgement on my part, obviously, and I'm not proud of myself. I was so fucked up after I came back from India that I just set about trying to distract myself as much as possible, and he was happy to help me do that. I haven't taken any of his calls since Loeb suspended him—I just want to stay the hell away from him.'

He purses his lips together and exhales sharply through his nose.

'So you have form when it comes to your bosses, I see,' he says.

'Jack! That's so unfair! It's not like that at all.'

'When were you planning on telling me?'

'This weekend. I promise. I'd made a deal with myself that I would do it by the end of the weekend; I never wanted it to come out like this.'

He holds his hands up. 'Did you not think,' he says, 'I'd want to know before I slept with you? Did you not think it would be a basic courtesy to mention it? Jesus, Emmy!'

'I know I should have,' she says in a small voice. 'But that night things happened so quickly, and to be completely honest—this is going to sound awful—I didn't dare risk it. I wanted to be with you so badly; I was so ecstatic you were interested. I knew if I told you I was pregnant you'd probably—'

'Go on,' he says. 'Say it. I'd probably what?'

'You'd probably walk away.'

'Wow,' he says. 'So you thought you'd make the decision for me, and you went ahead and fucked me knowing that you being *pregnant* would be a deal-breaker for me. For fuck's sake.'

His words are agony and make her eyes fill, but in a way they're also a relief because they force her to confront how far she's betrayed his trust. Despite the ugliness of the words, she can't argue with his interpretation of events.

'It sounds awful, when you say it like that.' Her eyes and nose are streaming and she scrabbles in her bag for a tissue. Jack leans over, wrenches open the glove compartment and throws a pack of tissues on her lap, all without looking at her. She blows her nose. 'Thanks. It wasn't as if I planned it all and set out to deceive you. But yes, you're right that in the heat of the moment, I was selfish. I acted on my feelings for you and just went straight for what I wanted—for what we both wanted, I think—and it was incredibly disrespectful to you not to come clean about the pregnancy. I'm so, so sorry.'

'Look.' He makes eye contact, but he still hasn't touched her since he withdrew his hand. 'I'm not sure whether to be more pissed off about you being pregnant or you blatantly deceiving me. I'm not some playboy, Emmy. I've done very little dating since Stacey left me. And I think you and I both know that this wasn't a onetime thing. We were only going to get in deeper, so for the love of God, I don't know why you thought keeping it from me was the way to go.'

He's using the past tense to describe what they have, and

it's agony. She opens her mouth to speak, and he holds up his hand. 'I'm not finished. If you'd told me before we kissed that you were pregnant, then you're right; I would have retreated quick-smart. I have four kids; you're expecting another. That's stalemate. I would have regretfully walked away, but you didn't do me the courtesy. You slept with me on false pretences. I know, you don't owe me anything and we're both adults, but I could really have done without spending the past couple of days with you if it wasn't meant to be.'

'I'm so sorry,' she whispers. 'I know how selfish it was. I've been so freaked out since I found out I'm pregnant—I'm terrified and I haven't wrapped my head around the idea yet that it will be me and the baby on our own. I wasn't expecting anything from you; I couldn't help myself. I've been so happy these past few days, and this has been eating away at me. I just didn't want to have to think about real life and how hard it's going to be.'

Jack turns on the ignition and does a U-turn, taking them back the way they came. Michael Bublé blasts out again and he turns the sound system off.

'I'm sure it's a difficult time for you,' he says stiffly, 'and I'm sorry you're scared. But you won't be alone. You have Rosa and David, at least. And you should let the father know; you'll need some financial support, I imagine. But you do need to start making plans and facing up to reality. And I'm afraid where you and I are concerned, I need to step away from this whole situation immediately and put some distance between us. You have a very specific journey ahead of you, so we should keep our relationship professional from now on.'

She looks over at his tense profile. The carefree look of a few minutes ago has gone; she's erased it. As they drive on in silence, she tries to think back to how she imagined this situation may play out. She never expected he'd be thrilled about it, but she hadn't expected him to feel this betrayed. It's not as though she thought he might welcome her and her baby into his life with open arms—she honestly hadn't thought that far ahead. But his wholesale rejection of her, and the tiny person with whom she now forms a package deal, feels like a death sentence.

24

SATURDAY, 14TH DECEMBER

They pull into The Lodge, the gravel crunching beneath the car's tyres. They should be soaring through the sky now, tethered to one another by the harness, experiencing something extraordinary together. Instead, a brick wall has appeared from nowhere and signalled the end of the road for them.

Neither of them uttered a word on the twenty-minute drive home. She's huddled on the far side of her seat and he can tell she's been crying silently given the number of tissues she's worked through. Of course, a large part of him wants to pull her into his arms, but she can't take back the revelation that changes everything: she's pregnant with another man's child.

He cuts the engine and they make awkward eye contact. Her nose is red and her eyes look swollen.

'I really am sorry, Jack,' she says, 'for messing everything up so spectacularly. You've been so lovely to me. I'm going to head to Rosa's for a few nights, get out of your hair. I'll see you on Monday.'

'See you on Monday,' he echoes ineffectually as she gets

out of the car and closes the door behind her. Fuck. He leans his head back and waits till she's gone round the side of the offices to access her flat. Having locked up the car, he strides across the courtyard and heads behind the house to the stables. His horses are the only beings who can provide comfort right now.

He enters the stables, and the warm, earthy smell of the animals draws him in. There are still a couple of grooms about, tidying up. On Saturday mornings, some local kids with physical and mental disabilities come in to ride the ponies, but those sessions are finished now. The three small ponies, Merlin, Dodge and Lisa, are quietly munching on hay in their stalls. He makes a beeline for Maggie, a beautiful, timid grey whose huge eyes have been fixed on him since he walked in. He can't remember how it started, but years ago he and Stacey decided it would be funny to name some of their animals after characters from *The Simpsons*. Their cheekiest pet, a little Jack Russell who was, appropriately enough, named Bart, has been resting under an apple tree in the garden for the past couple of years. Marge hasn't been the same since he stopped terrorising her.

Jack reaches in his pocket and takes out a couple of polos, which he feeds Maggie. She nudges him with her nose.

'No, sweetheart,' he whispers. 'Two's quite enough for you.' He drapes his arms around her and rubs his face into her neck. She stills and allows him to hug her. He closes his eyes; he can hardly process the curveball Emmy's dealt him. A few hours ago, he was curled around her in his bed, marvelling at the happiness and levity this woman brought him. He never imagined he could feel like that after his marriage failed. Now, it's as if someone's shown him a parallel universe and then slammed the door shut in his face.

Last night she fell asleep in his arms. He was lying on his back with one arm around her and she was curled in towards him, her leg over his, her arm flung across his chest, her face burrowed into his neck. He lay there, his other hand outstretched across the crook of her arm, listening as her breathing deepened and slowed to a constant rhythm, not wanting to move or disturb her. But he must have fallen asleep soon afterwards. He slept like a baby.

He moved far too quickly in every way—offering her a job the second he met her, sleeping with her within days of her moving in and starting her role. It was as if she'd cast a spell on him. On the evening they hooked up, she was playing on a loop in his mind on the way home from his Christmas lunch. He wasn't sure if inviting her over would amount to anything—he'd convinced himself he was imagining any interest on her part—but when he saw her sitting at his kitchen island, with that smile on her face, he knew their connection was real. Her smile told him she'd given up trying to hide her feelings and allowed them to shine through—it was guileless and inviting and joyful. It was the most beautiful thing he'd ever seen. And so he told her how he felt. It turns out, she wasn't as guileless as he took her to be.

He gives Maggie a final stroke and turns to Homer, his enormous chestnut stallion who, despite his name, is in great physical shape. He needs to work out some of his frustration and it will delight Homer to oblige. Once he's saddled him up, he grabs a helmet and leads the beast out into the yard. He mounts him and they head for the fields at the back of the house where there's a public bridleway.

He's furious with her. Absolutely fucking livid. Why

couldn't she have just come clean with him from the outset? Then his heart would still be intact, and he'd be suffering little more than some mild disappointment and sexual frustration right now. He doesn't know whether to believe her when she says she intended to tell him this weekend. Just as he'll never know how long Stacey was feeling trapped in their marriage before she hit a tipping point. It still mortifies him to think she was gradually becoming more and more unhappy, and he never really noticed. And Emmy was perfectly capable of joining him in the most intimate, charged moments without letting her enormous secret slip. He can't stand being lied to. Either he has zero emotional intelligence, or women are terrifyingly good at keeping secrets.

But as he settles into a canter on Homer, across fields that are hard and stubbly but not quite frozen, he remembers the look on her face when he told her he needed to walk away. It's far too convenient to paint her as a liar and a manipulator, but that's not accurate. She's scared and she made a poor judgement call. She's human. Aside from those imperfections, she's utterly lovely—she's given up the past few years of her life to work with the world's most marginalised women, for Christ's sake. It's such a fucking waste.

25

SATURDAY, 14TH DECEMBER

Emmy sprints upstairs and throws herself onto her bed. The loud, shuddery tears she's been holding in the whole way back come now, in great gasps. She howls into her pillow. Her cheeks and jaw ache from the tension of having had to hold the tears in. God, it hurts *so* much: his face in the car, the knowledge of how far she's betrayed him, and worst of all, the idea that she won't get to touch him or be with him again in any way that's remotely gratifying. He's made it painfully clear he's closing himself off to her, except in the most unsatisfactory, professional way. She thought this week at work was hard, pining for him before they'd got together, but next week will be a horror.

There's what sounds like the clattering of hooves outside, and she stands and peeks carefully out of the side of the window. Jack is on an enormous horse and they're heading out to the fields. His back is erect—tense, more like. Sweet Jesus, she could do without the Mr Darcy element. Granted, he's wearing a sensible helmet and a Barbour instead of a ripped shirt, but the idea of Jack galloping through the countryside to rid himself of his torment is tortuously erotic. She needs to get out of here ASAP. She calls Rosa.

'Hey.' Rosa sounds weary, sleepy, even.

At the sound of her big sister's voice, she tears up again. 'Oh my God, I've had such a shocker. I've made a total mess of everything. Can I come and stay for a couple of nights?'

'Sure,' says Rosa. 'I've had a shocker too. Bet I win.'

'Bet I win.'

'Mine's worse.'

'No, mine is.'

They've done this since they were little girls—competed on every front imaginable.

'Shoot,' Rosa says. Emmy detects a glimmer of amusement in her voice. 'Let's see what you've got.'

'Ok. I slept with Jack—well, we've been pretty inseparable, the past couple of nights. And today he took me on a surprise date but it was skydiving, so I had to tell him I was pregnant, and now he won't even look at me and he's told me he wants nothing to do with me outside of work.'

On the line, Rosa inhales through her teeth. 'Jesus. That's definitely an Emmy special. I'm going to need all the details, obviously. Ooh, I feel better already. Is he good in bed? Stacey always said he was spectacular in bed.'

Emmy flinches at the mention of Stacey as much as at the reminder of Jack's skills. A particularly graphic memory of him on top of her, pinning her arms above her head, flashes into her mind's eye.

'He is spectacular; thank you for reminding me what I'll be missing. Now tell me your fuck-up. It had better be worse than mine.'

'I think it is. Tallulah hijacked my phone on Tuesday and uploaded a video to Instagram Stories of her telling everyone to cancel me and calling out Volare—that Italian leather goods brand I work with? She posted images of snakes being skinned alive and accused them of animal cruelty. Anyway, the whole thing's gone viral, I've lost half a million followers and Volare is threatening to sue me for breach of contract. Plus, brands are ditching me left, right and centre.'

'Fuuuck.' Tallulah is a piece of work, alright. 'That's fantastically awful. So I'm pregnant and heartbroken, and your career may be in tatters. Fabulous. Mum'll be so proud. I wish we could get drunk.'

'Well, I'm going to drink without you,' Rosa says. Drinking on a Saturday afternoon is definitely not her sister's usual style.

'I'll come over on your bike,' Emmy tells her. 'I'll bring chocolate.'

~

It's a beautiful, crisp day and she should take herself off for a walk or something similarly bracing, but all she wants to do is hide away and veg with Rosa, David and the girls in their grown-up, festive home. She takes a detour to Waitrose on her way over and stocks up with mountains of the promised chocolate as well as minced pies, Stollen and some Waitrose Christmas canapes. This is one of the things she loves most about the festive season in the UK—the delicious, unhealthy party food that Waitrose and M&S do to perfection.

Walking into Rosa's home, with Mariah Carey playing and the abundance of fairy lights twinkling, made her feel once again like an errant toddler returning to the comfort of Mummy's lap. She dumps her rucksack in the hallway and takes the goodies through to the kitchen. Given what Rosa's told her on the phone, she's been expecting her to be an emotional wreck, but she looks weirdly content, if slightly unhinged. She has no makeup on and is in an admittedly stylish knitted tracksuit—it's probably finest cashmere, but still. It's nice to see Rosa let her hair down. Said hair hasn't even—shock horror—been tonged.

David walks over and gives her a bear hug. 'Men troubles, I hear,' he says. Emmy works on the assumption that whatever she tells Rosa, Rosa will discuss with David, so it doesn't surprise her that he already knows. She leans into him and nods tearily into his chest.

'Want me to have a word with him?' David asks, peering down at her. 'I can tell him to get over himself. He's already got four kids; what's another one?'

'Shh, David.' Rosa jerks her head towards Dolly, who's colouring at the kitchen table and not listening anyway, but her tone is softer than usual and Emmy notices she shoots David a smile instead of her usual scowl. Weird.

'Thanks, but no. He's seriously pissed off with me for not being straight with him. And he said I have a 'very specific journey' ahead of of me'—she makes quotation marks with her fingers—'that he's made clear he doesn't want to be a part of. So that's that.'

'I'm so sorry, Em,' Rosa says. 'That's really shitty. Are you gutted?'

'You girls go through,' David says. 'I'll make tea.'

As she and Rosa head through to the living room, Emmy says, 'I'm absolutely devastated. I've been in some kind of love—or lust—bubble for the past forty-eight hours and I've been dreading telling him about the baby, but it was even worse because I got forced into it and now he doesn't trust me at all. And I know this sounds dramatic, but I'm not sure how I go back to just being colleagues with him—I'm completely addicted to him.'

'How did it happen? I thought you were full of good intentions to keep things professional? Although, the chemistry between you two on Saturday night was smoking.'

'Yep. Well, it turns out that was impossible. He invited me over for chilli on Thursday night when he'd got home from a boozy Christmas lunch—he was pretty pissed—and he told me he couldn't stop thinking about me. Before I knew it, I was naked and we were having sex on the rug in front of his fireplace.' She shrugs as if to say *what can you do?*

'Wow, that's hot,' Rosa says. 'I happen to know that rug cost an absolute fortune. Stacey would be furious.'

'Well, it was worth every penny. It was very soft.'

'What are you going to do?' asks Rosa.

'About Jack? Or work? Or the baby?'

'All of them.'

Emmy considers. 'I'm going to make sure I keep myself very, very busy at work. Also, I want to do a brilliant job for him now, because I'm sure he's cursing the day he hired me. But I may have to think about whether I stay on in the new year. I can't imagine it getting easier, seeing him every day. At least there's only one more week before we close up shop for the holidays.

'He did give me a bit of a talking to, about Lorenzo, though. He said I should make contact with him and stop sticking my head in the sand where the baby is concerned. He probably thinks I'm really immature.'

'I'm sure he doesn't, Em. But are you ready to do that—tell Lorenzo, I mean?'

Emmy shrugs again. 'What the hell. I've lost Jack, I'm pregnant and I've spent remarkably little time this week actually facing up to that. Right now, 2020 is looking pretty scary. I suppose the first adult thing I should do is face Lorenzo. If you take away the fact that he's a dodgy fucker, he is actually a successful, ridiculously smart guy who's managed to keep two kids alive for a few years. And I need all the moral support I can get, even if it's from him.'

'How are you feeling about the baby? Rosa asks. She hesitates. 'Do you still think you've made the right decision to go ahead with it?'

'I had this awful thought earlier,' Emmy confesses, 'that this whole mess is the baby's fault, and if I'd just got rid of it, then Jack would never have known and I'd be free to be with him. Isn't that terrible? God, it's so selfish.'

'It's probably pretty normal,' Rosa says. 'You're scared and upset, not to mention hormonal.'

'Anyway, I'm still going ahead with it, and I need to take some time to come around to the idea that I'm going to be a mother and start making plans. It's just so surreal that this little thing that's causing all this drama isn't even something I can feel yet.'

'Would you like to look at some baby clothes?' Rosa asks. 'I have boxes and boxes upstairs and most of the newborn stuff is unisex. There's *nothing* nicer than looking at baby clothes. It might make it seem more real, but also, it's such a fun thing to do. I know it doesn't seem like it now, but having a baby is amazing. It's not all scary and stressful. Let's go have a play.'

~

In the second spare room, which acts as a storage room, they put down their mugs of tea and a box of Maltesers on a chest of drawers. The room is piled high with packing boxes and files. It's pretty civilised by Emmy's standards, but she knows it fills Rosa with a deep despair.

'This is my version of *The Picture of Dorian Gray*,' Rosa moans. 'The more Zen the rest of the house becomes, the more hideous this place gets.'

'It's totally fine,' Emmy assures her. 'Just think of it as a loft. That's what redundant spaces are supposed to be used for. But I can't believe you've kept so many baby things for this long.'

'I lived in hope of you getting pregnant,' Rosa says. 'Not like this, I have to say, but what the hell. Most of this stuff is Dolly's. I got so many gifts during that pregnancy, it was incredible. So your little baby will be very fancy.'

She picks up a box labelled *Newborn / 0-3m* and opens up the top, gesturing to Emmy. 'Go for it—take a look.'

Emmy edges forward and picks out a bundle of immaculately pressed and folded white clothes. She lays them reverently on the table and picks the top item up by the shoulders. It's an impossibly tiny white onesie, embroidered with gold stars. She looks at Rosa questioningly. 'There's no way a baby can fit in this, surely?'

Rosa smiles at her. 'Dolly wore that when we came home from hospital, and she was seven pounds. She only wore it a couple of times, but yeah, your baby should be able to fit it unless you have a nine-pound bruiser.'

Emmy stares at it. It's like a doll's outfit. She imagines a baby snuggled up in it, tiny, bunched fists emerging from the narrow cuffs, little legs encased. It's as if she's a step closer to being able to visualise her baby as an actual living being.

Rosa breaks her train of thought. 'Bear in mind, Dolly was born in November. Yours will be due in—June? So some of this stuff might be too wintry, but there are lots of little short-sleeved vests there too. Do you think you'll find out the sex?'

'I think I might,' Emmy says. 'I'm hoping it'll make it all feel more real, and I can be more organised with planning if I know what sex it is.'

They sort through the items, making piles of girls' items and unisex pieces. Everything is immaculate and tiny and inspires awe in Emmy. It's crazy to imagine that in six months' time she'll be pulling these items over a soft, downy head and fastening these poppers under a nappy. Some of them are spectacular—palest pink cotton dresses with smocked fronts and Peter Pan collars, and even some adorable cashmere cardigans. That seems like a high-maintenance option for something that will probably get covered in baby barf.

'You're right,' she tells Rosa. 'This is like therapy. I feel like we're playing dolls again. You were the bossiest mum ever.'

'I still am.' Rosa sighs. 'I actually came in here the other evening—I needed to get away from my phone, and I was struggling to understand how things could have gone so wrong with Tallulah. I brought in a glass of wine and just played with the baby clothes. Is that weird?'

'No,' Emmy says. 'I get it. It's funny—here I am, worrying about how the hell I'm going to look after a newborn, but given what you're going through at the moment, the baby days actually sound quite straightforward.'

'It's so true,' says Rosa. 'The great ironies of parenthood. David and I always said how tough it was having a newborn—especially with Tallulah, when we had no clue what we were doing—but Jesus, it's child's play compared to this shit.'

'So what's the latest with your crisis? I thought you'd be way more upset than you seem to be.'

'I'm dealing with it the only way I know how, by hiding at home and pretending it's not happening,' Rosa says.

'Sounds sensible—kind of like how I've been dealing with this baby,' Emmy points out.

'It's strange—things are still terrible, and every time I go to check my phone I feel sick, but then if I just put it down and focus on something in the house, I find I can kind of regain my equilibrium. David gave me that advice the other night—the night it happened. He said that what's going on right around me, here, is much more real than what's happening on my phone and it's really helped.'

'I knew he was a keeper,' Emmy says. 'So, what's the reaction been from the industry? Are people still freezing you out?'

'Yes, and I'm still getting scathing messages and press articles. Most of it seems to be around my authenticity—I mean, Tallulah basically called me a fake.'

'So what are they saying, exactly?'

'That I should be careful about the values I espouse on social media; that if even my thirteen-year-old daughter can smell my bullshit then I'm on thin ice; that people value authenticity above everything else these days.'

'That's a bit harsh, surely? Aren't they making any allowances for her just being an angry, hormonal teen?'

'Well, they seem to like her anger because at least it's real, I guess. And interestingly, the feedback around Volare is almost unanimous—that I shouldn't be in bed with them in the first place.'

'Can you get out of bed with them? Will they sue you, do you think?' Emmy cracks open the box of Maltesers and takes a few, offering the box to Rosa.

'Thanks. I don't know. My agency's lawyers are looking over the contract to see if they have any recourse, given that the comments were made on my social media channel but not by me, and they're also looking to see if I have any get-out clause based on my having signed the contract before any of these animal abuse rumours came to light.' She puts a few Maltesers in her mouth. 'God, how are these so good?'

'They're amazing.' Emmy shovels up some more of the little balls. 'Do you have a plan? Like, are you going to address it on Instagram? Or just hide away forever? Delete your account and retrain as a bookkeeper or something? Move to New Zealand?'

'Ha ha. I need to see where the lay of the land is with Volare first, then I can decide. But I'm running out of time; I need to take a stand by Monday or Tuesday at the latest. I did get a gorgeous email earlier, from the designer Astrid Carmichael. Do you know her?'

'I know the name,' Emmy says, 'but she's a bit out of my price range.'

'She's sponsoring an event at Sorrel Farm next Saturday night, which I'm supposed to be attending. Let me read it to you. Let's see... here we go. *Dear Rosa, I'm sorry to see you've had such a tough few days. I've seen the press and can only imagine how you must be feeling. Your daughter's stunt is one I can see my daughter Tabby pulling in a few years' time. I wanted to say that we are very much looking forward to seeing you and a guest next Saturday at Sorrel Farm if you still feel up to it. You have always been such a loyal supporter of my brand, and I hope to get the opportunity to toast your family's good health at the party. One of the team will be in touch on Monday to discuss sending you an outfit. Best, Astrid*. Isn't that sweet?'

'Wow, she sounds lovely,' Emmy says. Not at all like how she imagines fashion designers to be.

'She is,' says Rosa. 'And Sorrel Farm is incredible—it's in Kent. Do you remember Evelyn Macleod?'

'Should I?'

'She was all over the papers last year when Seb Macleod came out as gay—she's Seb's ex-wife. She ended up divorcing him, leaving their company and moving down to Kent—her best friend runs Sorrel Farm and Evelyn married the farm manager there, and she's their Commercial Director. I believe she's pregnant, too.'

'Oh, I do remember that,' Emmy says. Jesus. Poor woman. That scandal had made it out to India. 'I'm glad to hear it's all worked out for her in the end.'

'She's great friends with Stacey,' Rosa says. 'Stacey and I went to last year's party together—I'm sure she'll be going along this year. You should come with me! It might cheer you up. It's the most idyllic evening, I swear.'

Emmy rolls her eyes. 'You, me and Stacey. Cosy.'

'Don't be like that. I promise, it'll be a lovely soiree. Besides, you can drive us.'

'And there's the rub,' Emmy says. 'Ok, show me this Sorrel Farm place. If they have good food, I might be in.'

'Believe me,' says Rosa, 'it's all about the food at that place. Malteser?'

'Thanks. So. Look at us both. What the fuck are we going to do? Do you want to play the namesake game?'

'We don't have much to lose, do we? You go first. What would Emmeline do?'

They've played this game since childhood. For all the moaning they'd done over the years about the burden of having been named after such trailblazing women, this was something their mother instigated and it's proven a useful tool. She often played it with them at night, when the blackness outside drove them to give voice to their deepest fears and most bothersome worries.

'What would Emmeline Pankhurst do?' she'd ask. 'What would Rosa Parks do? I didn't name you girls after these women for nothing. Channel them. They're like your superpower. They'll tell you what to do.'

Now Emmy takes a deep breath. 'She'd accept that she was going to have the baby. She'd move on from Jack and she wouldn't be afraid to contact Lorenzo. She'd tell him exactly what she needed from him and make it very clear what she would and wouldn't tolerate. She'd kick ass in the job, no matter how sick and tired and pregnant and lovesick she was—well, she wouldn't be lovesick—and she'd be the best bloody single mother ever.'

'There you go!' Rosa says. 'That was brilliant. How do you feel?'

'A little more like I can at least pretend I'm not shitting myself about it all,' says Emmy. 'Your turn.'

Rosa inhales. 'Ok. Well, it's simple really. Rosa Parks would be on the side of what is right, and she'd stand up for it, no matter how awkward or painful or scary it was. She'd be unequivocal—for her there'd be no alternative.'

This game is good—it always, always works. 'And what's right?' Emmy asks her.

'Walk away from Volare.' Rosa shrugs. 'Use more of my energies to promote brands that are actually doing the right thing. And, fix my relationship with my glorious, fucked-up daughter.'

Emmy raises her teacup. 'To our namesakes,' she says. 'May they have our backs this week. We're going to need them.'

26

TUESDAY, 17TH DECEMBER

Stacey's eyes are closed. The fire is crackling and spitting, Mia is snuggled into the non-bandaged side of her body, Martha's making popcorn in the kitchen and she can hear Jack yelling at the boys to cut out whatever raucous play they're immersed in and give their sister some space. With her eyes closed, it's as if the past year hasn't happened and they're just a regular family.

It's been a momentous day. Not only has she had her lumpectomy, but all four kids broke up for the holidays this afternoon. She's a mixture of wrung-out and utterly content, except the contentment is tinged with a knowing, a sense of impermanence.

The procedure was, apparently, both uneventful and successful. Her memory of that first hour after she came round is fuzzy, but Jack was waiting for her in the private room they put her in post the operation. As she dozed and then rallied sufficiently to manage some tea and toast, he was there, sitting in a wipe-clean armchair, typing on his phone for the most part. On the way home he seemed unusually quiet, melancholy even. She assumed he'd found the whole experience draining.

They've previously agreed that she'll stay here tonight, and tomorrow night too if she's still feeling fragile. Jack said he'd rather she wasn't on her own after a general anaesthetic, and it's both a relief and a luxury to be with her family. She went up to their—Jack's—spare room as soon as they got back from hospital and grabbed a couple of extra hours sleep. Since he picked the kids up from school, she hasn't moved from the sofa, polishing off a generous portion of Carol's cottage pie on her lap and enjoying being in the thick of the action. There's something about the dynamic of having her and Jack both there that works. The kids have picked up on it too; they're already high from having broken up for Christmas, and having Mommy and Daddy together, in their old family home, has sent them into raptures.

Mia nestles in closer to her. She's the one whom the divorce hit hardest; when it happened, she was just five and unable to process why her parents split up and why Mommy got herself a new home. Although the custody agreement specifies that during term-time the kids sleep with Stacey during the week for the sake of consistency, it's been a wrench for them to leave their old home and it breaks her heart to know they still prefer it here.

'I like being here with you, Mommy,' Mia tells her now.

'I know, sweetie.' She flinches as Mia elbows her in the ribs and pulls her little daughter closer. 'It's fun to have a family sleepover tonight.'

'Why can't we all live here together again?' Mia asks.

Stacey keeps her voice artificially bright. 'We're lucky because we get two houses! And my pool is bigger than Daddy's pool.'

'But Merlin is here. And Marge.'

Mia has known Marge since she was a baby; the labrador guarded her crib from the moment Stacey brought her home from hospital. Stacey suspects she regards Mia as the pup she never had.

'They are, because Marge can't see so we can't ask her to get to know a new house. She's much safer and happier here, but you can visit her whenever you like. You'll get to spend lots more time here now it's the holidays.'

'But I like you being here too.' Mia's voice is almost inaudible, her face buried in Stacey's stomach. 'I want us to all be together.'

Stacey and Jack have, in her view, done an admirable job of divorcing. They followed the *conscious uncoupling* method, which essentially tells you to put your kids first, no matter how much you hate or despise your spouse or want to put a fork through their eye. And so they've put the kids first at every step, even when Jack was furious and disgusted by her, even when she wanted to run for the hills and start her new life. The children haven't seen them fight or been caught in the middle of any verbal bashing. It's healthier this way, but perhaps it makes it harder for the kids to understand why they're not together, if they get on so well.

'We'll all be together on Christmas Day,' Stacey reminds her. This is how civilised they are: they've even agreed to do a family Christmas lunch here, at Jack's. The kids will wake up at hers, where Santa will have stopped by, and then they'll head over here, to their childhood home, for a feast.

Mia's voice is still muffled. 'I want us to all be together every day.'

AFTER THEY'VE DESPATCHED the kids to bed, she and Jack sit

in front of the fire with a mug of herbal tea. Mia's heartbreaking attempts at emotional blackmail notwithstanding, it's been a special evening. It's extraordinary, the power that a physical location can have. When she's in her sleek, luxurious offices in Mayfair, she's one version of herself. Her incredible, glass-fronted new home is everything she wanted for this next phase in her life. It's where she entertains exciting new lovers like Antoine and finds the space she needs to be herself. She idly replays her Saturday night with him back in her mind, remembering that her predominant experience was of feeling unleashed when she fucked him in the pool.

But this house has another kind of power altogether. It has the power to conjure a montage of her old selves: the thirty-year-old self who fell in love with the old barn conversion project when she had a toddler and twin boys on the way; the many joyful, chaotic years of mothering four kids while building her own business and, more recently, the self who felt as though this beautiful complex was her prison and that she might suffocate behind its gates.

Tonight the darker ghosts aren't here. From her newly liberated vantage point, she simply feels the joy and warmth of the place. How many nights have she and Jack spent like this, watching the flames and sipping herbal tea? She looks over at him. He looks so handsome in the firelight. He's always had a great profile. For a moment, she recalls the headiness of those days at Oxford when they first met. He was still an undergrad then, an Oxford blue whose classical features were undamaged by his pursuits on the rugby pitch. They couldn't keep their hands off each other. They must have had sex thousands and thousands of times over the years. She'd come to the UK with the intention of laying as many Brits as she could, but until this year, she'd hitched her wagon to just one.

It was never about him—the divorce. He's perfect. He's gorgeous. It was about her; that awful phrase, *it's not you; it's me*, that's as hackneyed as it is true. It was this intrusive idea that got under her skin and coloured all her thoughts until she gave into it: that her life would be Groundhog Day until she cut her perfectly good ties with Jack and went looking for some variety. She'd been searching for a way to add excitement back into her life—she'd started shopping more, drinking more. Then one day, somewhere, she read something that made her stop in her tracks. *Stop thinking you have to play the cards you've been dealt. Just get up and move to another table.* She filed for divorce and moved to another table.

The first time she slept with someone else, it was extraordinary. She'd been worried that after spending so long with the person who knew exactly how to push all her buttons, being with another guy would be frustrating. Not so. She popped her post-Jack cherry with a guy who'd been her broker when she was at her last hedge fund. There'd always been unresolved sexual tension between them—UST, she calls it. They had a highly charged date in Claridge's Le Fumoir bar over a couple of vodka martinis before they grabbed a room and ripped each other's clothes off like they were in a movie. The sensation of having strange hands on her body and an unfamiliar mouth on hers was so freaking *hot* that she would have been a mess even if he hadn't known what he was doing. But he had. And he was the first of many to elicit the same intoxicating feelings of what was novel and forbidden.

It still thrills her, but she's not sure what she's looking for. Raphael was fabulous until Antoine came along. And she's not sure what she wants from Antoine, beyond a few hook-ups. He's been sweet and solicitous via WhatsApp this week, and her housekeeper has sent her a photo of the beautiful bouquet of white roses he's had delivered to her house today to wish her a speedy recovery. But he's not the kind of person she'd want sitting in a hospital ward, waiting for her to come out of surgery, even if she knew him better, even if their relationship was a few months down the line. She's pretty sure what they have is just sex.

Jack's the only person she'd have trusted with today's job. He's been amazing, driving her into and out of London, waiting around at the hospital for her, dealing with the kids and putting her to bed in the spare room earlier, when they got back. He even had to help her up the stairs because she still felt wobbly. He brought her her painkillers and a cup of tea when she woke up, and he's waited on her hand and foot this evening. He's done it all quietly, without being asked. He's just been there for her. He's always been there for her.

She looks over at him again and feels a powerful surge of love. She leans over and puts her hand on his. He looks up from his tea, startled.

'Thanks for today,' she says. 'You've been a rockstar.'

'It's my pleasure,' he replies. 'I wouldn't have wanted you to go through that alone.'

'Well, it made such a difference having you there, when I came round. Thank you for looking after me, and thanks for letting me stay tonight.'

'Stay as long as you need to,' he says. 'The important thing is that they got it all out and that it was benign. And we have to get you fully recovered and fighting fit again. We all need you, Stace. It would be unimaginable, raising these guys without you.'

Her eyes tear up, and she squeezes his hand. 'I'm not

going anywhere,' she says. But in truth, the events of the past week have seriously shaken her. What if the tumour had been malignant; what if she'd been destined to spend the next few years diminished and fighting for her health? Her entire bid for freedom in her personal life has been based on this view of herself as young and in her sexual prime. She knows she's in good shape for her age and she even has an appointment in the diary for next week with *the* most in-demand plastic surgeon in London, just to see where she can optimise herself and enhance her natural assets.

What she hasn't given sufficient weight to is the question of what she'll want twenty, thirty, years from now. By then, the fleeting euphoria that sexual dalliances bring will likely have paled and she'll put more emphasis on the quieter but more admirable prizes of companionship, trust and support. None of the guys she's hooked up with are contenders for that kind of relationship. Only one man is, and he's sitting next to her, and he's always been right next to her, except she walked away. She's exhausted and emotional, and today's the first time anyone's properly looked after her in a long time—since her divorce, really. She's not quite sure, but she thinks she wants her husband back.

27

TUESDAY, 17TH DECEMBER

Rosa checks her appearance in her phone one last time. Her hair is rough-dried and her makeup is minimal (though she draws the line at going makeup-free, obviously). She's aiming to look accessible, to strip away any artifice her social media followers perceive her as having. This is probably the most natural they've ever seen her. Her iPhone is propped up in the centre of her ring light, which illuminates her skin flatteringly. There's no other way to procrastinate now. She hits the record button on her phone's video and starts speaking.

'Hi there. Firstly, I'm sorry for having been quiet. The past few days have been challenging for me and I wanted to make sure I took the time to respond properly to the accusations that my daughter, Tallulah, has made against me, as well as the reactions from you guys and from the press.

'Obviously, accusations like these are very difficult to hear, and I'm upset that Tallulah betrayed my trust in the way she did. But she believes I've been betraying her trust and your trust too, over the last few years.

'My sister Emmy reminded me the other day that our

parents named me after Rosa Parks. She's named after Emmeline Pankhurst. Since we've been little, we've always played the namesake game. Whenever we're stuck, we ask ourselves, what would Rosa or Emmeline do? Well, I know what my namesake would do. She'd see having a voice as an extraordinary privilege, and she'd use that voice to share messages that further humanity and in turn give voice to others.

'Now, I'm well aware that I'm not here to change the world—I'm a fashion and lifestyle blogger. But at the very least, I can make sure I don't amplify voices or promote platforms that can be seen as negative or in any way causing suffering. I still believe it's valid and necessary to celebrate the things that bring us joy, and those things can include clothes and makeup and interior design. Beautiful things make us happy. That's ok. But it's not ok when the price we pay for these things is too high, whether in the form of human or animal suffering or damage to our planet.

'From today, you'll find me being far more selective about the values of the brands I choose to work with. It's going to be an exciting journey, but I'll need your help. Tell me what brands you love and why. This Instagram account wouldn't exist without you, and I want it to be a real collaboration.

'The last thing I want to say is that in light of everything that's happened this week, Volare and I will be parting ways. I've had a lot of fun working with them, and I wish them all the best.'

This isn't strictly the whole story. Giacomo and Patrizia are still out for her blood. They want to sue for breach of contract because her platform broadcast defamatory content about them, but the problem for them is that Melissa's team of lawyers have also found them to be in breach, should the animal cruelty claims be proven. It turns out that her contract with them contains a morality clause! Who knew?! Rosa certainly didn't give it any thought when she signed with them, but she is entitled to break their contract in the event of Volare committing an act of what can be reasonably deemed immoral behaviour. While they won't admit the charges of having had illegal animal skins seized, it's something about which they're keen not to prompt any further discussion and they have, incredibly enough, agreed with the agency to drop Rosa as an influencer without pressing charges. She can't quite believe it—it's like she's been granted a Get Out of Jail Free card.

~

SHE PICKS the girls up from school. Dolly is beside herself with excitement at having broken up for the holidays. She's clutching a pencil with an elf topper on it that's a gift from her class teacher, as well as an untidy sheaf of coloured papers, all evidence of her industrious festive crafting over the previous weeks. She's talking a mile a minute. Tallulah is quieter; she sits in the front next to Rosa on the way home and looks out the window as Dolly chatters.

When they get home, Rosa taps her on the shoulder and jerks her head softly. 'Can I have a chat for a minute, honey? I have something to show you.'

Tallulah nods sulkily and follows her through to the kitchen. Rosa sits at the island and pats the chair next to her. She takes her phone out of her bag and pulls up Instagram, handing it to Tallulah.

She nods. 'Take it—check out my Stories.'

Tallulah hits the illuminated avatar on Rosa's account

and watches as Rosa speaks on-screen. When the clip has finished, she turns to her mum.

'Seriously? You've ditched Volare?'

Rosa laughs. 'Well, it was a mutual ditching, to put it diplomatically. But yes. What do you think? About the video?'

'It sounds cool,' Tallulah says. 'You should be showing off brands that are run by good people. People listen to you so you have a lot of power.'

'You're totally right,' says Rosa. She taps the phone with her fingertip. 'You did this, you know? You brought this change about. Do you know what that's called?'

Tallulah looks blank.

'That's activism,' Rosa explains. 'It's *doing* something rather than just sitting on your backside like ninety-nine percent of the population. You made this happen. Now, your methods were another matter. If you ever pull a stunt like this again, you can say bye-bye to all your devices till you're twenty-one. Got it?'

'Got it,' Tallulah says, but she's grinning. 'Nice one, Mom. Now can I have my phone back?'

28

WEDNESDAY, 18TH DECEMBER

It's one week till Christmas and Emmy couldn't be feeling more shitty. She suspects the excitement of her feelings for Jack has been bolstering her over the past week or two, and now she's crashed. She's in a physical and emotional puddle that she can't drag herself out of. She even crept upstairs to her flat during the workday yesterday to have a lunchtime power-nap and avoid the plight of face-planting with exhaustion onto her laptop.

The past few days have been as emotionally wretched as they've been dark and cold outside. It really is the bleak midwinter. She crept into work on Monday morning, feeling apologetic in every bone in her body, and huddled as inconspicuously as possible at her desk. Jack's been staying firmly on the AscenSoar side of the room. He's sent a few Slacks around the Discite team, but he's been pretty quiet overall. She didn't see him much yesterday at all; he was out for most of the day. He looks pale and tired too, in contrast to the rest of the team who are gearing up for the holidays and on top festive form. Someone's draped the kitchen area in tinsel and *Now That's What I Call Christmas* plays on a loop in the background. It's a particularly annoying time to be miserable with all this festive cheer.

What she really wants to do is get up from her chair, walk over to Jack and wrap herself around him, lay her head on his chest and ask him to forgive her. This is so much more painful than last week. She learnt her way around his body during their short time together and her head and heart are flooded with memories of how he looks, feels, smells, tastes. She's not just going crazy with longing; she recalls innocent, intimate moments too, like when she looked up and caught him smiling at her in a way that made her catch her breath. Fast-forward to this week and he won't even make eye-contact with her.

She has a meeting in the diary with him and Natasha for tomorrow afternoon. The intention is to give them an update on their key NGO relationships, which Natasha will pass onto their biggest donors before they break up for Christmas on Friday. That should be a riot. She decided on Monday morning that her choice was clear: mope at her desk and drive herself crazy, or get properly stuck into the professional challenge at hand and start taking her pregnancy more seriously. As she told Rosa, she knows which path her illustrious namesake would take. If Emmeline Pankhurst could crack on with four kids and a dead husband, Emmy can presumably handle a broken heart.

Accordingly, she's ploughed through the lists of NGOs she showed Jack last week and has made visible progress. In the end, she contacted every NGO on her target list personally and had a decent response. She's been getting in early the past three days (she's glad she came back to Jack's flat for week nights) and scheduling as many Skypes as possible in the mornings while it's business hours in India. She's been surprised by how much she's enjoying the video chats; these are her kind of people and she can empathise with the challenges they relay to her. It's amazing how much you can find out just by picking up the phone (or digital equivalent) and listening to people.

She spends the afternoons writing up her notes and adjusting the lists with her recommended action points for each of their partners. She'll share the findings with Jack and Natasha tomorrow. Hopefully, her progress will put a smile on his face. She still wants to make him happy, wants him to think well of her, even if he doesn't want to be with her. Her minor work wins have also given her the boost she needed in terms of energy and confidence. She's found something she's good at and passionate about and it's been a while since she had this fire in her belly—it certainly wasn't there when she was processing receipts for the Loeb traders' benders with clients.

A commotion breaks her concentration, and she looks up. Several children have come into the office. There's Dolly! She recognises Mia from when she picked Dolly up from their play date earlier this month; that seems like a lifetime ago. There's a stunning dark-haired girl who is presumably Martha and two startlingly identical boys—Pitt and Augie. All four kids have Jack's colouring. Her heart twists. Behind them—shit—Stacey comes through the doors. What the heck is she doing here? She's swathed in various layers of cream and caramel cashmere and has that unmistakable polish that comes with wealth. She looks incredible.

Jack jumps up from his desk and bounds over to the kids. It's as if someone's flipped a switch inside him; it's the happiest he's looked since she dropped her bombshell.

'Hey!' She can hear his roar from the other end of the room. 'Who let you urchins in here? Someone, call security, quick!'

The kids fall about and screech with laughter. Jack picks Mia up and twirls her round, before putting her down again and ruffling one twin's hair. The boy grins up at him ecstatically. The hilarity is infectious and various members of the team get up from their desks to high-five the kids and greet Stacey.

'Come on!' Jack says, pointing down towards Emmy. 'I think there's a big box of Celebrations in the kitchen. Let's see what we can find!'

The children whoop—they are so noisy—and swarm in her direction. Fuck. She slides lower into her chair, but Dolly spots her.

'Emmy!' she cries. 'This is my *auntie*!' she announces proudly to everyone around her. She launches herself at Emmy, who hugs her soft, warm little body gratefully. She needs a hug like this, needs the boost that comes with this little darling being glad to see her.

'Hello, sweetheart,' she murmurs into Dolly's hair. 'What a lovely treat. What are you doing here?'

'I'm having a play date with Mia,' Dolly tells her. 'Because we breaked up from school yesterday. And we're going to ride Merlin and Lisa after this. But first Mia's mummy said we could come and see her daddy's office. I forgot you worked here.' Her brow furrows in confusion.

'Well, I'm thrilled to see you,' Emmy says. 'And thank you for the lovely hug.'

Mia, who's a sweet little thing with an untidy cloud of dark hair and huge, green-hazel eyes like Jack, hangs back beside Dolly, looking at Emmy as though she's an exotic creature in a zoo. 'Come and get some Celebrations!' she hisses theatrically at Dolly. 'Daddy said there's *loads*!'

Emmy laughs and, looking up, catches Jack's eye. He's hovering, waiting for the girls. He gives her a tight smile.

The next thing she knows, Stacey strides up beside him, a flurry of golden hair and blinding teeth and sumptuous cashmere. She throws her arm around Jack, who stiffens, and beams at Emmy.

'Emmy!' She sounds as pleased to spot her as Dolly was. 'It's so great to see you again! Rosa told me you'd started here! How are you enjoying it—is this one treating you well?'

She tightens her arm around Jack's shoulder and pokes him in the ribs with her other hand. Emmy glances from Stacey to Jack and back again. He looks as though he wants to disappear through the floor, but they are stunning together. What a gorgeous power-couple: glossy, good-looking and impossibly successful. She feels like a kid when she looks at what they've built together during their marriage: four beautiful children, a few uber-successful businesses and now a charity. She fixes a bright smile on her face and attempts to match Stacey's exuberance.

'Ha! Yes, he's been very kind thanks.' *You have no idea how kind.* 'It's a great charity; I'm really enjoying working here,' she manages.

'Fabulous! It really is great work you're all doing.' Stacey clasps her hands together in a manner reminiscent of Anne of Green Gables. 'We all stayed here last night, and I couldn't resist coming to say hi to the team. I miss everyone.'

'Oh, I see…' Emmy wills herself to keep her eyes on Stacey. *She stayed here last night?* 'That's nice.'

Stacey leans forward. 'I had a little procedure yesterday,' she whispers conspiratorially. She points to her breast. 'Lumpectomy. It's all good,' she adds as Emmy's eyes widen. 'Nothing to worry about. But Jack insisted I stay over after the op so he could make sure I was ok. He's such a great nurse.' She turns her beam on Jack, who squirms.

Emmy smiles weakly. 'I'm glad you're on the mend,' she says. 'What a horrible thing to have to do the week before Christmas.'

'I'm just relieved it was benign,' says Stacey. 'Hey, Rosa says you're coming to Sorrel Farm on Saturday?'

'Yes; I can't wait,' Emmy says. She's been googling it and the place looks wonderful. It's something to look forward to and to take her mind off her troubles: her broken heart and a baby she's not totally convinced about.

'Awesome!' Stacey squeals. She seems to talk only in exclamations. She's lovely, and Emmy feels sick at resenting her mere presence. 'Jack's on kid duty this weekend'—she winks at him—'so we can have the most fun girls' night. I can't wait to hang with you.'

~

SEEING Jack and Stacey play happy families is the last straw. She slips out of the office and heads upstairs to her flat to call Lorenzo.

He answers on the second ring. 'Emmy! How are you?'

His voice instantly transports her back to a world that, until now, has felt distant.

'I'm fine thanks,' she says. 'How are you getting on?'

'Oh, you know,' he says. 'Natalia is divorcing me. I tried to call you so many times, Emmy. Where have you been?'

'I didn't want to speak to you, not after all the dirt came out at Loeb. I was so mortified. I mean, you screwed Lara, for fuck's sake! Couldn't you at least have limited yourself to one woman per desk?'

'*Cara*, you know me. And she was a pest; she threw herself at me. It didn't mean anything. Not like—'

'Oh, God,' she says. 'Please don't try to tell me this meant anything to you. We both know what it was.'

'It was very, very good sex,' he says. 'I was very fond of you, my little Emmy. I still am, of course. I wanted to keep on seeing you after I left Loeb. But why have you finally decided to call me?'

'I need to talk to you about something,' she says. 'I don't want you to feel any obligation, but you have a right to know. I'm pregnant, and it's definitely yours.'

She holds her breath. There's a silence at the other end of the line, followed by a sharp inhale.

'Fuck,' he says. 'I wasn't expecting that.'

'I'm sure you weren't. I'm eleven or twelve weeks gone, but I only found out a couple of weeks ago. But honestly, I'm really just letting you know as a courtesy; I'm not asking for anything.'

'Emmy,' he says, 'this is amazing news!'

'Seriously?' The warmth in his voice is completely unexpected.

'Of course! Do you know how tough the past few months have been for me? I know, I know; it's all my own doing. But I've lost my job, my home and my family. I hardly get to see the girls at all. And now you're telling me we have a baby on the way? It's a miracle!'

'Um,' she says. She hasn't prepared for the eventuality of him being happy about the baby; she expected him to be dismissive at best, hostile at worst. 'I suppose it is. More like an accident. Do you remember any of the condoms breaking? Because this definitely wasn't in my life plan.'

'Oh, Emmy,' he says. 'When will you learn that as soon as you try to make plans, life will laugh at you and upend them all? I'm telling you, this is a great, great thing. Where are you? Are you still at Loeb? What kind of help do you need?'

'I'm all good, thanks,' she says quickly. 'I left Loeb. I'm in Surrey for a bit, near my sister, and I'm doing some consulting work for a charity. We'll see how things go in the new year, but for now I'm fine.'

'If you are doing consulting, you won't get paid maternity leave,' he says.

'I wouldn't have got it at Loeb either—I was on a temp contract. So either way, I'm screwed. But I have accommodation thrown in here so I'll just save as much as I can before the baby's born.'

She won't mention that she might not be able to hack working at Discite for much longer and that if she throws in the towel, she'll be jobless and homeless.

'Well, I want to help,' he says, 'of course. Can I see you? Can we meet to make some plans? When is the next scan?'

Jesus. She wasn't expecting such an effusive reaction, and she had little interest in sharing her pregnancy with Lorenzo. But it's a welcome change to have a man in her life be so positive about the news that a baby is on its way.

'That's very sweet of you,' she says carefully, 'but I don't need any help. I'll manage fine. But if you want to come to the scan, then I guess that's okay. It's the first week of January—it'll be a bit late just because of Christmas. I'm hoping to find out the sex then.'

'Emmy,' he says in a voice filled with emotion. 'This is going to be wonderful. After all the shit of this year—to know that next year will bring new life; it is amazing. Amazing. *Grazia, cara*, for making my Christmas.'

29

THURSDAY, 19TH DECEMBER

'The Riordan Foundation has been asking about utilisation rates on the tablets we've got out in the field; the guys are perplexed as to why they're not higher.' Natasha raises her perfectly shaped eyebrows challengingly at Emmy and sets her mug down on the table. They're sitting with Jack on a couple of sofas near the office's main entrance. Unlike the rest of the team who are in jeans, hoodies and Christmas jumpers, Natasha looks immaculate as always in a slinky black dress that skims over her body, showcasing her incredible figure.

Emmy herself is in skinny jeans, Uggs and a dark green sweater that she knows goes well with her hair. She's been trying to walk the tightrope of looking good but not overdone since the weekend. It would be nice if she could remind Jack what he's missing, but no amount of bronzer or mascara is going to distract him from the deal-breaker—a deal-breaker that's apparently the size of a lime this week. She rubs her stomach—she's found herself doing this quite a lot recently, although she still can't feel anything move inside her—and, catching Jack's eyes on her, stops. He's wearing the same cream fisherman's sweater he had on at the nativity play, and he looks so handsome.

He turns his gaze to Natasha. 'I'm sure Emmy has some updates for us from the NGOs that will provide The Riordan Foundation with some reassurance,' he says evenly. 'Emmy? Why don't you tell us what you've been up to?'

She slides a print-out over to each of them with her proposed changes to the list of partner NGOs and fills them in on her calls. She hasn't been in touch with everyone, but she's had enough conversations to construct a useful picture of what's going on. She outlines her conclusions. The long tail of NGOs is worth culling. The vast majority of those in charge of a low number of tablets are struggling to find the time and headspace to focus on getting them up and running with kids. She's unsure whether Discite would write off or recall those tablets, but that's not her decision.

The conversations with NGOs who have a large number of tablets have been far more enlightening. Of those who haven't activated enough of them or who have low utilisation rates, most of these have claimed they're not getting enough support from Discite. She attempts to phrase this diplomatically.

'I know what it's like for these guys. It's not a nice, orderly working environment like it is here. For most of them, it's a total shit-show and I'm afraid the tablets are only one part of what they're trying to juggle out there. They'll be dealing with all sorts of annoying crap that we're not aware of, like teachers falling ill or not turning up, absentee rates among the kids, school buildings flooding or being structurally unsound... Every day brings a new challenge to distract them from getting the most out of our tablets. They've all signed up because they're so inspired by you, Jack, and excited about the product. But the key to getting the tablets working really hard is making it as easy for them as possible.'

'What do you mean?' Jack asks. 'Did they give you suggestions?'

'They said the product is great, and easy for the kids to use. You don't need me to tell you that. But occasionally they have technical issues and I guess they feel a bit... removed... from your support team? They seem to feel like they're in a vacuum, that once they get the tablets, they're on their own.'

'Well, we can't have that,' Jack says. 'There shouldn't be many technical issues, but we do need them to feel supported.'

'I get the impression,' Emmy continues, 'that they need a bit more moral support, something to boost their morale and keep their eye on the prize. I had an eye-opening conversation with The Mistri Foundation, which has one of the highest utilisation rates. They suggested that they'd be happy to share best practices with other NGOs, and I wonder if we can create some kind of community for all our partners—maybe a Facebook page, maybe a Slack channel; I don't know. But somewhere that they can share wins and anecdotes and also air their questions or frustrations. The important thing is keeping everyone focused on using the tablets as much as possible, so they don't just sit there and gather dust.'

She's rewarded with the first real smile Jack's given her since she leant across to him in his car and dropped her bombshell.

'That's a fantastic idea,' he says. 'I can't believe we didn't think of it. Of course we should hook them all up with each other. Can you liaise with them and see what platform would work best for them? If that's an effective way of giving them moral support and the chance to share best practices, it's an easy win for us. Nice one, Emmy.'

It's like the sun's come out after a long, icy spell and she basks in his goodwill. She can't help but grin back, but then she feels her face go slack as, over Jack's shoulder, a man walks through the door in a smart navy coat. It's Lorenzo.

LORENZO STOPS and looks around the room. He clocks her and makes a beeline for her. How the *hell* did he find her here?

'Shit,' she says and stands up.

'What is it?' says Jack, looking behind him.

'I'm so sorry, guys. I may need a minute, if that's ok, to—'

Lorenzo reaches her and kisses her on both cheeks, then folds her into his arms. '*Ciao, cara*,' he murmurs. This is beyond mortifying. She wriggles free.

'Lorenzo, I'm in a meeting,' she manages.

He looks around. 'Excuse me. Lorenzo Beneventi,' he says, and offers his hand to Jack. Oh, Jesus. Jack stays seated and shakes it, introducing himself tersely. Lorenzo turns to Natasha and his face lights up.

'*Ciao*,' he says, and holds out his hand again. '*Piacere*.' Natasha stands up gracefully and takes it without breaking eye contact with him. Emmy has never seen such a come-to-bed look in anyone's eyes; it's extraordinary, and presumably a handy talent to have. She's in awe.

'Natasha Greene,' she purrs. 'How do you do?'

Lorenzo grins at her for a beat too long before remembering why he's here and letting go of her hand. 'Emmy,' he says. 'Can we talk?'

Emmy looks at Jack who nods and says, 'Of course'.

'I'm so sorry,' she says again as she puts her notepad on the table. 'Give me five—I'll be right back.'

She hurries after Lorenzo, who's already striding out of the building. Outside, she folds her arms over her chest and hunches her shoulders. It's bloody freezing. She takes a minute to study him. He looks really well; being out of work suits him. While Jack's looks are clean-cut, wholesome, glowing with health, Lorenzo's are more exotic and wolfish. It's surreal to see him here, outside of their normal environments of the trading floor or a hotel room. He steps forward and brushes her stomach.

'You don't look pregnant yet,' he says. 'Just beautiful.'

She rolls her eyes. 'How did you find me? Lottie?' Lottie was Lorenzo's PA at Loeb, and she and Emmy have stayed in touch; the assistants there were a close-knit bunch and Lottie is particularly lovely.

'Yes,' he says. 'You were avoiding me yesterday on the call; I could tell. I didn't want to wait until some scan to see you. We are having a tiny baby together, *cara*! This is an amazing thing! I had to come to see you and tell you how ecstatic I am.'

She laughs, despite herself, at the enthusiasm on his face. It's actually very sweet. She hasn't seen this soft side of him before.

'I had no idea you'd be this excited about it,' she says.

'Of course I'm excited! I'm Italian. Family is more important than anything else to me.'

'Oh, please!' she scoffs. 'Don't stand there and feed me bullshit like that, Lorenzo. Your wife is in the process of leaving you because you fucked, or attempted to fuck, every woman in Loeb. I know about them all, not just the ones you succeeded with, like Lara, but the ones who turned you down, like Isabella Whitney.'

He flinches. 'That was all blown out of proportion. Look, I like women, Emmy. Correction: I love women. But my daughters are the two most important people in my life. And my son will be too. I want a relationship with him.'

'We don't know what it is yet,' she protests.

'It's a boy,' he says. 'I know it. The reason I came down is that I think you should come back to London. I can get you a flat and then, when the baby is born, I can see him often.'

This is crazy.

'Lorenzo.' She holds up her hands. 'That's extremely generous, but firstly, we're not a couple. You don't get any say in what I do or where I live. Of course you can see your baby, but we won't be bringing him or her up together. Secondly, you've lost your job and you're getting divorced. You're not in a position to be shelling out on flats for all your mistresses and their illegitimate children.'

'Come on,' he says. 'I was in the City for twenty-five years; I have plenty of money. And I'm not trying to tell you what to do, but I do want to be involved. In a few months you may feel grateful for that. What are you doing here, anyway?' He gestures at the Discite offices.

'I'm working for an amazing charity that provides educational tablets for children in Third World countries,' she says. 'I'm liaising with their partner NGOs. It's much closer to what I was doing before in India than the Loeb gig was, and I absolutely love it.'

She realises it's true; while this week has been a low-point emotionally, the work, and particularly the interaction with the NGOs, has given her a huge kick. She can make a difference here; she knows it.

JACK WATCHES Emmy walk away with the dickhead who's responsible for this entire mess. If he hadn't got her knocked up while he was busy committing sex crimes elsewhere, nothing would stand in Jack's way of being with her. He twigged who Beneventi was before he'd even introduced himself. Everything about him screamed City arrogance, from his walk to his clothes and the way he spoke. When he grabbed Emmy, Jack felt like punching him. He's spent the past ten minutes on the sofas—the past four days, in fact—struggling with every fibre of his being to avoid looking over at her or making any sort of contact, and it's killing him. This meeting has been the first time they've managed any sort of normal interaction since the weekend, and then Beneventi had to ruin that.

He knows she's been back in the flat this week, but he's kept his curtains drawn and his brain busy. Having Stacey and the kids here has helped enormously; the house has been full of laughter and warmth, and Stace has rallied brilliantly. The days have been harder, knowing Emmy is a glance away. He's never avoided the kitchen area so steadfastly. He had a few stolen seconds to watch her interacting with Stacey yesterday—it was uncomfortable watching them together, but a huge relief to be near her for a minute or two. She still doesn't look pregnant; he would never have guessed her secret. He's dreading how he'll feel when she starts to show. Some of his friends were freaked out when their wives' bodies adjusted to pregnancy; he absolutely loved it, all three times. Stacey looked like a fertility goddess and something tells him it will be the same with Emmy.

Natasha interrupts his train of thought. 'Do you know who that is with Emmy?' she demands. He caught the way she reacted to Beneventi; it was highly amusing. She's a piece of work.

'I think he's her—ex boss,' he says carefully. 'And a—friend, too. Do you want to run me through the draft email for the donors while we wait for her?'

Emmy returns, alone, five minutes later and slides back into her place on the sofa, eyes lowered. 'Sorry about that,' she mutters.

'All ok?' he asks, making his tone non-committal.

'Fine, thank you.' She picks up her notebook. 'Now, where were we?'

'Who was that?' Natasha asks her.

Emmy looks up at her. 'My old boss from Loeb.'

'Is he single?'

Jack grins inwardly.

'Oh, he's single, alright,' Emmy tells her. 'He's getting divorced.'

Natasha squares her shoulders. 'Would you mind passing my number onto him, please? Just, you know, in case he's interested.'

Emmy hesitates. 'I'd be happy to, but… he's bad news, Natasha.'

'I'll be the judge of that,' Natasha says sharply. 'I can look after myself, you know.'

'Ok,' Emmy says. 'I'll pass it on. I'm sure he'd love your number. But be careful. He's just been fired for sexual assault and misconduct. Oh, and he's also knocked me up. But if none of that bothers you, feel free to go for it.'

Natasha's face is a picture. Her jaw drops comically open. Jack's amazed Emmy's shared her news so freely.

'You're pregnant?' She looks at Emmy's perfectly flat stomach and then over to Jack, who shrugs.

'Eleven weeks,' says Emmy calmly. 'That's why he came to see me; I told him yesterday on the phone. But I promise you, there's nothing going on between us now, so please, be my guest.'

It takes a lot to floor Natasha, but she looks completely dumbfounded. She gathers up her phone and notebook. 'I have to get on with this email,' she says. 'Emmy, could you please write up some summary bullets on the NGOs that I can paste in? And you can give Lorenzo my number if you're sure'—she nods towards Emmy's stomach—'about everything.' She sashays across the room, leaving Jack with Emmy.

She raises her gaze to meet his and gives him a small grin.

He settles back on his sofa. 'And may they live happily ever after,' he says.

Emmy giggles and he grins with relief at having broken the tension. 'Seriously,' he says, 'I suspect they deserve each other.'

'They're definitely both fast workers,' she says. 'Don't say I didn't warn her.'

'I didn't expect you to tell her your news,' he says.

She throws her hands in the air. 'Honestly, Jack, I couldn't give a shit whether she knows or not. Natasha's opinion of me is way down my list of things to worry about right now, believe me.'

'Did it all go ok... with him?' he asks. 'Not that it's any of my business,' he adds hurriedly.

'It was fine,' she says. 'He's very excited and happy about the news.' She raises her eyebrows at him imperceptibly, but her barb is clear. *Touché*. Well, it's that guy's baby; it's quite right that he should be supportive.

'I'm glad to hear it,' he says, not rising. 'Look.' He lowers his voice and leans forward. 'This week's been difficult. I know we've been staying out of each other's way. And I know you have a lot on your mind; I don't want to make things tougher for you. You're doing a great job, honestly. I'm feeling better about our distribution than I have in a while. I'd love you to finish updating me if you're not in any rush. What do you think?'

He lets his gaze roam over her face. What he wouldn't give to be strolling across the courtyard to The Lodge with her shortly, knowing that an evening by the fire, on that blessed rug, lies ahead of them. Instead, he'll be rattling round in his big house alone and she'll be upstairs in the little flat. The sense of things being utterly wrong hits him once again.

30

THURSDAY, 19TH DECEMBER

When he heads over to the house later, it's with a lightness he hasn't felt since Saturday. He and Emmy ended up having a long and highly enjoyable discussion around the challenges of the NGO community. It's clear she brings a much-needed perspective that will allow them to understand the needs of these parties. He's been treating the NGOs as a homogenous mass of semi-automated distributors, and listening to Emmy, he realises how misguided that's been. They need to show a lot more love for and gratitude to these guys immediately, and she's the perfect person to represent them. They've even developed their idea of an online community for their NGOs further, including a proposed global community where the guys in Tanzania can share their successes with the other, less established regions.

There's nothing like an engaging chat to lift the spirits, but the real reason for his levity is that they've broken that horrible tension that's existed the past few days. Going from being with her as much as possible to cold turkey was devastating, but seeing his own crippling misery reflected in hers this week has been worse. If he doesn't have the right to whisk her off to bed anymore, then perhaps he can learn to enjoy her friendship and the talents and passions she brings to her job. Thank goodness there's only one day left of work. In the new year, he'll work on rebuilding their relationship in a more professional way.

Once he's treated himself to his customary infra-red sauna and ice-bath, he settles down with a pint of water to watch a documentary about Tony Robbins. At least the kids will be over here from tomorrow night and their shrieks and silliness will bring the house back to life. Meanwhile, thank heaven, he has Marge, who sits curled up in an enormous ball next to him on the sofa.

The buzzer for the front gate goes. Marge looks up and grizzles before reluctantly lowering herself onto the floor. They pad across the hallway together. He presses the button on the intercom.

'It's me.' Stacey's voice comes through clearly.

'Hey,' he says, and releases the gate. He's not expecting her. He and Marge go to open the front door and watch as she steps out of her car. She's all dressed up in heels and a big furry coat; she must be on her way to a party. She brandishes a bottle of champagne as she approaches.

'This is for you,' she says. 'Thanks for looking after me this week. I'm not sure how I would have got through that without you.'

'Any time, Stace; I mean it,' he says as he stands back to let her through the door. He shuts it and takes the bottle she's offering. It's Krug. They stare at each other.

'Are you off out somewhere?' he asks.

'No,' she says. 'I wanted to come and see you.'

She slips off her coat and drops it on the bottom steps of the staircase. Underneath, she's wearing a little black, silky dress edged with lace. It's more like underwear than clothing. She looks sensational.

She takes a step towards him and puts her hand to his cheek.

'Oh, sweetie,' she says, smiling at him. 'I've been such an idiot. I think I made the biggest mistake of my life, leaving you.'

He freezes. 'What?' he says dumbly.

'This week, being here with you and the kids, was wonderful. It felt right, having us all back together.'

'It was lovely,' he says, fighting for time so he can work out what exactly is going on here. 'But you made a decision, Stace. *We* made a decision, and a couple of fun family evenings together doesn't change that. What about that guy you're seeing?'

She shrugs. 'He's fun, but he's not a long-term prospect. But look at you. You're the love of my life; I don't know why I thought I'd be better off without you. It was crazy.'

She tilts her face and kisses him softly on the lips, then again. Years and years of kissing her have forged a habit as instinctive as breathing, and he opens his mouth and slides his free hand around the silky fabric at her waist and up her back. As he does so he recognises that kissing his ex-wife is extremely pleasant but not earth-shattering, and she's not the person he wants to be doing this with. Bloody Emmy, with her bloody crooked, kissable little mouth. He pulls away.

'Jesus, Stace.' He runs a hand through his hair. Phew. That was a close call. Another minute or two and he would have been lost in her. 'This is not a good idea,' he says now. 'I think we need to open this bottle. Come through.'

He heads through to the kitchen and she trails behind. When he turns to her, she has her arms crossed tightly over her chest and she's twisting her mouth. He puts down the bottle and folds her into a brotherly hug, kissing her hair.

'It's ok,' he says, releasing her. 'Do you want some PJs or something? We can have a chat in front of the fire.'

She nods, and he jerks his head towards the stairs. 'Go and help yourself.'

When she returns, she's in his ancient Oxford hoodie and tartan pyjama bottoms.

'Better,' he says, and grins at her. 'Less temptation for me. You looked stunning in that dress.'

She takes the compliment with a relieved smile and accepts a flute of champagne from him.

Once they're settled on the sofa he says, 'Ok. Why don't you tell me what's really going on?'

She sighs and takes a swig of her champagne. 'I'm not sure... the breast lump terrified me, you know? Reminded me I'm not superhuman.'

'I'm sure,' he says.

'This whole bid I made for freedom—it just feels shallow and immature in light of the past week. I mean, what if I'd had cancer? I walked away from you—you were my whole life. And I arrogantly thought I'd be young and healthy forever, and I could do whatever the fuck I wanted. But when illness or death come into the equation, it doesn't look like such a smart move.'

'That's always been part of the marriage contract, for me,' he says carefully. 'You commit to someone and you hope to be there for each other when you get old or sick or you need your adult nappy changed...' He smiles at her to show her he's not lecturing her. 'But at the same time, you can't stick with that person if you're not happy just so you have a nursemaid on standby if you need one.'

'I didn't mean it like that,' she says, shaking her head. 'I didn't mean that was all I wanted from you. It's more that the past week has made me question what's important in life. I've been on a quest for excitement and variety,'—she's avoiding his gaze—'but surely having a loving family to come home to is worth more than all that.'

'I can't answer that question for you,' he says. He knows Stacey; she's impetuous and passionate, and he'd hazard a guess tonight's visit is more of a spontaneous stunt than a well-conceived plan. 'But you have a loving family. You have four kids. And we're still co-parents; you haven't lost me.'

'But it's not the same,' she says, and tears glisten in her eyes. 'When I was sitting right here earlier this week, and I looked over at you, I thought I'd never seen such a sight for sore eyes.'

'That's very sweet, but it's been an emotional week for you,' he says. 'For me, too. But you didn't think that when we were still married, Stace. You couldn't bear the sight of me in the end; you couldn't wait to get away. It's natural that you feel closer to me this week after what you've been through, but don't do yourself the disservice of undoing all your hard work over the past year. You've got a new home; we went through all the pain and shittiness of the divorce. You've been very clear for some time as to what you wanted from life. Have some faith in yourself. You're young and healthy and gorgeous. That life of freedom and adventure you wanted, you can still have it, you know.'

She takes a deep, shuddery breath and sighs. 'You think so?'

'Yes, I do. You can have whatever you want. Think of it this way—we've got the best of both worlds. We're definitely the happiest divorced couple I know; we're spending Christmas Day together, for God's sake! So you have me and the kids. But you also have the chance to get out there and take another shot—at love, at happiness, at world domination. Whatever you want. And so do I, I guess.'

He takes a sip of his champagne and looks up at her. She's studying him intently. 'What?' he asks.

'Is there someone else?' she asks.

'No,' he says. 'What makes you say that?'

'Hmm.' She narrows her eyes at him. 'I just came by half-naked and threw myself at you. The Jack I know isn't that gentlemanly.'

She knows him far too well. 'There was someone,' he says. 'But it's not going to happen—I won't go into why. More to the point, I'd like to think I'm decent enough not to sleep with you if I don't intend it to amount to anything.' He pats her leg. 'No matter how gorgeous you are.'

31

SATURDAY, 21ST DECEMBER

Sorrel Farm looks like a winter wonderland when they sweep up the driveway. A uniformed man directs them to a car park and Emmy pulls the car to a halt. As she walks through the resort with Rosa and Stacey, she's filled with delight that places like this exist. She takes in the surroundings: the up-lit fruit-frees bedecked with white fairy lights and a huge old barn from whose vast windows spills warm, golden light. Another staff member welcomes them and gestures towards a walled garden, where the festivities will kick off, and from which direction the strains of Christmas choral music are wafting.

When they walk through the old wrought-iron gates into the walled garden, a festive tableau greets them. The ancient walls are illuminated, a choir stands on a platform at the far end of the turquoise pool and a long bar, dressed as if it's part of an old Christmas market, is off to their left. Colourful guests throng in the foreground and people are hugging, laughing and drinking. There are a couple of enormous fire pits giving off an unmistakable woody scent and some healthy flames.

'Let's go get a drink,' says Stacey, pointing at the bar. They make their way across the grass to the bar and Stacey screams.

'Evelyn!'

She throws her arms around a stunning brunette in a huge brown furry coat. Stacey spent much of the journey here regaling them with a colourful take on Evelyn's story, from her split from her mega-famous chef husband, Seb, to her dramatic move to Kent and her fairytale romance with the farm manager here, Angus. Apparently Evelyn and Angus have got married and are expecting a baby. Stacey also mentioned that Seb Macleod will probably be here with his husband, Gino, which gives Emmy a thrill. This is by far the most glamorous event she's attended in living memory, although Rosa is used to this type of thing. Indeed, it's so magical to be here that even her pain over Jack and her worries about her pregnancy are ebbing away.

Evelyn breaks away from the people she's speaking to and comes to join them. She's even more beautiful up close. Her skin is radiant, and she has the warmest smile. A well-built, good-looking man follows her over and stands beside her. Something about his demeanour instantly reminds Emmy of Jack. His eyes crinkle as he grins at them and kisses Stacey.

'This is my gorgeous friend Evelyn Macleod-Rutherford, and her equally gorgeous husband, Angus Rutherford,' Stacey announces. 'What you see tonight is all Evelyn's doing, and Angus manages the farm here. Guys, the place is looking incredible.'

'Thank you, darling,' says Evelyn. 'It's so lovely to have you all here. We're determined to make it the least bleak midwinter's night possible. When the choir has finished, we'll move into the Main Barn for a good old feast.'

'Evelyn's friend Zoe is the chef here,' Stacey tells them, 'and she's so talented. And obviously she has great produce to cook with, thanks to Angus.'

'That's right.' Evelyn beams at her husband. 'You'll get to sample it all tonight.'

'How's the bump, Evelyn?' Stacey asks.

In response, Evelyn pulls open her coat to reveal a shapely bump beneath a sleek cream ribbed dress. *Pregnancy goals*, thinks Emmy.

'The bump is great, thanks,' Evelyn says. 'Twenty-three weeks and counting; it's going like a dream. She's a great little girl.' She pats her belly.

'Just like her mother,' says Angus, and he puts his arm around his wife. She nestles into him, her hand stroking her bump, and looks up at him adoringly while he gazes at her as if he might burst with pride and happiness. It's a heart-warming scene and a harsh reminder of how different her own pregnancy will be, with a baby-daddy who's utterly dodgy and a boss she adores, who doesn't want to know her. It's going to be lonely as hell. Instinctively, her hand slips under her coat to her stomach. Rosa, not always the most emotionally aware, catches the gesture and presses her lips together as if in sympathy.

Rosa looks fantastic tonight, in a huge baby-pink faux-fur coat and matching Sixties-style hat that are apparently by Astrid Carmichael, as is the rest of her outfit. She looks like an elegant marshmallow. Emmy's aware that this is a big night for her; it's her first work event since she redrew her rules of engagement on Instagram. She's nervous, but she's good at hiding it.

A waiter comes over with a tray hanging from his neck, bearing sausage rolls and shot glasses of what turns out to be oxtail soup. Emmy helps herself to one of each; the heat of the soup flashes through her body as she swallows and the sausage roll is the best she's ever tasted. She's wondering if she can sneak another one off the tray when there's a slight commotion and an extremely glamorous blonde woman joins them, accompanied by a familiar-looking, radiantly pretty brunette. Stacey and Rosa flock to the blonde woman.

'Hi Astrid,' Rosa says, kissing her on the cheek.

'I recognised your coat from the other side of the garden,' says Astrid, smiling. 'It looks gorgeous on you.'

Astrid is wearing a long, off-white coat with a matching fur collar and cuffs. It's immaculate, and not something Emmy would dare to wear on a farm, of all places. Her hair is styled in a chignon and she looks like a silver-screen movie star.

Stacey leans in to kiss her. 'I have to ask, Astrid,' she says. How did the date go with that hot compatriot of mine?'

Astrid blushes and jerks her head into the crowd. 'It was amazing. He's here—he's come over for Christmas. You'll have to meet him later.' Emmy can't see who she's referring to.

Then Astrid says, 'Sorry, I'm so rude. This is my friend Natalia Beneventi. Natalia's doing some consulting for us at the moment and she helped me pull together the vision for this event.'

As she speaks, it's as though she's getting smaller and smaller and her voice sounds further and further away. Now Emmy knows why the woman with Astrid looks familiar. She's seen photos of her on Lorenzo's phone. Natalia is Lorenzo's wife.

32

SATURDAY, 21ST DECEMBER

'Jesus,' a man's voice says, and someone catches her as her vision narrows to pin-pricks. 'Are you ok?' he says.

She's nauseous and her legs feel like cotton wool; her hands are shaking and she may have dropped her shot glass. She hangs her head and breathes in great gulps of air; it's so cold it burns the back of her throat. For one horrible moment, she thinks she's going to throw up and then it passes. She should have eaten more before they left Surrey.

Slowly, she straightens her legs and her body. Evelyn's handsome husband, Angus, is still holding her and everyone in their circle is staring at her. This is mortifying. She holds her hand up. 'I'm fine,' she says.

'I'll take you inside and get you warmed up,' Angus says. 'Do you think you can walk on your own? Take your time.'

'Do you want me to come?' asks Rosa.

'No,' she says. 'Stay here; I'll be out in a minute.'

She walks slowly through the garden with Angus, whose arm is still hovering near her in case he needs to catch her again. He leads her out into the main courtyard and into the large barn they passed on the way in. It's beautifully decorated but empty aside from waiting staff hurrying back and forth. There's an enormous fireplace on one side of the room and Angus pulls up a chair for her right in front of it.

'Sit,' he says. 'What can I get you? Food? Brandy?' Water?

'I'm pregnant,' she says. 'But thanks. Something hot? Tea or hot chocolate, please? And some food, if possible. I probably had a blood-sugar crash.'

'Ok,' he says. 'Give me a sec.' He calls over a server and asks her for a hot chocolate and something sweet to eat.

Emmy rubs her hand over her face. 'God,' she says. 'I'm so sorry about that.' She feels unaccountably weepy and fragile, all of a sudden. It's probably down to this lovely man showing her some sympathy. A tear rolls down her cheek.

'Oh my goodness,' he says. 'We can't have that. Here.' He looks around and pulls a napkin off a nearby table. 'I'm sure you gave yourself a bit of a fright. Fainting is always a horrible experience. But how lovely that you're pregnant. How far along are you?'

She closes her eyes to stem the tears that threaten to spill over onto her cheeks. 'Nearly twelve weeks,' she says. 'But the whole situation is pretty horrific. I'm not with the father and—there are other problems too. Not with the baby, with my life.'

He leans forward. 'I'm sorry to hear that,' he says. 'Thank you, Cora.'

He accepts a mug of hot chocolate on her behalf, and a plate laden with brownies and cookies. She takes a brownie and bites into it—good lord; it's sublime.

'You're very brave, doing it on your own,' he says. 'I'm sure it must be daunting.'

'Thank you,' she says. 'Do you know that lady with Astrid—Natalia Beneventi?'

'No,' he says. 'I just met her earlier this evening, when they came to set up. Why?'

Emmy takes a breath. 'Her husband, or soon-to-be ex-husband, is the father of my child. We worked together. And it never in a million years occurred to me I'd come into contact with her.'

Angus grimaces. 'Shit,' he says. 'That's awkward. Does she know about you?'

'No—at least, I'm pretty sure she doesn't. But as I understand it, they're getting divorced because he was unfaithful to her with lots of women, so I suspect she's not under any illusions. But I'm having his child—my baby will be her daughters' half-brother or sister. That's so weird. Surely I should come clean?'

He laughs, kindly. 'I'm not sure I envy your situation. But it does seem serendipitous, doesn't it, that you've both turned up here tonight? Perhaps it's a good chance to bite the bullet?'

'Hmm,' she says. 'I'm sure you're right. But given I just fainted upon hearing her name, I'm not convinced I have the strength! Jesus, it's all such a mess.'

'Take your time,' he says. 'Load up on sugar and see how you feel. Would you like me to call a doctor?'

'Oh, God, no,' she says. 'I'll be totally fine. It's amazing the effect guilt can have, isn't it?'

'So, are you a friend of Stacey's?' he says.

Now it's her turn to grimace. 'Not really. She's good friends with my sister, Rosa. But I'm afraid that's all very messy, too. I got involved with her ex-husband, Jack—Stacey doesn't know. But he found out I was pregnant and he went ballistic and now he wants nothing to do with me. Also, he's my boss. And I think I might be in love with him.' She's not sure why she's telling him this. Maybe because he's kind and solid and reminds her of Jack. She buries her head in her hand, and when she looks up, he's staring at her.

'Good lord,' he says. 'Have you thought about selling the film rights to this? You poor thing. What a tough time you're having.'

'Tell me about it.' She shakes her head and takes a sip of the hot chocolate. It's delicious, as though Belgian chocolate has been melted into milk.

'I've never met Jack,' Angus says. 'They split up around the time Evelyn and I got together. But as far as I know, it was all Stacey's doing. I thought she was thrilled to be single?'

'I think she is,' she says, 'but it's still awkward.'

'I don't know about that,' Angus says. 'At our age, it's like a game of musical chairs. Why shouldn't you and he be happy if Stacey's moved on?'

'I don't think he feels like that,' Emmy says. 'He thinks I've betrayed him. Plus, he's got four kids, and he made it clear that he doesn't want to be involved with anyone who's got another one on the way.'

'Hmm,' he says. He offers her the plate again. 'Go on. Evelyn said Jack was an amazing guy; she was very cut up when Stacey walked out on him.'

'He is,' Emmy says. 'He's incredible—he blows me away.'

'His reaction sounds a little disproportionate,' says Angus, 'though of course, I've only heard your side of the story. Maybe he was just hurt and shocked. People do funny things when they're feeling defensive; their ego rears up and they lash out. Would you consider trying to reason with him? I guess what I'm saying is, if he means that much to you, then it may be worth risking a little hurt pride?'

She crunches into a cookie. He's right in that the main obstacle to pleading her case with Jack again is her fear that he'll knock her back again, that she'll see that look in his eye a second time as he spells out to her that he's not interested in her and her tiny, apple-sized baby.

'Maybe,' she says cautiously.

'I nearly lost Evelyn,' Angus says, and she jerks her head up in surprise. 'I'd made this assumption that when her summer at the farm was over, she'd go back to her jetsetter life in London, and I didn't even have the courage to ask her if my assumption was right, or what she wanted. And she totally blindsided me. She negotiated the sale of her stake in Seb Macleod Limited and the purchase of her stake in this place without even telling me, and Jess—who owns the farm—announced it publicly at a dinner. You could have knocked me down with a feather. I've always felt so grateful to her for being courageous enough to make the grand gesture, but it still horrifies me to think about how things could have ended if she'd been as useless and apathetic as me.

'And now I wonder what I was thinking. Was pride, or fear of rejection, really worth weighing up against my entire future happiness? My life has been transformed; we have three sons between us and a daughter on the way. So my philosophy these days is: grit your teeth, screw up your eyes, and jump. You might end up with a bruised backside and some hurt pride—or even a broken heart—but God knows, fortune really does favour the brave.'

33

SATURDAY, 21ST DECEMBER

Rosa is busy taking photos and videos for her Instagram Stories. Tonight represents the first sign to the outside world that she's coming in from the cold. Astrid Carmichael is a big deal in British fashion, Seb Macleod is a big deal around the world, and Evelyn has really put Sorrel Farm on the map in the past eighteen months. To be here, at one of the most sought-after events of the festive season, is a privilege. A couple of weeks ago the Sorrel Farm invitation was merely the highlight in a busy December calendar; now she's not sure she's ever felt so grateful to be included.

The incredible surroundings make her job easy. She takes some clips of the choir singing *In the Bleak Midwinter.* It's a carol that always makes her skin prick, but here, standing in the smoky air, its solemnity and purity takes her breath away. She even pockets her phone briefly and closes her eyes to let the choir's exquisite voices wash over her. Her mind flits to Emmy—her poor little sister. She deserves to catch a break. She hopes she's ok—she's in safe hands with Evelyn's husband.

The other details are equally stunning—the large wooden trays carried by servers dressed as elves, their straps bedecked with bells; the enormous eucalyptus wreaths adorning every window in the Main Barn when they wander through to the main courtyard, and the horses pulling cheerful red carts which will take guests for a tour of the resort. As they walk, Evelyn gives Rosa and Stacey an update on the status of the farm.

'We've really expanded the managerial side,' she explains. 'It was partly self-serving—I don't want Angus to have to get up at four-thirty every morning! But hiring a few people underneath him means he can spend more time on long-term planning, especially on the shift to a real biodynamic approach—rather than getting caught up in the reeds of the daily problems. We don't just want this to be an organic farm; we want it to be as restorative as possible for the landscape and as conducive as possible to wildlife flourishing.'

As she talks, Rosa's aware of an unfamiliar glow of warmth. It's the pleasure that comes from knowing she's on the right side of something. These are decent people with an important vision; they're making a difference to the planet through this wonderful place, and they're improving people's health with their beautiful produce. There's no hard sell here; there's no need for her to quench any deep-down distaste she has about her job. This place sells itself, but whatever she can do to help them promote it, she will.

Her cup runs over when Seb Macleod himself materialises. With him is his husband Gino, instantly recognisable from the amount of press coverage the two have had. Gino worked for Seb and Evelyn when he and Seb got together, and the tabloids had a field day. They married this spring with a lavish event in Positano that the great and good of Instagram seemed to attend.

'Hey, gorgeous,' Seb says, wrapping his arms around Evelyn as Gino grins. 'Great event—you've pulled in an even bigger crowd than last year. Perhaps it's time for me to admit that Zoe's a far better draw as a chef than I am—she's certainly better looking.'

'She is,' Evelyn retorts, 'and everyone will get a signed copy of her cook book in their goodie bags when they leave, so maybe you can learn something.'

Seb turns to Stacey. 'Jesus, Stacey, are you ageing backwards? You look incredible.'

Stacey laughs and hugs him. 'I definitely am not. I have a little visit booked to a very discreet plastic surgeon on Monday, so ask me next time I see you.'

'I hope you're still misbehaving terribly,' says Seb. 'I loved your stories at Evelyn's wedding. Do you have any more for me?'

'As long as you're not feeling squeamish,' Stacey says, winking, 'I have plenty of stories for you, honey.'

It's a relief to see her on such good form. On the way here, she updated Rosa and Emmy on the status with her lump. It clearly gave her a scare, but she's doing a great job of putting on a brave face.

Gino steps forward. 'Ladies. You all look gorgeous. Let's get a photo of Seb with you all; I'm in charge of his Instagram tonight.'

Seb shrugs. 'He doesn't even work for me anymore, but it's the perk of having a husband who's an Insta ninja. He can't help himself.'

He moves between them, and they pose. Within minutes, this will be going out to Seb's forty million followers. It shouldn't matter, but it does. She's lost followers that she may never get back; she's alienated or scared off brands who prefer to follow the crowd. But there are decent people and wonderful brands and inspiring causes out there, and they haven't abandoned her, and she won't abandon them.

~

Emmy and Angus only stop talking when the other guests file into the barn. She's mortified for having kept him so long at his own event, but he's extremely gracious.

'You're doing me a favour,' he tells her. 'All that small-talk and mingling isn't really me. I'd much rather have a nice chat with you in the warmth and eat biscuits.'

She wonders what it must be like to have someone like Angus by your side every day, to know that he's unfailingly there beside you, whatever life throws at you. Lucky Evelyn, to be facing pregnancy and new motherhood with him. It's not the most progressively feminist way of thinking, but she can't help it.

As the barn fills up with the sound of excited chatter, she reluctantly takes her leave from him.

'I'd better find my sister and Stacey,' she says. 'And, I guess, Natalia. Thanks for the pep talk and for looking after me. I really appreciate it.'

'Good luck with it all,' he says. 'I hope to see you back here next year with Jack and your little one.'

An unhelpful image flashes into her mind: her and Jack, all wrapped up in coats and scarves and beanies, with her infant strapped to her front in one of those Baby Bjorn things. For a second she feels Jack's hand in hers and the life-affirming warmth of her baby snuggled against her. She blinks and stands up.

She spots Natalia near the food, which is piled high on

huge platters along an enormous trestle table and looks spectacular. Despite her brownie consumption, she could definitely make a dent in this, but she'd rather get the tough conversation over with first.

Natalia is still with Astrid, who has now shed her white coat and is in an equally pristine cream sweater and cream trousers. They're with a tall, dark-haired man who has his arm around Astrid's shoulders and must be the new American beau she and Stacey were discussing. She approaches in a state of dread and clears her throat.

'Hi—Natalia?'

'Oh, hello,' says Natalia. 'Are you ok? You didn't look too well out there. We were all worried.'

'That's very kind,' Emmy says. 'I'm absolutely fine, thanks. Um—I was wondering if I might steal you for a quick word?'

Natalia looks surprised but has the good manners to cover it up. 'Of course,' she says, and gestures away from the buffet. She's probably only four or five years older than Emmy and very pretty. Lorenzo is such a shit.

'This is extremely awkward,' Emmy begins, 'and I'm sorry to hijack you here, but—you see—I know your husband, Lorenzo. We worked together at Loeb.'

Natalia's demeanour shifts and her face closes up. 'I see,' she says.

This was a terrible idea. What was she thinking? Why couldn't she just have left it to Lorenzo to tell Natalia? She pushes on.

'The thing is,' she says, 'we had a brief relationship before he was fired.'

Natalia frowns. 'Did he hurt you?' she asks.

'No! God, no. I'm afraid it was completely consensual and I have absolutely no way to justify my behaviour except that I was a bit messed up at the time. But it's no excuse. One of the things I wanted to say to you was how sorry I am that it happened.'

'Look,' says Natalia. She pauses and then continues, 'I'm not sure what to say. But let me tell you this. I've sat down with a woman whom my husband assaulted, and that was one of the most horrific conversations I've ever had, so you telling me you had a consensual fling with him is quite mild by comparison.'

'Isabella?' Emmy ventures.

'Yes. The way he treated her was unspeakable. But still, I'm not sure why you're telling me this.'

'Because I'm pregnant,' Emmy says. 'And I wasn't sure if he would tell you. My baby will be your daughters' half brother or sister and I guess they'll meet at some point down the line… if you're comfortable with that.'

Natalia's gaze flicks to her stomach and back. 'You're pregnant? How far gone? Does he know?'

'I'm nearly twelve weeks,' Emmy says, 'and yes, I told him this week—I saw him. But that was the first time I've had any contact with him since he got suspended—I left the firm after I found out I was pregnant.'

'Wow,' Natalia says quietly. 'Ok—that's a lot to process. How did he take it?'

'I was dreading telling him, but actually he seems excited about it,' Emmy says. 'I think he sees it as part of a fresh start, maybe? I definitely wasn't expecting him to be supportive; I want to do this on my own.'

'He is a decent father, when he's not, you know, molesting women and being unfaithful,' Natalia says. 'I can see why he might see this as good news—perhaps it'll be the kick up the arse he needs. So you don't want a relationship with him?'

'Oh, God, no,' Emmy says. 'Sorry—no offence.'

'None taken,' Natalia says. 'I don't blame you. Well, if you're going to have a little brother or sister for my girls, I guess it's good we're in touch. Fuck knows whether Lorenzo would have bothered telling me.'

34

SATURDAY, 21ST DECEMBER

Stacey leans her head back against the headrest of Rosa's car. Emmy's driving and Rosa's in the back, already asleep. Tonight has been exactly what she needed after the week she's had, the lumpectomy and wholesale rejection by Jack being the low points. This evening was about wonderful hospitality with good friends in magical surroundings. Not for the first time, she feels a pang of envy for Evelyn. She's hit the jackpot, but there's no doubt Sorrel Farm's recent success has been squarely down to her ability to whip it into shape and maximise its potential.

'I may need to unzip my pants,' she tells Emmy. 'I ate so much. That roast chicken was like the tastiest bird I've ever had. And those desserts! It was all sublime.'

'You should be like me and wear elasticated waistbands whenever possible,' Emmy says.

'Oh, darlin', I did that for years with my pregnancies,' Stacey says. 'It's a slippery slope.'

She closes her eyes. She could easily nod off after all that red wine and food.

Emmy is silent. Then she says, 'Well, I may get to pull off the elasticated waistbands for a bit longer, because I'm pregnant.'

Stacey's eyes shoot open in time to see Emmy glance over at her.

'Holy shit!' she says. 'I can't even tell. Early days?'

'Nearly twelve weeks,' Emmy says.

'Who's the baby-daddy? Can I ask?'

'My old boss from Loeb,' says Emmy. 'Lorenzo Beneventi. I had a bit of a shocker tonight because his wife was at the party and I had to tell her.'

'Jesus!' says Stacey. 'Go girl! He's hot—I was a client of his when I ran equities for a hedge fund. I have to say I'm envious, though I see from the press he's been a bad boy. Are you guys still hooking up?'

'Definitely not,' Emmy says. 'And yes, he is hot, but he's also dodgy as fuck. Although he seems very excited about the baby, which is good, I guess.'

'Excited is way better than hostile or in denial,' Stacey says. 'Believe me. Does Jack know?'

'Jack?' Emmy spits out his name and whips her head round to look at her.

'I mean, because you're working for him. I don't want to put my foot in it and mention anything in case you're not ready to go public with the news at work yet.'

'Oh, I see, sorry.' Emmy sighs, a long, shuddery exhalation. 'Yeah, he knows.'

'I hope he's being supportive? Encouraging you to take naps? Napping is so important in the first trimester; it's exhausting.'

Emmy makes a little groaning noise. 'Stacey.'

'Hmm?'

There's a pause. 'I got involved with Jack. I seem to be on a roll with confessions tonight so I may as well tell you.'

She *knew* it—she knew someone had gotten under his skin. He couldn't have been less interested in her the other night. She looks at Emmy again. Her profile is beautiful—there's no doubt she's gorgeous—but she didn't see this coming. It's hard to tell what your ex's type is when you're the only person you know whom they've loved.

'You're shitting me,' she says now. 'I could tell he had someone on his mind, but I didn't realise it was you.'

'Believe me, it's not me,' Emmy says. 'It only lasted a couple of nights. I'm sorry, Stacey. I know it's a bit close for comfort.'

Stacey draws in her stomach and rallies. Now is not the time for self-pity. She should never have come onto Jack the other night. Given what she put him through with the divorce, it was despicably selfish. She's self-aware enough to realise the fact that he's now off-limits was part of the attraction, and she's also evolved enough to admit she's glad he stopped things before they got out of hand. She allowed herself a little daydream this week, but that's no reason to undo all the hard work they've both done to keep their relationship as positive as possible for the sake of the kids.

Besides, she likes Emmy. She and Stacey are very different people, but maybe that's what Jack needs. Jack and Stacey were always in competition with each other, seeing who could succeed the most and climb the highest. It was a huge part of their chemistry, but it was exhausting a lot of the time. Emmy seems more... mellow, more balanced. She'd be good for Jack. Stacey can see the attraction she must hold for him.

'So what happened?' she asked. 'You're not that into him?'

Emmy gives a dry little laugh. 'No, I'm very, very into him. Unfortunately, I was so eager to be with him I failed to tell him I was pregnant when we hooked up. I promised myself I'd tell him last weekend, but then he surprised me with a skydiving trip and I had to come clean. He was furious, and he just cut me off straight away.'

This is all classic Jack: the grand gesture and the self-righteous overreaction.

'Oh, Jeez,' she says. She scoots round in her seat so she can face Emmy. 'Yep, I can see him going apeshit over that. What did he say, exactly?'

Emmy's voice is small. 'That he would never have—you know—got involved with me if he'd known I was pregnant and he felt really betrayed and he already has four kids so he would never date someone who has another on the way.'

Stacey snorts. 'Oh, pur-lease. Jack is baby-obsessed; did you know that? He wanted us to have a fifth when Mia was just two. A fifth! He's amazing with babies—and kids, obviously. I think we both know what's going on here; it's not his, so he's shot straight up the moral high ground. Jack's a great guy, but he can be a self-righteous pain in the ass when he wants to be. But you really like him?'

'I'm completely crazy about him,' Emmy says. 'But I'm aware I'm not the most attractive proposition at the moment.'

Stacey considers. 'How are you guys getting on at work?'

'Better. The beginning of this week was awful but we've made some headway and actually he seems pretty excited about the stuff I'm doing with the NGOs.'

'He was miserable on Tuesday when I had the op,' Stacey says. 'He moped about all day; I thought he was worrying about me, but he seemed miles away. He must feel strongly about you if you've had that effect on him. Let me talk to him. I'll see if I can knock some sense into him.' This is something she can do for Jack. She left him high and dry and then tried to fuck him up again with her ill-judged proposition this week. The least she can do is try to sort out his love life for him and save him from his own bullshit. If she can give him his Happy Ever After, the guilt that's eaten away at her since she left him may finally fade.

35

SUNDAY, 22ND DECEMBER

Jack's just finished the washing up after producing an enormous cooked breakfast for himself and the kids. They've had bacon, eggs, sausages and American-style pancakes cooked on the AGA's griddle. It's a Sunday tradition when he has the kids: brunch followed by a full roast late in the afternoon, before they go back to Stacey's. This week is slightly different; Stacey has some doctor's appointment tomorrow so the kids will stay here tonight. Tomorrow he's taking them to Winter Wonderland in Hyde Park. They're all very excited about Christmas and he's had to field innumerable questions from Mia regarding Santa's logistics. She's particularly concerned that he won't know which house to find her at. The other kids do a superb job of playing along and humouring her before craftily moving the conversation along to which cookies they should bake for him.

His phone goes; it's Stacey. He hasn't seen her since she left his house on Thursday night, but they have too much history for things to be awkward. They've had far more excruciating conversations than that one in their time.

'Hey,' he says.

'You're a fucking idiot; y'know?' she says, but her tone is affectionate.

'Nice to hear from you too,' he says, moving away from the kids into his study. 'What have I done now?'

'I spent yesterday evening with Emmy and we had a very interesting chat on the way home. C'mon, Jack; what are you playing at?'

'I don't know what you mean,' he says. 'She's pregnant with someone else's baby and she didn't have the decency to come clean about it up-front. Both those things are huge red flags for me—I'm better off steering clear.'

'Why?'

'Because it's not my problem! I'd rather not get involved.'

'That's not what you said when I called you about my breast lump,' she says.

'Come on, Stace! You're the mother of my kids. Of course I wouldn't let you deal with that on your own.'

'I don't know, sweetie. I walked out on you and yet you were there for me last week when I needed you. Emmy hasn't abandoned you—you've abandoned her. That's not the Jack I love. You've devoted the past few years to helping thousands of people whose problems aren't your problem.'

He's silent for a moment. 'She lied to me. How can I trust her after that?'

'Oh, for fuck's sake,' she says. 'Stop being such a sanctimonious prick.'

He's used to Stacey speaking her mind, but this hurts. It's deeply unfair that she should give him a hard time for walking away from someone who deceived him. He's not the party at fault here.

'I'm not,' he protests. 'Is it wrong that I want to protect myself from getting hurt again?'

'Ouch,' she says. 'Ok, that's understandable. But it's not right—I don't want you knocking about in that house by yourself till the end of time, because you're afraid to take a chance on someone again. As far as I can tell, she lied to you because she liked you and she knew you'd flip when she told you.'

'Exactly,' he says. 'She withheld information. It's hardly the basis for a healthy relationship.'

'What does she seem like to you at work? Trustworthy?'

'Totally,' he says. 'She's a star.'

'Well, there you go,' she says. 'She's unlikely to be a sociopath, is she? What would you have done if *you'd* knocked her up?'

'I would have fully supported whatever she wanted to do,' he says. 'You know that, Stace.'

'So, if she'd wanted to keep it, you would have stood by her.'

'Of course I would!'

'I knew it,' Stacey says. 'It's all about your ego. Just because it's not your kid, you have a hissy fit and kick her to the curb.'

'That's grossly unfair,' he says. 'It's a big ask, to take on someone I hardly know and her baby who'll be with us in six months' time. I'd like a girlfriend, yes, but is it too much to ask to have a normal courtship, without the pressure of an imminent baby? I mean, I can't mess her around here; she needs to spend the next few months getting herself sorted.'

'Sometimes timing is shitty,' says Stacey. 'Doesn't mean you can't make it work. You love babies, sweetie, and you're an amazing father. You've got five horses and four kids and a dog—what's one more in the menagerie? At the end of the day, it's another living being that will love you. We can all use as much love as we can get.'

He allows himself, for a second, to imagine himself and Emmy on the sofa with a sweet-smelling baby cooing at them. Can he even do this again? It's been thirteen years since he became a dad and six years since he did the newborn thing.

'Why are you so set on this?' he asks Stacey.

'I want to see you happy. I made a promise to you and I broke it, and I want to fix things. Besides, I like Emmy. She's a cool girl and you seem to have a lot in common with your philanthropy stuff. Let me ask you something. If she wasn't pregnant, on a scale of one to ten, how interested would you be in her?'

He closes his eyes and sees her face, her hair, that crooked smile. He imagines sliding his hand through her hair and down her back, and pulling her to him. He's been telling himself he can't trust her, but really the problem is that she couldn't trust him. She couldn't entrust her predicament to him, so she withheld it to get closer to him. What a mess.

He clears his throat. 'I suppose—um, a ten, really.'

She sighs. 'Wow. You're one of the smartest people I've ever met, sweetie. Don't you think you have your answer? You can have a miserable fucking Christmas or you can go get your girl.'

HE ENDS the call and trudges through to the kitchen. One of the kids has put *Last Christmas* on the Sonos system and the boys are dancing with the girls. Augie's looking up at Martha, who's much taller than him, and Mia is attempting to stay standing on Pitt's feet. She's laughing so hard that she keeps falling over. Augie is singing the wrong lyrics at the top of his voice. They're so magical; vitality streams from them. They don't know any other way to be.

Can he go through this again? Not just the newborn stage, but—he shudders—the toddler years, the Terrible Twos? Mia nearly broke them at that age. Then he looks at his boys. They were tubby little tanks when they were younger; now they're on their way to becoming lanky teenagers. Mia will be that age in a few years. She'll probably insist on boarding—she's already furious that she's the only one of the four of them who can't—and the house will be empty.

If the past year has taught him anything, it's that he doesn't do well in an empty house. This place wasn't meant for a lonely bachelor; it should be filled with life and laughter—and love. When they were breaking up, Stacey often talked about her desire for a second chance. What if Emmy and her baby are his second chance?

He scoops Mia off Augie and throws her over his shoulder. She shrieks with delight, far too close to his ear, and hammers ineffectually at his back with her small fists.

'You're coming with me, you little scamp,' he tells her, and marches out of the house and around the back to an outhouse they use as storage.

'What are you doing, Daddy?' she asks as he sets her down by the door.

'In here,' he says, 'are lots of your baby things. I wanted to see what state they're in. Shall we take a look?'

'Cool!' she says.

He unlocks the door and turns on the light. It smells musty but not damp. On one side are the now-empty boxes that usually store their Christmas decorations. On the other is a jumble of kid-related stuff: several old push-chairs (including the twins' double buggy; why did they never get rid of that?), a high chair, a wooden cradle and boxes and boxes of clothes, towels, changing mats and the like. This is the problem with having a surplus of storage space; it's made him undisciplined.

'Look at that.' He points at the cradle. It's an old-fashioned rocking one, mounted on a wooden frame.

'Was that mine?' She peers into it.

'It was,' he says. 'You used to sleep in that next to Mummy in our bedroom. Look, it rocks. You had a little pink and white striped gro-bag, and in the mornings your cheeks were always rosy. You'd gurgle and coo and chatter utter nonsense and we'd lie completely still and hope you didn't really want to wake up. But then we'd give in, because you were too adorable to resist, and we'd put you in our bed, between us, and cuddle up to you. A Mia sandwich. You were like a little hot-water-bottle.'

She's beaming at him; she loves hearing stories about when she was little. They all do.

'I can sleep in your bed tonight!' she announces. 'Like a hot-water-bottle! Please, Daddy?'

'No way!' He tickles her. You kick too much and I don't have a gro-bag big enough to keep those long, kicky legs in. I'll be black and blue in the morning. We'll all get a better night's sleep in our own beds; big day tomorrow, you know. Why don't you see what's in that box?'

She scoots over to examine the hoard and he looks down at the cradle again, swinging it gently with his hand. Those days of looking down at his baby girl seem so long ago. She was always, without fail, ecstatic to see him; her gummy smile would almost break her little face when he came into view. What would it be like to have another little baby in here, nodding off to sleep as they rocked him or her and stirring to wakefulness, tiny fists jerking and flailing?

He closes his eyes and sees, for some reason, a little dark-haired boy. Well, Beneventi's very dark; that makes sense. This baby has huge brown eyes with feathery lashes and a downy cap of dark hair. He's in a dinky blue vest that fastens under his nappy, and his little legs are ringed with circles of fat. Jack remembers the heaven of blowing raspberries on legs like that. A pang of longing hits him, so potent it makes him wince. He can't tell whether it's for Emmy or her baby; he suspects it's for both of them—the precious package deal he so cruelly and swiftly dismissed.

Stacey's right, as usual. He's made this complicated, and it's very simple. He wants to be with her, or, more accurately, he can't be without her. And the fact that she's having a baby has somehow morphed from being a poison-pill to a wonderful blessing. His hand shoots to his phone in his pocket, but this isn't a job for WhatsApp. He needs to do her the courtesy of showing up, cap in hand, and asking if she'll forgive him, if she'll give him a chance to prove his commitment. The kids are heading back to Stacey's on Tuesday. He'll do it then. As his wise ex-wife has pointed out, it's time for him to go get his girl.

36

SUNDAY, 22ND DECEMBER

'Fortune favours the brave,' Emmy tells herself as she dabs some of Rosa's Tom Ford Illuminating Primer onto her face. 'Fortune favours the brave,' she repeats as works her mascara wand into the roots of her eyelashes. Angus' words of wisdom have had a clarifying effect and have galvanised her into action. The past week has been utterly miserable, even though she and Jack seem to have reached a place where they can coexist professionally. There's only one thing she wants—to be with Jack—and she wants it badly enough that she'll take Angus' advice, even if it's terrifying. He's right: it's worth putting her heart and her pride on the line to make a play for the thing that will bring her the most happiness in life.

She can't say she's feeling confident. It's hard to produce a line of argument that will cause him to throw out his original horrified reaction to her pregnancy and welcome her and her baby into his life with open arms. But she has to do something. She has to know that the decision rests with him and that she's done everything in her power to make amends. She'll emphasise how unreal the pregnancy seemed in those early days and how she didn't want to taint what they had by acknowledging her predicament. She'll apologise again. She'll promise that she'll never deceive him again, and she'll emphasise that she's not expecting any help or support from him. The thought has crossed her mind that he may have suspected she was after him for his money. She's penniless and pregnant, after all, and he's clearly loaded. That he might think this breaks her heart.

All she can do is go to him with her truth and ask him to listen to her. Then it's out of her hands. She wonders if Stacey's talked to him yet. It's comforting to know that she's on board and willing to try to 'talk sense' into him, but it may not make a difference. She's already seen that Jack can dig his heels in when he wants to.

She comes downstairs. She's wearing a very soft, white cowl-neck that Rosa's kindly lent her. Rosa's been amazing. She was intrigued and amused to hear Emmy's rundown this morning of her conversations with Angus, Natalia and Stacey. 'Your life is like a soap opera,' she said. But she's seen how devastated Emmy is and she suggested again that David has a word. Emmy declined. Nothing was likely to rile Jack more than her sending in a bunch of allies to talk him over. It's best she goes to see him herself. She can make her own case better than anyone else.

'I'm off,' she says, grabbing her parka and David's hi-vis vest from their hooks. 'Wish me luck.'

'Do you want me to run you round to his in the car?' Rosa asks. 'I'm popping to Waitrose.'

'No, thanks. I'll take your bike if that's ok. I want to be able to make a quick exit if it all backfires horribly.'

'Ok,' Rosa says. 'Here, I'll follow you out. Good luck. See you later—or maybe not, if you get lucky.'

'Ha,' says Emmy. 'Let's not get ahead of ourselves. If he even lets me through the front door, it would be a result.'

She takes Rosa's bike out through the front gates and hops on, helmet fastened. She turns on her blinking bike light and waves goodbye to Rosa, who's unlocking her car. It's four-thirty in the afternoon and pitch-black. The Lodge is a ten-minute cycle ride away along the back roads. She cycles along, keeping as close to the hedgerow as possible because there's no path. A minivan is coming towards her and another vehicle approaches behind her, its headlights sweeping across the road ahead. The noise of the engine intensifies; it feels too close. She swerves hard into the mass of twigs that is the hedgerow at this time of year, but she's out of space.

An impact so hard it knocks the breath out of her.

Flying.

Then nothing.

~

ROSA EDGES OUT of the driveway, looking left and right. To her left, she sees what must be Emmy up ahead, but a car is approaching on the right. Its headlights are on full, momentarily blinding her. It streaks past, and she indicates left and follows it out.

'Idiot,' she mutters.

As she straightens up, the unthinkable happens. The car in front swerves to avoid an oncoming minivan and a doll-like figure in a hi-vis spins through the air before crashing down out of sight. It's Emmy. She can't see her. She screeches to a halt and automatically flicks on her hazard lights, jumping out of the car. The minivan on the other side has stopped and the driver is getting out too. Then she sees someone lying in the pool of the minivan's headlights and notices that the car that hit her has gone, racing away.

'Hey!' shouts the minivan driver at the retreating vehicle.

Rosa runs towards Emmy. 'That's my sister!' she screams. 'Emmy! Emmy!'

The man puts out his arm to stop her. 'Don't try to move her. I'll call 999.'

Emmy's lying awkwardly on the tarmac, her face turned to one side and her eyes closed. She looks terrifyingly lifeless. Rosa thinks she might throw up. The man is talking on the phone and pulling off his coat. He lays it on top of Emmy and Rosa realises that, of course, they need to keep her warm. She kneels down.

'Emmy?' she whimpers. 'Emmy? Sweetie, please wake up.' She gingerly puts her hand to Emmy's face. There's dirt and blood on her chin and around the neck of the jumper. Her face is cold, but wind-cold, not dead-cold. She very carefully puts her own face towards the ground and pulls her phone out of her handbag, turning on the torch. She can see Emmy's breath steaming in the freezing air.

She looks up at the man on the phone. 'She's breathing,' she says. 'Tell them to get here as quickly as possible—she's twelve weeks pregnant.'

He screws up his face as if it's too much to take.

Rosa snaps into over-functioning mode, her default in any crisis. She calls David.

'David,' she says. 'Emmy's had an accident; she's been knocked off her bike just outside the house. Fill a hot-water-bottle, quickly; tell Tallulah to grab hers and bring it and the big furry throw from the den out here. Yes, the ambulance is on its way; there's another driver here who's on the phone with them right now.' She sits back on her heels and holds her sister's hand, squeezing it tight, willing her to be alright.

~

WHEN EMMY COMES ROUND, she seems to be lying on a road. Rosa is there, and some paramedics. The pain and the cold strike her at the same time.

'You were knocked off your bike by a car,' the female paramedic tells her. 'In a moment we're going to turn you onto your back and put you on a stretcher so we can take you to hospital. Do you understand?'

She murmurs yes, but really, she doesn't understand anything. She closes her eyes again and submits to the pain and indignity of being slowly, slowly turned and put on something hard and plastic.

'Oof,' she says.

'You did brilliantly,' says the male paramedic. 'Your sister's going to come with you in the ambulance, ok? We're going to Kingston.'

'Arm,' she whispers. Everywhere feels sore, but her left wrist is throbbing agonisingly.

'Your left arm?' he asks. 'It looks like you landed on that wrist. We'll be able to give you some morphine for that in the ambulance, and we'll x-ray it when we get to Kingston. I'm Gavin and this is Saima. We'll get you there as quickly as we can—Saima's a speedy driver, and I'll be in the back with you. You ready? Ok.'

It's not until she's lying in the ambulance, strapped down with plenty of blankets around her, Rosa stroking her hair, that she has the thought—the thought that hits her with such violence that she gasps.

'The baby,' she blurts out. 'I'm pregnant. I'm twelve weeks pregnant. Is the baby ok?'

Gavin and Rosa exchange a look over her head.

'Your sister told us you were pregnant,' Gavin says. 'I promise that's one of the first things we'll check when we get you into A&E. We'll give you an ultrasound. I know it's difficult, but try not to panic too much.'

Her eyes fill with tears. Her baby. What was she doing, cycling around in the dark? She seems to have survived this, but what if the baby hasn't? It should be as big as an apple this week; it's still small enough to be wrapped up deep inside her, isn't it? She's noticed herself filling out; she's bloated, as if she's eaten a huge bowl of pasta. Perhaps the bloat will be like bubble-wrap, insulating her precious little apple from whatever the hell just happened.

'We're just a few minutes away,' Gavin says. 'Can you remember what happened?'

She recalls coming out of Rosa's driveway and then... nothing. She shakes her head.

'A car nicked your bike as it overtook you,' Rosa says. 'We don't think it hit you hard, maybe just your handlebar, but it was enough, obviously, to upend the bike and you went flying. I was behind the car; I saw it all happen. It was so awful, sweetie. I'm so glad you're alive.'

'Did the car stop?' she asks.

'No,' Rosa growls. 'Fucker. But the car coming the other way did; he gave you his coat and called 999.'

'Saima will call this in as a hit-and-run,' Gavin says.

Emmy closes her eyes. Right now she can't even be angry. The morphine seems to be kicking in; the pain in her wrist is melting away.

In the hospital, she submits to everything and keeps her eyes shut as much as possible to avoid staring directly into the blinding lights overhead. They shine torches in her eyes and take her pulse and pick out the gravel that has apparently become embedded in her chin and jaw. Rosa's with her the whole time, even though Emmy tries to persuade her to go off and get herself a coffee. In a few minutes, she's told, she'll be taken down to Radiology for an x-ray of her arm and ribs. But there's only one person she wants to see, and it turns out to be a tiny woman with kind brown eyes, who introduces herself as Poorni.

'Are you ready?' she asks Emmy.

Emmy bites her lip and looks at Rosa, who squeezes her hand.

Poorni tucks a piece of blue paper into her waistband and pulls up her sweater. She spreads cold gel on Emmy's stomach and presses with her probe. She turns to Emmy and her smile is warm.

'We have a healthy, normal heartbeat,' she tells her. 'Take a look—your baby is fine.'

The rhythmical, underwater whoosh of the heartbeat and the flashing light on-screen are gifts from heaven. Emmy bursts into tears.

37

MONDAY, 23RD DECEMBER

'Here you go, Emmy,' says Tallulah, coming into the den with a tray. She lowers it gently to the coffee table. On it are two crumpets with butter and marmite and a huge mug of foamy hot chocolate.

'Wow,' says Emmy, raising herself up gingerly on the sofa with her right hand. Her ribs aren't broken but are badly bruised and her left wrist is fractured. It's in a temporary cast until she gets her fibreglass one next week, but it could have been worse. Rosa yelled at the doctor who did the bandaging, telling him there was no need for him to encase most of Emmy's hand in the plaster. She didn't realise at the time what a good call it was on Rosa's part, but now she can wiggle her fingers and even make a pincer grip.

She smiles up at Tallulah, though it hurts her chin under the dressing to do so. 'This looks delicious, thank you darling,' she says, and is rewarded with the sweetest smile. 'I should get injured more often if I'm going to get spoilt like this.'

'Oh, please don't,' Tallulah gasps. 'We were all so

worried. Dolly was so upset that she had to sleep with Mom and Dad.'

Rosa stayed with her in the hospital until around ten o'clock, when they'd finished examining her and bandaged her up. They then kicked Rosa out but kept Emmy in overnight for observation because of her loss of consciousness after the accident. Ironically, there was no fear of her falling into a deep sleep in that place and getting concussion; she spent most of the night in painful wakefulness thanks to the bright lights, constant noise, lack of privacy and the regular prodding and taking of her pulse. When they finally discharged her at eleven this morning, Rosa ran her a huge bath and put her straight to bed. Rosa's also ordered a waterproof sleeve to go over her cast so Emmy can shower; hopefully Amazon will get it to her sooner rather than later amidst its Christmas rush because right now, Emmy feels useless and frustrated. But, as David pointed out over a late lunch, it's a lesson in forced relaxation. It's Christmas week, the office is closed and all she can and should do is rest, for her baby's sake as much as for her own.

'Are you ready?' she asks Tallulah now and picks up the remote control. She's going to follow David's advice and vegetate, today at least. Tallulah collapses down beside her and Emmy turns on *The Wizard of Oz*. She and Rosa used to always watch it at Christmas, but today Rosa is manically prepping for Christmas lunch, which she's hosting. Their mother is coming and Emmy will wait till Mum is a few glasses of champagne down before revealing her news. God knows how she'll take it.

The Wizard of Oz is one of those movies whose every word and gesture is blessedly familiar, and she watches with half her brain while the other half replays the horrific events of last night. Her cast rests on her belly as she recalls that sickening moment of realisation in the ambulance that she may have killed her unborn child. Before now, her attitude towards her pregnancy has been a weird, undulating mass of ambivalence, resentment, denial and vague fondness, with each emotion taking centre stage at some point depending on circumstance and her mood. Yesterday, lying in the ambulance in that stretcher, it was as if someone had spun her emotions in a centrifuge and out of the vortex came absolute clarity: her baby is all she cares about. He or she is all she has. He's more important than Jack, more important than even Rosa, because he's the only being she can absolutely guarantee will stick around for her.

The movie progresses and draws to a close. Emmy watches Dorothy's face as, in the process of running after Toto, she misses the hot-air balloon and her only chance to get home to Kansas. It's heartbreaking because Dorothy's moment of clarity has come too late. *Now* she finally knows what she wants—she wants to go home—and she's literally missed the boat. A chill breaks out all over Emmy's body as Dorothy weeps. It took this crisis to make Dorothy understand what's important to her, just as it took being hit by a car and thrown across a road to bring home to Emmy what this tiny, miraculous baby means to her; this baby who was never meant to be and who must have fought like hell to find her. The accident was her very own hot-air balloon moment, and it could have come too late. It could have taken a miscarriage to make her see sense.

In another, *Sliding Doors*-type parallel universe where the accident didn't happen, she could be entwined with Jack on his sofa right now with two working wrists. However, she'd likely be sitting there with a vague feeling of resentment brewing over the inconvenience of her pregnancy.

Instead, she's here, alone with Tallulah. Except she's not alone. She has her baby with her and she feels the most profound connection to this fledgling life inside her. She'll never again take her baby for granted; she'll never again dare to put anyone or anything ahead of him. If Jack can't see a future ahead of them with her baby in the picture, then he's not right for her and she'll move on without him. All she knows is she'll never apologise for her baby's existence again.

~

ROSA'S PHONE rings as she's chopping onions for the stuffing. David has taken Dolly out for a walk, and Tallulah and Emmy are in the den watching a movie. She has the kitchen to herself. She dabs under her eye with the back of her hand. Bloody onions. She's exhausted from the distress of yesterday evening and the broken night that followed. It was impossible to sleep when she knew Emmy was lying in a hospital bed. Dolly's kicks and wriggles all night didn't help either. But really, what kept her from sleeping was that sight of her sister flying through the air like a rag-doll, over and over again. It was the most surreal thing she's ever seen, and she can't forget that moment when she thought she'd lost her. So, if the stuffing's not quite up to scratch on Christmas Day or the house isn't looking as Instagrammable as it should, she won't give a flying fuck.

She picks up the phone. 'Rosa Hamilton.'

'Hi, Rosa,' says a voice. 'This is Victoria calling from Stella McCartney. Are you free to speak?'

She stands up straighter. Stella has never courted her, unlike most of the other British brands in the luxury space. Her currency is on the rise again after her appearance at the high-profile Sorrel Farm event. The society pages all picked up on it and many ran the photo of her with Seb Macleod. Perhaps Stella has seen it and it's piqued her interest.

'Hi Victoria,' she replies. 'Of course.'

'I'm sorry to call you so close to Christmas,' Victoria says. 'We're firming up a childrenswear campaign for the new year on eco-warriors, and your daughter Tallulah's recent activity on your Instagram feed caught our eye. We admire her stance on animal cruelty, and we think she'd be a great fit for the campaign. As far as I'm aware, she doesn't have her own agent and so I thought I'd approach you directly. What do you think?'

You can't make this shit up. Rosa has to laugh. Only Tallulah can pull a stunt like that and emerge with a modelling gig for one of Britain's hottest brands. But it will be amazing for her. It will validate her in her own eyes and give her the endorsement she needs to pursue her many passionate causes.

'I think she'll be perfect for Stella's brand,' she says. 'Can you do me a favour and send me over a PDF of the offer letter? I'll give it to her on Christmas morning.'

38

MONDAY, 23RD DECEMBER

The waiting room has the same layout as every Harley Street waiting room Stacey has ever been to—high ceilings with elaborate coving and enormous windows—but the similarity ends there. This space has white walls, and a huge circular Damian Hirst installation of butterflies adorns one end. There's no standard-issue durable carpet, instead the floors are polished parquet. The immaculate blonde receptionist brings her an espresso, and she settles down into a Roche Bobois sofa. Now she knows why this guy's fees are so stratospheric. At least he has taste; she should probably take comfort in the fact that his eye is so uncompromising.

Mr Ariel Bloch is the ultimate in cosmetic surgeons—he's as discreet as he is effective. Stacey came to hear about him in the best possible way; she had drinks one night with a woman who is on the board of a FTSE 100 company despite not looking a day over thirty-five. Stacey prides herself on being able to tell exactly what procedures women have had, and she would have put money on this woman, Monique, having had nothing done at all beyond a little light Botox like Stacey herself. Imagine her surprise when Monique admitted to being forty-five and having had the full works done. By the time they'd drained their fourth cocktail, Stacey had Mr Bloch's number.

All she knows about him is that he's Israeli, educated at Harvard Med School and impossible to get an appointment with. She booked this months ago; it'll be her Christmas present to herself and her reward for seeing her company through another record year. Today's just the initial consultation. Mr Bloch will examine her and talk her through her suite of options. She's well-versed in the most innovative procedures available, but she'll put herself in his hands. He is, after all, *the* expert on this side of the pond.

A few minutes pass while Stacey sips her coffee contentedly. Her mood today is very different from that horrible wait for the breast consultant a couple of weeks ago, just a few blocks away. She scrolls through some photos Jack has sent through of Winter Wonderland. The kids are having a great time and there's one of Mia holding a stick of cotton-candy that's almost as big as she is. Her grin is wide and dried-up streaks of pink sugar encrust her cheeks. She's heaven. She texts Jack. *Have you put on your big boy pants and called E yet?* He replies straight away. *Tomorrow. I promise. Kind of busy with your kids right now, woman*. She laughs. *K*, she responds. It's a start. Things seem to be back to normal with him. Thank God. She's still kicking herself; how the hell could she have done that to him after walking out on their marriage once? It must have been her heightened emotional state after the op. She's heard of general anaesthetic doing seriously weird things to people. One little scare and she ran straight for security.

She hasn't contacted Antoine either. While she can see now that running back to Jack was an extreme reaction, somehow Antoine seems the opposite extreme. Too obviously just sex, perhaps; so no-strings-attached that it feels clinical. Having her mortality flash before her eyes, even briefly, has proven a useful mirror through which to assess her life choices.

'Ms Fisher?' The blonde appears in front of her. 'Mr Bloch will see you now.'

Stacey stands and folds her coat over her arm, click-clacking down the wide corridor and into a light-filled room.

A man is sitting at a large desk, bent over a laptop.

He raises his head and stands up, holding out his hand to her.

And time stops.

An electric shock runs through her, so palpable it lingers on her skin and causes the hair on her bare arms to stand on end.

He's beautiful.

He has dark hair, cut short to disguise a receding hairline. His skin is olive-coloured and his eyes are black and so heavily lashed that it looks as though he's wearing eye-liner. At a guess, he's mid-forties. In a second, she appraises what it is about him that's caused this physical a reaction. He's presumably highly intelligent, ambitious, an expert in his field. So far, so on-point for her. But he also looks utterly comfortable in his own skin. This is his domain, and he fixes her with a gaze that's supremely assured. If Jack's spirit animal is a labrador, then this guy's is a panther, or a cheetah, perhaps. On top of all that there's something she can't articulate, except to say that when she looks at him her heart hurts. He's triggered something in her that's undeniably carnal but also feels spiritual.

She steps forward to take his hand, and the shock

happens again; her stomach flips like she's on a Winter Wonderland ride with the kids.

He smiles at her and his face softens, and her heart hurts a little more.

'Ms Fisher. How do you do? I'm Ariel Bloch. Please. Take a seat.'

His accent is slightly broken and transatlantic. It's extremely hot. He gestures at the seat between them and she sinks into it in what she hopes is a graceful, sexy way and crosses her legs. Thank God she's wearing her favourite Astrid Carmichael shift dress, the dress that says *fuck me* and *don't fuck with me* in equal measure. She still hasn't spoken. Seriously, get a grip.

'How do you do?' she murmurs. Her heart and mind are racing; she needs to find some way to rescue this situation. Doesn't the Hippocratic oath say a doctor can't get sleep with his patient? In an instant, all thoughts of his cosmetic wizardry go out the door. She just wants him.

'So,' he says. An amused smile plays on his lips. She must seem a hot mess. 'Why don't you tell me a little about why you've come to see me today?'

Her palms are sweating. She discreetly wipes them down the sides of her dress. Jeez. She says the first thing that comes into her head.

'Are you my doctor already? Like, this second?'

He frowns. 'Are you having second thoughts?'

'Maybe.'

'That's natural, and of course there's no obligation for you to go ahead with anything that we discuss.'

She leans forward. 'But is this a doctor-patient relationship yet, technically speaking?'

'Technically speaking, no. I haven't issued you with any

medical advice at this point. So you're very welcome to walk out of here if you'd like.'

She takes a deep breath. He's not going to make this easy. There's no way around it. She's hit on plenty of guys since the divorce—Raphael, for instance—and it's been fun. But the stakes are high here because she's not sure she's ever wanted anything so much in her life.

'Look,' she says. 'I'm just going to say this.' *Shit*. Here goes. 'I don't want you to be my doctor because I want to date you. If you're single, that is—I don't see a ring. If you're not, forget I said anything.'

She sits back in her chair and folds her arms, almost afraid to look at him. But she does.

'I see,' he says. He puts down his pen and mirrors her body language, sitting back in his chair. He keeps his gaze on her.

'Fast decision-maker,' he says. 'I like that.'

'Well,' she says, 'I had no choice. Another few minutes and you would have been my doctor and the decision would have been made for me.'

'Fair,' he says. 'Yes, I'm single—divorced, at any rate—and I felt something too, when you walked in. So I agree; it's probably best if I don't take you on as a patient.'

He grins at her and she smiles back at him, and it's as though her heart is radiating waves of warmth beyond her body and through the room. So is her groin. She squeezes her thighs together more tightly.

'What do we do now?' she says in a voice that makes her feel about sixteen.

'I tell you what.' He looks at his watch. 'You're my last appointment of the day. How about you go and find us a table somewhere? The Dorchester? The Lanesborough? I'll be right behind you—give me twenty minutes. I just have some paperwork to put to bed here.'

She laughs at his mention of bed—it's a nervous reaction—and he grins again. He has a beautiful smile. 'Clumsy choice of words,' he says. 'I'll have Celia call you a cab. Here's my card. Give me a shout and let me know where to find you.'

'The Lanesborough,' she says. 'The Library Bar.' It's one of her favourite places and the bar is usually quieter and more discreet than those of the more central Mayfair hotels.

He nods his approval. 'I'll see you there,' he says.

He stands to see her out, but before he opens the door, he leans over and grazes her cheek with his lips and it's all she can do to stop herself from turning her head and pulling him towards her.

'I look forward to it,' he murmurs in her ear.

THREE HOURS LATER, she lies with him in a room at The Lanesborough, an arm and leg draped across him, attempting to catch her breath after two energetic and earth-shattering encounters.

'You didn't have to go to all this trouble,' she murmurs. 'I would have fucked you on the couch in your office—or even on the desk.'

'I know you would,' he says, tracing a line down her stomach, 'but I thought it might be fun to have an actual bed to hand, the first time. Call me an old romantic.'

'It's a beautiful room,' she says. 'Thank you. But will you fuck me in your office next time?'

'Let me guess,' he says. 'Doctor fantasy?'

She exhales. 'Oh, yes.'

'I can definitely oblige,' he murmurs. 'I have all sorts of gadgets in my consulting rooms that may appeal.' He traces the outline of the dressing with his finger and she shivers.

'Lumpectomy?' he says. 'All ok?'

'Yes,' she says. 'Last week; it was a fibroadenoma. I'm totally fine.'

'Good,' he whispers, and kisses her. His finger continues to trace lazy lines around her breasts and over her abdomen. 'You would have been a lousy patient,' he says. 'There's nothing for me to work with here. You're perfect.'

She shoves him gently. 'I bet you say that to all your patients,' she says, but the compliment makes her glow. Luckily, she was too consumed with lust earlier to remember to be self-conscious about being butt-naked in front of a cosmetic surgeon.

'Seriously,' he says. 'I mean it. But I could have told you that before I took your clothes off. Right when you said you wanted to date me, I was whipping through a mental Rolodex of my colleagues to see if I could persuade you to transfer to someone else. You just beat me to it.'

'Easiest call I've ever made,' she says.

He eases onto his side to face her and his hand moves round to her back, tracing her spine up and down, up and down.

'Your hands are incredible,' she says. 'You're seriously —dextrous.'

'You don't want to know how much they're insured for,' he says. 'But you're getting all the benefits of my professional skills for free.'

She giggles. 'Today sure is working out well for me.' She can't believe she's lying in bed with him. When he looks at her, she spirals into a vortex that's a heady combination of base lust and pure transcendence. 'Why are you even working this close to Christmas?' she asks. 'And isn't it Hanukah already?'

'I'm a terrible Jew,' he says, 'despite having the most Jewish name of all time. And my ex and I don't celebrate the Jewish holidays with our kids—she's a British Protestant. Besides, the NHS side has been crazy this year, so today was a good opportunity to see some private patients. I'm done now for the holidays.'

'I didn't know you did NHS stuff,' she says. 'So I can get a boob job for free?'

He laughs. 'You do not need a boob job. No, I only do reconstruction on the NHS—mainly facial, mostly for burns victims or post-trauma work. But juggling the two is full-on. That's why my wife left me, a couple of years ago. She said I prioritised my work over her and the kids. She was right.'

'I get it,' she says. 'I work hard too.'

'I know you do.' He kisses her. 'I got up to speed on you on the cab ride over, to make sure I wasn't falling into the lair of some total predator.'

'And it turns out you were,' she says.

'Indeed. And I'm very happy about that. But I read all about your company. You are an amazing woman; you've achieved so much. It's extremely sexy.' He wraps a leg around hers and buries his face in her neck, and she thinks she may die of happiness.

'Why did you get divorced?' he asks, his voice muffled.

She shrugs. 'I got bored. Not with him, but with marriage, really. We got together very young.'

'Wow,' he says, pulling away so he can look at her. 'Poor bastard. Are you guys friends?'

'Totally,' she says. 'He's the best. He came with me last week when I had my op.' She doesn't mention her little wobble after the op. Thank Christ Jack didn't humour her when she threw herself at him; that would have put her in an unimaginable position when she met Ariel.

His fingers skim down her back and over the curve of her butt, lighting up all her nerve endings. He kisses her eyelids softly.

'I promise,' he says, 'I will do everything in my power to make sure I don't bore you.'

Her eyes prick. 'There's literally zero chance of you boring me,' she says.

39

TUESDAY, 24TH DECEMBER

Emmy's trimming a mound of Brussels sprouts, a low-skill task she can just about manage. She's sitting at the island in the kitchen with a large mug of tea while Rosa, acting as head chef, barks orders at everyone and David lovingly stirs his bread sauce for tomorrow on the hob. Tallulah and Dolly are sitting at the kitchen table, constructing an elaborate gingerbread house from a kit. It appears more Smarties are making their way into their mouths than onto the walls of the house.

It's amazing the difference a decent night's sleep can make to her outlook on life. She slept like a baby mostly, despite waking a few times when she tried to turn over on top of her broken wrist. Her sense of fragility is wearing off and in its place is quiet resignation and a mounting feeling of resilience. With a good night's sleep behind her and the knowledge that her baby is safe and well, she can do anything. Anything except call Jack. She's spooked now; could the universe give her any stronger a sign than hurling her off her bike when she was on her way to reason with him? What will it do next time? Spontaneously combust her phone?

The doorbell goes.

'I'll get it,' David says cheerfully, turning off the gas under the pan. 'This baby is perfection.'

His cry of delight floats through from the hall, alongside a murmur of male voices, and he comes back into the kitchen, grimacing apologetically. Behind him is Jack in his Christmas jumper. He stops as soon as he sees Emmy.

'Good God,' he says, staring at her. 'What happened to you?'

She must be a right sight, with her arm in a sling, and her face bashed up. She still has a dressing along the length of her jaw and under it the cut is bloody itchy. At least she managed to shower and vaguely wash her hair this morning, thanks to the waterproof sleeve having arrived. Darling Tallulah, thrilled to have a real-life mannequin to work on, combed and blow-dried her hair beautifully, so at least one part of her looks glamorous.

'A car knocked me off my bike,' she says, shifting on her bar stool. 'I'm ok—I fractured my wrist but I'm fine.'

He's still staring at her, a haunted look in his eyes.

'And'—his glance flicks to the girls at the table and back to Emmy—'what about...' He points to his stomach.

She nods. 'All good. I had a scan.'

He blinks. 'Thank fuck.' The last time he said that was right after he'd kissed her for the first time. What a difference a couple of weeks makes.

'Jack!' Dolly squeaks, belatedly alerted to his presence. 'You sweared!'

'Hey Doll,' he says, flashing her a smile. 'Yes, I did—sorry about that. Don't tell Mia, will you? She'll be cross with me.'

'Can I get you a tea or coffee, mate?' David asks him.

'Thanks, mate, but no; I'm fine,' says Jack. He returns his gaze to Emmy. 'Do you think we can have a chat?' he says.

Her stomach is doing somersaults. She hasn't seen him since the office closed on Friday and the impact of him has hit her all over again, especially in that jumper which has serious memories attached to it.

'Sure,' she says, clambering inelegantly down from the stool and picking up her mug of tea.

'Use the den,' says Rosa. 'It's nice and cosy in there.' What she means is that it's private. Emmy throws her a grateful smile and awkwardly leads the way into the den.

Once inside, she sits down next to Jack on the sofa, pulls off her sling to give her neck a break and rests her cast on a cushion. She turns so she can face him. He is heart-stoppingly handsome; the reality of him is such a relief after her endless thoughts about him.

'So, how are you, really?' he asks her.

'I'm ok,' she says. 'I spent Sunday night in hospital, which I could have done without, but they kept me in because I briefly blacked out after I hit the road. But otherwise I'm fine; just trying to get to grips with this thing.' She holds up her wrist.

'I'm so sorry,' he says. 'I had no idea. I would have come earlier if I'd known. How did it happen?' He's staring at her so intently that she looks down at her tea.

'It happened right outside of here actually,' she says. 'On Sunday afternoon. I decided I'd be brave and go to see you, and a car nicked the side of the bike and threw me in the air. Rosa was pulling out of the drive and saw it happen, thank God, and came with me in the ambulance.' She looks up at him. His face is filled with horror.

'You had an accident coming to see me?' he says. 'Oh,

Jesus, I'm so sorry.' His voice quietens. 'Why were you coming to see me?'

She can't decide whether to look at him; her gaze is flitting all over the place. 'To apologise,' she says. 'To try to persuade you to give me another chance.'

He inhales sharply, and she continues. 'I had a long chat on Saturday night with Angus—Evelyn's husband—at Sorrel Farm. He told me he'd nearly lost Evelyn because he was too proud and scared to go out on a limb for her, and what he said persuaded me I should try talking to you. I figured it was worth a shot, and at least I'd know that if I didn't end up with you, it wasn't for lack of trying. I'm so sorry about—'

He puts his hand up and cuts her off. 'Emmy. You do not need to say you're sorry. I'm the one who's behaved like a total twat. No, let me speak; it's important. May I?'

He goes to take her mug and she nods, watching as he puts it on the floor and takes her good hand in his. The warmth of his skin on hers is bliss; it's like coming home, and hope rises in her.

'Look,' he says. 'I don't know why I had such a strong reaction to you telling me you were pregnant. Well, I do. It was good, old-fashioned jealousy. My ego was outraged that another guy had got to you first. I'd put you on some kind of pedestal and when you turned out to be mortal, I punished you for it and it was unforgivable. I was hurt and pissed off, and I lashed out at you, and I'm ashamed of myself. Stacey told me I was a sanctimonious prick.'

A gasp of laughter escapes from her mouth.

'Yeah,' he says. 'No one's ever had the balls to call me that before.'

'Not to your face, anyway.' She raises her eyebrows at him.

'*Touché*,' he says. 'But she was right. I don't know why I got my knickers in such a twist. I made it out to myself that it was all very complicated and there was no way I could be with you. But really, it's all quite simple. I miss you so much, and I'm fucking miserable without you. Everything else is just details.'

He's running his thumb back and forth over her knuckles as he utters these magical words, and she wants to sink into him. But she made a promise to her baby in that hospital bed.

'I miss you too,' she says. 'I've been devastated that you wanted nothing to do with me. But if this accident has taught me anything, it's that my baby is my highest priority now. I can't tell you how wonderful it is to hear you say those words, but if you can't handle the fact that I'm having a child then that's not just a detail; that's a major problem for me.'

His eyes widen, and he smiles at her. 'I wouldn't expect anything less, and obviously, I've been giving that a lot of thought. I realise it's early days and we've only known each other a few weeks. But I believe this is worth fighting for. The timing's not ideal, no. I'd rather have got to know you without the pregnancy factor being at play so soon, if I'm completely honest. But all I want is to be with you, and if things work out as well as I hope they do between us I'd be honoured to be a part of your baby's life.'

'Phew.' She exhales and looks into his beautiful eyes. 'That's a very generous thing to say, but do you really mean it? A baby's a big deal, Jack.' *Please say you mean it. Please say you mean it.*

He grins. 'I'm well aware. I went through our old baby stuff on Sunday—I thought we could use some of it for your little one, if you'll take me back—and it made me realise how quickly time passes. Mia's shooting up so quickly and she had no recollection of her wooden swinging cradle, even though I have so many precious memories of her in it. So if another baby wants to come into my life and make fresh memories, I will consider myself a lucky bastard.'

His eyes are wet and he's gazing at her in a manner that makes the blood rush to her head. That he was sorting through baby stuff for her child, right while she was gathering up the courage to go and see him, is overwhelming. She extricates her hand from his and puts it to his cheek, then leans forward and kisses him. He opens his mouth and cups his hand around the back of her neck; he tastes like Jack, like home, and the relief is sublime. She hoists herself up to sit on his knee, and he wraps his other arm around her waist in a vice.

'Mmm,' she manages when she comes up for air, 'I've missed this.'

'I've missed you,' he says between kisses.

'You're wearing my favourite jumper,' she says, pulling back far enough to see his face.

He looks sheepish. 'Well, it worked for me once, so I figured I'd give it another shot. I needed all the help I could get.'

'Maybe it's my least favourite jumper,' she says, sliding her hand underneath it and up his bare back, 'because whenever I see it, all I want to do is take it off you.'

'Ah, the mark of a fine jumper,' he says. 'If you want to undress me, does that mean I'm forgiven?'

'You're forgiven,' she says. 'And I realise I'm not blameless here. Just—don't stonewall me again, ok? I'm serious. You shut me out in the cold and you refused to even discuss your decision with me. It was devastating. Next time you're pissed off with me, promise me we can talk about it?'

'Oh, God, sweetheart,' he groans. 'I'm so sorry. That's more than fair, and you have my word. I'll never shut you out again. It's been just as hideous for me, if it's any consolation.'

'Are you sure you're good with this, though?' she says. 'Soon I'm going to start showing; do you really think you can handle being with me while I'm pregnant with another man's baby?'

'I can't wait for you to show,' he says, sliding his hand over her breast, 'and right now you could be having Donald Trump's baby for all I care, because you are going to be such an unbelievably sexy expectant mother that I won't care about anything else. I mean, you already are an unbelievably sexy expectant mother.'

She giggles and squirms on his knee, kissing him.

'If David walks in here and finds me with a boner, I'm in serious trouble,' says Jack. 'What are your Christmas Eve plans—can I persuade you to come back to mine?'

'I have no plans, except for being Rosa's sous-chef,' she says. 'We're having Mum over for Christmas lunch tomorrow and I have to tell her I'm pregnant, so whatever you have in mind to distract me from that would be wonderful.'

'That works,' he says. 'Stacey and the kids are coming for lunch tomorrow, but I'm free until then—they'll do stockings at her house in the morning. I have several distractions in mind for you, and if you spend another second thinking about your mother, I'll consider it a spectacular failure on my part.'

'That's good enough for me,' she says. 'Let me grab my stuff.'

40

TUESDAY, 24TH DECEMBER

Jack sweeps into the driveway of The Lodge and squeezes her hand. 'Home,' he says.

It does feel like home. As soon as she walks over the threshold into his enormous hallway with its twinkling tree and scent of oranges and cloves, she has the acute sense that all is good with the world.

Jack puts her rucksack by the base of the staircase and walks over to her, unzipping her parka and painstakingly easing its sleeve over her cast. She puts her arm back in the sling hanging around her neck.

He bends his head and kisses her softly on the lips. 'I can't tell you how happy I am you're back,' he says. 'I'm so sorry I didn't come to my senses sooner; if I'd pulled my finger out of my arse, you wouldn't have had that accident coming to see me.'

'It's ok,' she says. 'I'm fine; the baby's fine; I'm here with you now.' She kisses him more intensely and feels him respond; he presses himself against her and wraps his arms tightly around her before pulling away.

'I'm worried I'm going to hurt you,' he says. 'You're like a baby bird with a broken wing.'

Fuck that.

'I'm not a baby bird,' she says. 'I'm perfectly fine, except for this bloody cast and a very unattractive dressing on my face. Don't hold back; I'm going crazy over here.'

'Really?' he says.

'Really. What do you expect? You abandoned a horny pregnant woman and now I need a good seeing-to. Can you help me or not?'

She's rewarded with a grin of utter delight. 'Fuck,' he says, shaking his head at her. 'Come upstairs. Right now.'

IN HIS BEDROOM, he's all business. He strides over to her and kisses her, his hands raking through her hair and pulling her in towards him as his tongue twists in her mouth. She's already trying to resist the urge to moan. He backs away and tugs off his sweater and t-shirt and then she does moan, nuzzling her forehead and nose into his shoulder. She's missed his skin more than anything else.

'Let's get you naked,' he says softly, and he unhooks her arm from the sling. She's wearing a loose silk shirt Rosa lent her for its accommodative shape and he unbuttons it slowly. She watches his face while he undresses her; he's wearing a small frown of concentration, which is adorable. He slides the sleeves off and, catching her eye, shoots her a smile.

'Look at you,' he says, caressing her shoulders and her back and her stomach before unhooking her bra and sliding it off. He bends and sucks one nipple and he rolls the other around with his thumb. They're not as sore as they were a couple of weeks ago, but they're just as sensitive and she whimpers with pleasure. At the sound, he comes up and kisses her harder while he undoes the flies on her jeans. He bends and slides them down and she puts her good hand on his shoulder for support while he pulls them off, first one leg, then the other. Still crouching, he covers her stomach in tiny kisses while he slides one hand up between her thighs. The other slips around the back and inside her knickers. Oh, Lord. She digs her fingers into his shoulder as he strokes her, agonisingly slowly, before pulling her knickers down her legs.

'Aaah,' she moans.

He stands up and she grabs his belt-buckle, unfastening it and his jeans as quickly as she can.

'You,' he says, 'are so fucking heavenly that I don't think I can wait any longer.'

'Me neither,' she says, tugging his jeans and boxers down. He's naked now, and she puts her arms around him and rubs the length of her body against him.

'Dear God,' he says, arms encircling her. 'Right, on the bed so you don't do yourself any more injury. I take it I don't need a condom?'

She giggles. 'Nope. That ship has sailed.'

He shakes his head and tuts in mock disapproval as he climbs on top of her, taking a pillow and stuffing it under her bum. She luxuriates in being back here, in—on—Jack's bed, watching this naked god above her.

'A good seeing-to,' he drawls. 'Was that the turn of phrase you used?'

She wriggles in amusement and embarrassment, but mainly in anticipation.

'Yes, please,' she says.

'I see,' he says. 'Legs up.'

She lifts her legs, and he leans forward so they're over

his shoulders and he's pushing them back towards her. His weight's on one of his hands beside her head and he runs the other hand across her breasts and down her stomach before he pushes into her. She gasps—it feels so bloody incredible that she could bawl her eyes out.

'Ok?' he asks.

She nods and closes her eyes to intensify the sensation.

He moves agonisingly slowly, pulling almost all the way out of her and in again.

'Oh, God,' she says.

'Do you like it like this?' he says, and she opens her eyes and nods at him before closing them again to focus on the blissful sensation.

'Or like this?' he says, and he slams into her, hard. It's so intense that her eyelids fly open and she cries out.

'Good?' he says.

'Yes,' she groans. 'Harder.'

'Ok, gorgeous,' he says, and he pushes harder and faster. At this angle, the intensity builds rapidly until she's over the edge and falling into oblivion, her body shuddering and jerking as she tries to arch her back. He comes right after her and collapses on top of her, gasping. She turns her face to kiss him and he lifts his head and finds her mouth. They're both slick with sweat and she hooks her good arm around his neck as they kiss.

He raises himself up onto his forearms and grins at her. 'Did I see to you sufficiently?'

'That was amazing,' she says, beaming. 'Exactly what I needed.' She stretches luxuriously. 'Sorry I wasn't a very active participant; I just lay there.'

His expression is serious. 'You just lying there, as you put it, was so sexy I can't even... it was amazing for me, too.

Fuck, Em, I'm so happy we sorted things out. This is looking like the best Christmas ever.'

'Best Christmas ever,' she murmurs in a contented stupor as he pulls out of her and rolls her onto her side and into his arms.

41

WEDNESDAY, 25TH DECEMBER

5.24am

DOLLY: Mummy! MUMMY! Santa's been! SANTA'S BEEN!!!

ROSA: Oh, good lord.

6.31am

ROSA: Merry Christmas, Lulah darling.

TALLULAH: OMG Mom, you got me the rose gold one! OMG OMG. It's sooooo beautiful. Thank you. I love you so much, Mom.

ROSA: I love you too, sweetheart. Now, open this one.

TALLULAH: *Opens it.* What is it?

ROSA: It's a letter from Stella McCartney. Her team thought that your little hijack stunt *<pokes her in the tummy>* was very impressive because it shows how passionately you care about animals. So they want you to model in their kidswear campaign around eco-warriors next month. What do you think?

TALLULAH: *Face crumples.*

DOLLY: Can I come too?

6.51am

STACEY: Ok, this last one is for all of you to share.

PITT: Is it from Dad too?

STACEY: No, this one's just from me. Dad will have presents for you later. Let Mia open it.

AUGIE: She always gets to open things just cos she's the youngest. It's not fair!

PITT: Shut up Augie!

STACEY: Hey! Do the honours please, Mia.

MIA: It's a photo of a puppy. Aww! He's so cute! Why did you get us a photo of a puppy?

MARTHA: Ohmigod Mom, did you get us a puppy?

STACEY: Yes. We are getting a puppy! We'll all go together next weekend and pick her up, ok?

General mayhem ensues.

8.07am

JACK: Merry Christmas, baby.

EMMY: Mmmm. Merry Christmas, gorgeous.

JACK: It seems I have a present for you.

EMMY: Giggles. Yep, it's poking me in the back!

EMMY: Ok then, you'd better give me my present.

8.22am

EMMY: Oh my God. Oh my God. Oh my *God!*

~

10.05am

EMMY: Jack, I need to get my arse in gear and get ready for Rosa's. Seriously. Mmmm...

~

10.35am

ARIEL via WhatsApp: *Merry Christmas beautiful. FaceTime this evening?*

STACEY via WhatsApp: *Merry Christmas! Have a great day! FT definitely xxxx*

ARIEL via WhatsApp: *I'll make it worth your while x*

STACEY via WhatsApp: *You'd better x*

~

12.12pm

ROSA: Where the fuck is Emmy?

DAVID: Give her a break. Don't you remember what we were like when we first got together? We didn't leave your flat for days. Speaking of which, you look extremely hot in that little black dress.

ROSA: Pour me a large glass of champagne and then you can flirt with me all you want. *Kisses him in a manner that suggests she's not entirely displeased by the flirting.*

DAVID: God, I love my wife.

~

12.20pm

EMMY: Thanks for the lift.

JACK: My pleasure. I'll call you when Stace and the kids have gone, ok? Then I'll whizz around and get you and we can have a cosy evening in in front of the fire.

EMMY: On *that* rug? I know your game.

JACK: Oh, yes. On *that* rug. *Breaks into song.* ChestNUTS roasting on an open fire...

EMMY: Oh, God. I'm getting out. Wish me luck.

JACK: Good luck, baby.

3.01pm

EMMY: *Washing up.* So, Mum, I have something to tell you.

JEANETTE: What is it, darling?

EMMY: Well, I've met a guy. Called Jack. He's great. He's a good friend of Rosa and David's.

JEANETTE: That was quick work. You've only been down here a fortnight!

EMMY: Four weeks.

ROSA: And he really is great.

JEANETTE: Well, if you're happy, I'm happy. What lovely news.

EMMY: There's something else, too. Um—I'm expecting a baby. In June. I'm twelve weeks gone.

JEANETTE: *What?*

EMMY: Yes. And it's not Jack's; it's an ex-colleague's actually. But the father's been very supportive, and Jack's on board, and, well, I'm very excited about it. The accident really shook me up, but the baby's healthy and—

JEANETTE: Did I teach you nothing? How on earth did you let that happen?

ROSA: Mum...

JEANETTE: You're only just back in the country and you've thrown away any chance of getting a career off the ground by letting yourself get pregnant!

EMMY: It was just one of those things—I don't know. We were careful, but these things happen. Anyway, Mum. Try to be happy for me, please.

ROSA: MUM. Emmy's had a tough week and we're all really relieved the baby is healthy. Jack's an incredible guy. He's also, for your information, rich as sin and a philanthropist; Emmy's working with him on his charity to educate children in India, and I know the two of them will achieve amazing things together. So please be supportive and don't ruin Christmas Day for us all.

EMMY and JEANETTE: *Speechless.*

5.30pm

STACEY: We had a great day, thanks, sweetie. That lunch was amazing.

JACK: Carol prepped most of it, but I'm glad you enjoyed it. The kids are on brilliant form. You sure about that new puppy?

STACEY: No, but they are so excited! Fuck knows what I'm doing but they're great kids; they deserve it. Hey, I've been dying to ask you all day. Did you patch things up with Emmy? Oh my God, look at that smile! You did, didn't you! Do you have her stashed in a bedroom upstairs somewhere?

JACK: I ran her back to Rosa and David's about twenty minutes before you guys turned up.

STACEY: Check you! I thought you'd been super cheerful today. Nice work. You happy?

JACK: Ecstatic. So happy it's revolting. Thanks for giving me the push I needed.

STACEY: Good on you! Seriously, you deserve it. I met someone too, and I know he's gonna be a keeper.

JACK: Did you? When? What about the French bloke?

STACEY: Nah. I'm telling you, this guy is the bomb. He was supposed to be my plastic surgeon and—

JACK: You're having plastic surgery?

STACEY: Well, I was considering having a few little things done, just to, you know, cheat time. But that went out the window as soon as I saw him.

JACK: I didn't think you wanted a relationship?

STACEY: Me either, until I met Ariel. It's funny how things work out, isn't it?

JACK: *Kisses her on the forehead.* It really is.

~

7.36pm

LORENZO via WhatsApp: *Buon Natale Natasha xx I look forward to our 1st date next week @ Claridges*

NATASHA via WhatsApp: *Merry Christmas Lorenzo.*

NATASHA via WhatsApp: *Please be aware that I will not take any shit from you if we start dating. I know all about you.*

NATASHA via WhatsApp: *I'm looking fwd to our date too and I have no intention of wearing any underwear, FYI, so you may want to book a room.*

NATASHA via WhatsApp: *xx*

LORENZO via WhatsApp: *Holy shit <hands in prayer emoji>*

8.12pm

ARIEL: Where are your kids?

STACEY: Watching a movie downstairs. I've locked my bedroom door.

ARIEL: Excellent. Take off your dress.

STACEY: Yes, Doctor. *Takes off dress.*

ARIEL: Good girl. Now, take off your bra.

STACEY: Sure thing, Doctor. *Takes off bra.*

ARIEL: Holy fuck, I wish I was there with you. Take off your pants.

STACEY: If you say so, Doctor. *Takes off pants.*

ARIEL: I do say so. Jesus. Now, do exactly as I tell you...

8.47pm

EMMY: Erm, I think this rug may need a dry-clean after that.

JACK: Fuck the rug. You look so beautiful by firelight, I can't even tell you.

EMMY: Your arse looks particularly fine by firelight, too.

JACK: Emmy, I—

Loud crash from the kitchen.

JACK: Oh fuck, don't tell me Marge managed to get to the turkey. Marge! *Marge!*

*** THE END ***

Discover the story of Astrid, Lorenzo, Natalia and others in *Parents and Teachers*, my FREE ebook, which is available here:

saramadderson.com/free-book
Discover Evelyn and Angus' story in *Food for Thought* which is available in ebook and paperback on Amazon and as an ebook from all major ebook sellers here

AUTHOR'S NOTE

I've read many books on the craft of writing and one of my favourites is *GMC: Goal, Motivation, and Conflict* by Debra Dixon. Dixon uses the balloon incident from the climax of *The Wizard of Oz* to illustrate the power of those moments that show us exactly what we want in life.

I thought this was a wonderful example of the gut punches life can deliver, and couldn't resist adding Dorothy's revelation into Emmy's fictional narrative. Thank you to Debra Dixon for the inspiration.

SM

Printed in Great Britain
by Amazon

58338153R00187